Thom Cree is the author of several novels and stories, written under multiple pen names. His work has been published in literary journals worldwide, and his science fiction novella, *Eidetic* features in Temple Dark Books' *Channel The Dark Anthology*. His unique graphic writing style uses sparse punctuation and attribution.

*'Cree's **The Man Who** is a fascinating literary piece, drawing the reader immediately into the piqued perspective of a protagonist who sees everything and is longing to tell us all about it. The writing is certainly unusual, a sort of 'punctuation-less' approach which invites subjectivity to its interpretation. I found it difficult at first, but with a little focus the writing became fluid, alive, inspired, reading more like poetry disguised as prose, giving it an otherworldly sense of immersion and pace. The minutiae in the descriptive brings this wild vista to the forefront of the reader's mind, and we explore with the protagonist (Gilchrist) a merciless landscape of fleeting aspiration and mournful beauty, populated by animals as indifferent to his passing through as the people he encounters are to the morals he fights to uphold. Witnessing the cycle of violence in these lawless lands, Gilchrist traverses a land in which people are either struggling to survive or exploiting others for their own survival, with Cree all along treating us to a stylized vernacular to further aid the immersion into this arid and unforgiving tale of evil men and the endless fight to set them straight; and perhaps of the relentless cycle of reprisal that keeps us from sharing our world.'*

Ronald A. Geobey, Author of the Kiranis series

*'Thom Cree shows great skill at depicting such savage acts of violence with such lyricism and viscerality of style. **Capstone**'s beauty lies in exactly how the language is deployed, namely in that acts of horrific violence and trauma are rendered so eloquently on the page.'*

Daniel Wade, Author, Playright

*'It is indeed a unique talent to construct a taut, interesting tale, but to write it in such a way that the reading of it creates delight, page by page. Cree is such a writer. I simply revelled in the text and constantly wished to slow down and savour the language. Cree certainly demonstrated knowledge of the intelligence community. **Stalemate** is, to recall a phrase, a "good story well told." Strongly recommended.'*

Chris Maddix, Author

THE MAN WHO

A COLLECTION OF STORIES BY

THOM CREE

Matador
Unit E2 Airfield Business Park
Harrison Road, Market Harborough
Leicestershire LE16 7UL
Tel: 0116 279 2299
Email: books@troubador.co.uk
Web: www.troubador.co.uk/matador
Twitter: @matadorbooks

ISBN 978-1-80514-053-5

British Library Cataloguing in Publication Data.
A catalogue record for this book is available from the British Library.

Printed and bound in Great Britain by 4edge Limited
Typeset in 11pt Minion Pro by Troubador Publishing Ltd, Leicester, UK

Matador is an imprint of Troubador Publishing Ltd

Thank you sincerely Eugen Gorean, Ronald Geobey,
Daniel Wade, and my father.

for Z. H.

CONTENTS

HISTORICAL WESTERNS

For Taylor Sheridan, Sam Elliott, LaMonica Garrett, Nick Cave, Warren Ellis and Max Richter

CONTEMPORARY

COLD WAR ESPIONAGE

Dedicated to Shaun Evans, E. M.
i.m. David Cornwell

'And some there be… who are perished, as though they had never been; and become as though they had never been born…'

Ecclesiasticus

CAPSTONE

THIS CHILD. Twelve years since his birth. Small boy of raven hair. Skinnier than a prairie muskrat. His spotless eyes observe the labour of his folk while they harrow down the scorched purlieu in the white heat of the dry noon sun but his father has been a minister. A dozen years. Preaching the good book before tenet stanched by doubt and bare conscience. He is Texas born. His wife halfbreed. And while the black sky casts pinpoints of light the boy watches his mother suckle the infant by stentorian blue flame as wolves slank the ambit with unsilent howl. He watches his father enter a void of thought prohibited by living man as he draws circumspect on his clay pipe. On a certain day they are humbled by a weekly dose of wrathful tongue and the auguries of the reverend fall upon his listeners like a plague of hailstone and the boy shuts his ears watching the faces of the congregation gathered. He sees fear in their eyes. A fear he will later feel on their journey homeward. He sees a small girl perched on a makeshift hassock regarding him with her halcyon eye, her hair as gold as the dawn or a dying solstice sun. She smiles but he does not return it and her mother vents disapproval, moving her towards that dour voice of contention. The rain has been falling during the extent of the reverend's sermon and the boy listens to the patter as it strikes the canvas tent and he likens the sound to that colony of ants he had watched on the prairie scuttling about the nest mindlessly.

The rain stops as has the homily and his father makes for the livery stable to untether the horse and flatbed wagon. He walks it to the rear of the tent and they ready themselves for the several mile journey ahead. The boy is cold and buries himself beneath the pallet in the wagon and falls asleep to the motion of the scantling shifting and fraying over the dark loam earth. They reach a small creek and the boy is woken by the sudden jolt of their standstill. He opens his eyes but does not move.

What is it you want? he hears his father say. His escopeta lies across his thigh and he indicates to the riders of their prising it. You can take this here rifle. Just don't want no trouble now. They offer no reply and he is made uneasy by their presence and the cradled infant begins to cry as if summoned by some spectral prediction and the folk bid her hush while the ominous faction look on with their faces slathered with almagre and mounted on their horses like monoliths. A band of carrion birds drop weary black notes upon the motionless scene and a lizard scratches about on the parched dust, for there has been no rain there and the creek trickles effortlessly through rock and eelgrass but nothing is still said and at length a brave appears up on the ridge above them waiting as if there for the view.

The father attempts to whet their appetite with scant pickings of his wares and as he reaches for them into the wagon he pinions his son to stay put with his large firm hand. The goods are spread out on the ground before them and the Comanche survey the chattels with mute indifference. One of the four braves astraddle a white stallion points to the rifle and the man tenders it with both hands from bended knee hoping above all hope a neutral trade can be determined. This same brave perhaps the chief is clad in buffalo hide and a feathered headdress, his long braided hair in a scalp lock with beaver fur and the sole tribesman of the four in such attire. As he dismounts his horse a hundredhead riders unite from the kerfs of the ridge overhead and like a herd of antelope they descend the talus slope and wheel round the creek to flank the wagon. The chief aforementioned walks towards the man takes the shotgun and surveys it turning it over in hand then pitches it to one of the tribe behind him while the infant continues to cry. Without warning he unsheathes a large blade proceeds forward and cuts the man's throat ear to ear and the woman screams a terrifying shriek of fear yet still the boy does not move. The chief then places the blade to the dead man's scalp and yanks it clean from his head with little labour and the bloody skull lies tonsured flooding the dust-slaked earth beneath him. His next move is a sudden one for he tears the infant from its mother, taking it by the throat and with all his strength of barehand scrags the child until entirely dead. The woman now desolate with grief climbs down from the wagon falling to her knees and gathers the remains of her crushed child from the fouled earth as the trammelled heat beats down on her and as she embraces it in sodden agony the natives look on insensate and unyielding.

The unseen boy has rank terror in his eyes and this fear he has never known weighs heavy on him as if gravity itself depresses his small thin frame. A red-tailed hawk soars overhead shedding uneven symbols above qualified prey then a drove of arrows release and they are each unerring in ambition. The first cleaves through the woman's left eye, the rest a retardance through torso and limb delivering her to the blood blackened dust where the dead child lies. A pandemonium of ungodly syllables spew from the flanked Comanche as they circle the dead with speed raising clouds of victory dust to the firmament while the chief clutches the dead woman's hair, winding it round his left arm then cleaves the scalp clean off. Another of the four untethers the horse from the wagon and ties it to the trailing reins of his horse before he hobbles the limbs of the dead folk and fastens them to the recruited horse, then a torrent of gunfire erupts and the hundredhead horses stampede the turf balefully and as they exit the territory they torch the pilfered wagon blind to the boy nested there. The flames surge quickly and the boy is squirrelled with fright. He feels the burning heat through the pallet swell as the terror takes root of his soul. Attempting to flee he makes for the opening of the wagon with the pallet trussed to his back and with the flames ablaze he at length jumps from the pyre unscathed and beaten.

IT WAS DUSK and the heat had not abated. The residual smoke from the wreckage lay waste and everything once familiar to the boy had gone, abandoning him to the corrosive elements of the desert. He had been crying for hours and was crouched behind a shale ridge in the creek beset with hunger. There was a laggard wind with voices being carried from the south and from the sage scrub a spotted towhee flit to and fro its brood. The drunken voices drew nearer and the boy edged further into the bluff. One of the men dismounted his mule and staggered to the edge of the creek. He unholstered his gun and fired it aimlessly into the night air. Puta pistola, he said then reholstered the gun. He then pulled out his implement and started urinating in the creek.

Estupido culo, said the other man from his mule. Stop. No mear en el agua!

Callate Pendejo. It won't kill nothin.

Why you gotta piss on everythin? Some stoopid hombre might take to drinkin it.

Y qué, so what. Their problem ah?

The two men laughed and the second man dismounted. He looked round the terrain and saw the blistered remains of the wagon some yards away then walked over to it to forage for chattels. The man standing in the creek was staring up at the crescent moon while the coral sun was setting behind the ridge then he seemed to lose balance and fell into the creek.

Mierda, he said laughing to himself. Hey Tavo! What you doin? Come dip your ass in the water. It's freezing my cojones.

Tavo ignored him. This here wagon is no long been torched, he said.

Qué estas diciendo? I can't hear you.

Campa! Get your skinny ass over here. There is wagon and no horse. Burnt to wattle. Qué demonios? You think it's redskins?

If the horse is gone. That redskins amigo. Comanche socio. Then he spat.

The two men walked round the wagon and looked over the patches of ground where the scalping had taken place and the blood had darkened into a black mass, coagulating the desert floor. Demonios, said Campa. It look like two or three scalpings. Comanche loco ah?

Look like el cabron bushwhacked them sons of bitches.

Taken dead with em too. Any forage?

Nah, nothin. Just some tools de basura over there.

Some loose shale tumbled from over where the boy was standing and the Mexicans turned quickly to consult the movement. Tavo put his hand to his holstered pistol and edged towards the ridge slowly. Salga! he said. Where we can see you.

The boy pushed himself further into the gully but as Tavo drew nearer he came clear into view. Eh chico. What you do in there? Salga. Come out pequeño.

Qué es, Tavo? Then again in Spanish, is it merchandise?

Cristo, Campa! He might speak Español. Imbecil.

Removing his hand from his holster he slunk closer to the boy while attaining some lanyard from his back pocket. Campa flanked the boy from the rightward curve in the crag and the boy remained mute.

What happen here muchacho? The boy gave no answer. Was it injins? Tavo earned no claim further then he pointed to the bloody causatum fouling the dust over by the wreckage. This here yer folk ha? Es esta tu gente? They leave you alone, eh? Where is your casa? Your house? We take you there, si?

No trouble for us amigo, said Campa. We collect yer things and take you with us. Fort Union. Find you safe place.

You want come with us? Get your possibles. No stay here chico. Getting dark. Dangerous for hombrecito.

The boy looked downwards then up again at the two strangers as if to weigh his fate. Then gave a spry nod. Bueno, said Tavo. The two men were then deep in discourse contriving some wily filching for their trouble then with a sudden move he tied the lanyard round the boy's wrists and hove him over to his mule, attaching the other end of the rope to the pummel of the saddle. You stuck with us now tonto.

Aprenderás chico. You will learn. Never trust no borracho Mexican el perro. If we no steal or cheat, we kill. So better watch your back hijo de puta.

The two strangers gave a baleful laugh then Campa picked up a stob of mesquite and harried it into the boy's mouth. This shut you up till we reach your casa tonto. Ni una palabra. No speak, comprender? Muéstranos. Dónde está? Show the way mestizo. Move!

IT WAS DARK when they reached the jacal and the terrain was as deserted as the compound and it was strange for the boy to look upon his home that night, like visiting a dignitary's grave or souls lost that were once familiar. They were benighted there.

The Mexicans halted their mounts and climbed down and tethered the trailing reins to the hitching rail. Tavo untethered the boy then they uncinched the saddles and carried them into the hut leaving the boy alone outside. At length the boy trailed behind them and stood doubtful on the wattled portico questioning the face of the impregnable darkness. The sky was cloud-sprent and the moonlight bled through with the odd burning star and the trees were silhouetted against the endless vault as the coyotes croaked from the desert floor, somewhere in an unnamed district. The boy entered the hut and looked over at the stove where he had stoked the fire that morning and he had come to feel the palpable truth he had fallen victim to parricide as he watched the Mexicans pilfer the place with divested deed. They foraged and befouled like a company of rancid vultures at their vittles leaving nothing untampered or undefiled and they would not profit from this shelter that night and the boy knew it as he set to gather his possibles. He rolled up a pallet with a blanketroll and packed some clothing. For his journey would be unknown to him or any man and it would reek of savage bloodoaths and hostilities of senseless war. He took a large rawhide pouch from the pantry and filled it with pinole then took a couple of canteens and sated them with fresh water. The Mexicans were seeing to their equipage while the boy untethered his father's pony from the barn, and the food prepared by his mother that day had been swallowed or bagged for their progress. Seeing the Bowie knife in the stalls the boy stowed it under the fender of the saddle then walked the pony out where he would join partisan to lawless company, contesting the torching of the jacal which was once of his father's labour.

They mounted and rode on and the boy looked back and watched the flames scale and roar and the black smoke tower overhead as if it were being sucked into oblivion through some occult agency, and it was there the boy lost all innocence like a skinshedding serpent, casting childhood and name into the angry fire. Their progress was slow and a grey fox had been following them the past mile or so weaving in and out of their trail with no prospect and Campa took his pistol and shot inanely at the ground near the animal which became some base amusement till it scampered off into the dark. By and by they reached the foothills of the Sangre de Cristo where an army of bristlecone stood giant and sentry hissing in the vast unknown and a nighthawk gave a nasal peent from a remote perch. There a gang of elk harboured further still among all manner of creatures and they made camp and sat wordless by the fire which had been the first show of silence since starting off.

The Mexicans glared anodyne into the fire chewing on some cribbed cured meat while the boy watched whittling on a random stob, then Tavo asked the boy of his name to which he rendered no answer and since that had so far been his enterprise they determined mute would become his name. Mudo. As the night wore on the two contested themselves on mescal which inebriated them tellingly and Campa made product of stories heard of the Comanche tribe to unsettle the boy in his orphaned state and he began by feasting on the demise of the boy's folk and of their final resting place which he said would come after a fashion. He remonstrated a bloody battle among Osage and Comanche which reduced both sides of their men slain and the few fallen into the hands of the Osage suffered sacrilege by Comanche law. They secured the heads of some by hewing or clove the scalps of others, casting the corpses to the haggard carnivores. In turn, he said the Comanche brought the bodies of the dead Osage to camp then clove them before broiling and boiling then eating them. Some roasted a foot or hand like it were some regale and as he spoke this truth the boy's eyes widened and the Mexicans laughed malefically then added his folk had most likely met the same end.

The boy did not sleep that night nor many a night after and a myriad of thoughts haunted him as he lay in nag while his eyes catalogued the white stars colossal in their scads and the mules snuffed, the men snored and a solitary wolf strained its cry as if to echo the boy's reasoning. A long night was spent in wait and come daybreak the boy had led his pony down to a firth for a sup before the Mexicans would rise and when he had returned to the camp he found Campa standing over Tavo with his pistol cocked and the barrel plumb centre of Tavo's forehead.

Get up puta or I drill a hole in your head. He chuckled.

Valgame dios! You crazy ass son of a bitch. Get your jodido pistol outta my face! Then with ferment he toed him in the rear with his boot. Campa continued laughing and dragged himself laggardly over to a sumac where he proceeded to urinate before dropping his trousers and crouching in the bigelow. Tavo hauled himself up and extinguished the last of the embers by urinating on them then turned to Campa and spat.

Make sure you no wipe that guano in your face el cabron. You go blind amigo.

The fools laughed and the boy looked on berating them mutely while eating the last of the flapjack. They decamped and rode on and their jornadas was silent and solitary save the odd blue grouse or ptarmigan and they ascended the heavily forested slopes of pinyon, aspen and limber pine in the pregnant heat of the day. The timberline stretched for miles up into the Pecos and stood as still as a regiment steeled for battle and a dull tread of hooves echoed through the talus slopes and cliff rocks where neither animus nor device of man had yet polluted. They halted for water in a stream and the boy used a narrow spray to joust cutthroat trout for the first meal of day while the Mexicans rowelled him on and the mules stood kneedeep in water while they ate the boy's catch in the shade. By and by they trailed northeasterly and reached the Saddle peak which towered over the Pecos Baldy lake where a herd of bighorn sheep grazed in a meadow and the boy scanned across the endless peaks and broad mesa tops in hallowed awe.

It was late afternoon before they gained the deep and narrow canyons where they took the winding switchbacks leading down to the desert floor and they anguished the white heat in lassitude as a sequence of kek notes fell from a passing Northern Harrier with its wingspread full and motile. They came upon several wickiups beside a freshwater lake, some with brushwood intact others carbonised to its truss and they saw smouldering poles of tepees and rangy carcasses of horses and burros laying foul in their arterial blood. Death was regnant in this landscape with the Choctaw hacked and mutilated with their scalps clove tonsured to the bone and the company stood side by side confounded, looking upon the bloody entrails strewn across the silent purlieu. The Mexicans dismounted pistol in hand and advanced the wickiups for forage and the boy stalled in his saddle with tears issuing his inviolate eyes and in this purgatorial decay he saw portents there in what would fast become his future odyssey.

THEY HAD DESCENDED the narrow switchbacks and come upon Sapello on an endless plain as far as the eye could stretch and larkspur was plentiful here among great swales of grass. They rode past an adobe mill by a creek with the protean ebb of the sack hoist and hatches and waterwheel wading with agency, and a man halted his labour and stared at them as they rode on slothlike in their address. The boy hobbled behind with his mind turning over the hellsprent ordeal aforewitnessed and the Mexicans heckled vamanos as they slanted their pistols his way. It was dusk before approaching the tradingpost which they reckoned was about half a mile off and they came upon a solitary burro confused in its bearings, flyblown and granular as if it had been hove across the desert floor and a man lay a few feet away facedown with his head kicked in and he groaned in all his malaise.

Agua, he said. Water por favor, and Campa dismounted. He slunk over to the injured man and stood over him canteen in hand.

This what you want chico? The man nodded and croaked the words por favor in a hiss. You pretty dirty amigo. You bleedin. What son of a puta do this t'you eh? Some stinkin white dogs creo que?

Si, the man answered. They take my horse. At this particular moment Tavo dismounted and examined the man's possibles while Campa turned the man over on his back. He unscrewed the canteen then feinted to move it towards the man's mouth then drank from it himself laughing.

Look like you luck no change amigo. We no Bueno pilgrim. We some coldhearted pelados who help no stinkin people. Unless somethin in it for us entendido? So what in it for us amigo, eh? The Mexicans exchanged a brief look while the boy berated wordlessly then Tavo shouldered the man's chattels and mounted his mule. Campa pitched the canteen at Tavo then flung out his implement and started pissing on the man's head and he was cackling and giving forth a string of Spanish words no man could comprehend. The man was now gagging on the urine and raised his arm aloft to shield the mockery then Tavo took the saddlepistol from the scabbard, seated a pistolball in the chamber levered it home then aimed at the burro's head and fired. The mules shied and shifted about as the shot echoed in that barrenland and the burro's legs folded underneath it and dropped stout to the ground.

Well amigo, we must to go now, said Campa as he mounted his mule. Adios. Take it nice n slow getting up tonto. That head a yours look nasty.

The Mexicans rode on but the boy dismounted and gave his canteen to the man then towelled the expelled blood away with some damp crop of cloth, for the boy could relate to their motive no more than he could the savage Comanche and he questioned his purpose and what was forthcoming. The Mexicans halted and turned in their saddles to look back at the boy. Hey mudo, said Tavo. Basta. Vamos! They rode on leaving the injured man lying there.

As they commenced upon the tradingpost a lone horse bolted past them with its saddle mounted and the trailing reins hanging loose heading south towards where the injured man lay. Shortly after, the queerest sight ever beheld by the boy was charging towards them of a man in a woman's dress painted face and a pitch wig. The man enquired politely of the whereabouts of his horse, his accent fell unfamiliar to the boy and the Mexicans thumbed him casually on southward.

In the darkness stood a large timber hut bedim before them and would be the first tradingpost for miles and the portico was narrowly lit by tallow lamps where an old woman was crouched smoking a pipe. Several horses were tethered at the hitchingrail and a couple of fetid curs harried and scuttered about them gnarling and jerking without claim and out in that wild unrest coyotes howled and slunk mindless in their enterprise while distant campfires burned in that starless black postured sky. The sign on the door read Stayout. They hitched down and tethered their rides then proceeded forth into the bodega where an assemblage of gruff looking pelados sat idle in a game of dominoes. Along the back wall of the hut was a broad limber pine bar where a posse of men stood smoking and liquored up and they each of them turned to qualify the intruders unhurriedly. Over on the left was a stock of merchandise and an open livery where three mature horses stood cropping and set behind them in the farthest corner was a family of five Mexicans sitting on their pallets just staring. Various tables scattered the right side of the hut with escorbuto vagrants gathered about them smoking their cigarillos.

The cantinero sized up the customers at the door while swabbing down the surface of the bar halfassedwise and a guitar was being played from somewhere unseen. Tavo handed the boy a couple of monedas and pushed him towards the bar with his boot then the Mexicans laboured over to the tables and sat down. A tall man wearing an oilcloth slicker was abreast as the boy approached the bar and he picked up his glass and moved to one side shuffling the posse further down the bar. The barman looked at the boy without expression. Digame, he said. The boy held up three fingers and the barman stared at him then held up two. Te refieres a dos? The boy frowned and the man in the slicker rested his forearms wearily on the bar and took a sup.

Leave him be, Benito. Give him cider. Caint see no harm in it.

No. Le leche es major, said one of the posse and the men laughed.

The boy put the coins down on the bar and nodded to the man in the slicker. This man the boy heard the posse address as Creed and the other man that had spoken Simp and he was looking on at the boy mighty strange with his dark menacing eyes as he chewed and spat his tobacco. Quires chupar muchacho? he said to the boy.

Enough, said Creed. Git on with yer whiskey.

El es Lindo. He pretty as a chica. And ye know I no resist no hermoso chica.

I said that's enough! Creed struck his glass on the bar and seized Simp's left arm then drew a military knife from his person swiftlike and castigated like some predatory arachnid then slapped that same hand flat on the bar with the point of the blade ingress to the dorsal. Gouts of blood gave forth as Creed bore down with a wrath more hideous than a Tanakh God. Simp let out a scream of discord and every man woman and child fell silent in that place save the horses. Creed stared primitive into the Mexican's eyes commencing autonomous.

Next time I hear that kinda talk comin from yer mouth God help me I'll flay that there pizzle a yers clean off. Ye hear? The Mexican nodded with abjection as the posse and every pilgrim therein observed that black contention then all returned to their deed as if nothing singular had occurred. The boy stood rooted and mute as he watched on and Creed withdrew the knife from the trammelled hand with the ease of drawing from a scabbard and Simp keeled over cupping his hand hissing through his teeth and cursing in Spanish then bolstered it with his right. Creed tore a crop from the bar towel and handed it to the partisan.

Best stanch that there wound up afore it turn rancid. He poured the remainder of his whiskey on the wound then bound the cloth fast to his hand. The boy took his purchase from the bar and Creed touched his hatbrim then watched him walk towards the company yonder and as the boy looked back Creed was leaning back on his elbows against the bar with a blithe grin recondite across his furrowed face.

After seeing to his pony and pocketing his knife the boy headed over to the jakes at the rear of the premises and a prairie dog scuttled past on to the cooling desert floor as he drew near. He took a lit match and entered the jakes where an almost spent tallow was there for the lighting and the boy commenced to do his business with bats scudding about aloft the wattled roof.

After a short time he heard the tread of movement from outside the shed which he took for the prairie dog back for forage then a rowelling whistle followed which claimed the baring of his Bowie. With his trousers about his ankles he sat silent and quaking and he was delirious with portents like an auger before a scourge and the tread from the perimeter drew nearer and the voice called out primordial from the darkness. The door of the jakes swung open and the Mexican Simp stood before him with his appendage held forth and a priapic grin brandished and without pause took a slow lope towards the boy.

A scuffle took place in that confinement and a strife entirely unknown to the boy would haunt him for many a year before him and he reached for the Bowieknife with wretchedness during that endless black reckoning and he struck out with that blade like a feral cat and he berated and struggled as it commenced. The essay was almost at defilement when the sound of gunfire broke and it lofted forward a pistolball which made its final ruin in the rear truss and the boy turned his head and watched the eyes of the man Simp roll back into his head and the blood spew from the clean puncture of the ball leaving some great judas hole in his skull. As his dead weight fell forward on to the boy he saw the man Creed standing fast pistol in hand with that same recondite grin upon his face.

NOT ONE SINGLE pilgrim inside that place contested the gunfire for they would sooner rest in their niches and assume ignorance than tender defence in some deadly dual. The Mexicans were busy commandeering merchandise and when they returned to their mules it would seem Creed and his retinue had confederated to trek on to Fort Union with them. They mounted up and rode on into the night in silence with mutual autonomous and there above them hung a gibbous moon which soused the riders and desert floor in blue and the moonlight threw terrific and unearthly shapes which stretched out across the stark plain where wolves slank the unclaimed quarters in solitude or in packs.

The partisans were five and they were a queer melee of timadores. There was an American named Hite who had escaped jail in Chihuahua by bribing his way out with stolen gold; Rube a black man who rarely tendered a word good or otherwise; and the two Mexican brothers called Lugo. These men Creed had acquisitioned in El Paso and they were known bounty hunters who killed mindlessly with neither creed, colour nor gender to thwart them. They rode for an hour or so and the boy hung back from the column still shaken from the ordeal and the Lugo brothers were asleep in their saddles muttering incoherently while the other men smoked and spat.

Creed took to wheeling his horse to the rear and came up abreast the boy's horse to tender something near amenity, albeit unnatural to him. Yer a brave kid, he said. No mistakin. The boy looked at him nettled then cast his eyes elsewhere. I seen that there predilection in Simp fer sometime. But aint never seen him give to actin on it. He spat. Guess it were just a matter a time. Don't make it right. This here posse are nothin short of a assemblage a wilddog reprobates. Shoot ye soon as look at ye. He fished in his pocket for a cigarillo then gripped it between his teeth. And what that make me ye might give question? Well. He struck a match on his boot and corralled the flame to the cigar. Guess that would have te make me their equal. Caint deny it. Gotta be some mean son of a bitch te curb this here crew. The boy listened. There was a long silence. Yer kinda quiet aintcha boy? Nothin there criminal in that. Reckon yer smart too. I can see them there cogs clickin away behind them eyes a yers. Defended yerself with agency back there. Somethin righteous prosperin gainst such a miscreant.

The boy stared off ahead and they watched the cobalt lightning tendril across the sky from about ten miles away. Ye got a name boy?

El no tiene, said Tavo. Hasn't spoke a word since we pick him up. Lo llamamos mudo.

Mute ay? I'm guessin that aint no natural disposition fer ye. Probly got good reason fer it. The boy stared on at the sky with its great kerfs of light splitting the angry void and sighting meteoric shapes of distant mountains sketched sable against the vault. Then blackness. You've somethin halfbreed bout ye son. Measure a Cherokee I'll wager. Which a yer folk is the mongrel? The boy ignored him. How's a kid like you fall foul a this pair a pelados? You a runaway?

Hey, que te jodan! said Campa in a drunken torpor.

Well. Queerest bunch a rejects I seen this side a Mexico that's fer sure. Creed spat. Bout as regular as seein a flathead catfish in a juniper tree. The men crowed in their saddles and even Rube declared a gnarly smirk. Yep. Aint nothin queer as folk. Say, that cause me some recollectin a yer kin Lugos.

Thems asleep, said Hite.

Caint see as they'd holler if I recollect the tale to the boy. Creed turned in his saddle slightly to face the boy. Now, this here happenstance occur fore you was born and the desperado plumb centre a the story suffer some coalblack reckoning fer his deeds. This Mexican by name a Murieta speculated himself wild te venture in line a prospectin and jus like all them crazy mining folk he sets off te Californy from Mexico with heedless action. His mind was dead set on stakin a claim in them goldfields but when he find himself in that there country there be a foreign miners tax jus bin passed. Now this here tax requisition foreign folk te pay three dollar a month fer the privilege a cripplin their backs in labourin them mines and Murieta aint no law abidin citizen so he makes it his business te turn a deaf ear. This don't sit right with certain white neighbours a his and since thems none too cordial with the likes a Mexicans they contrive some writ claimin it was illegal fer Mexicans te stake any claim in them parts. Well, that Murieta give it no credence an he jus keep on diggin and them white folk took te fallin in with guns and warnin him off te head south if he don't fall in with the law. And that here writ sets off some vicious fire in that belly a his so he claims action and rustles up a set a mean Mexican miners who've find themselves dispossessed and they take to raidin them goldfields killin white miners and plunderin their gold.

From about a mile ahead they could see fires burning and spalls of flickered light in formation and as the periodic lightning harried the citadel was proselytised in the darkness. Creed went on. Among this band a desperados was his proxy Threefingered Jack and he was some treacherous son of a bitch who'd sooner trade his own mother fer a hunk a gold and Murieta led his retinue on some seditious swell a crime that snatch them above hundred thousand dollar in gold, near hundredhead horses and nineteen dead men in all their maraudin. Now these here Lugo brothers had them cousins a theirs join Murieta and his gang and all their lootin and pilferin and eludin pursuit of them lawdogs fer more than two years, but they find themselves in some filthy scrapes and even lynched some three officers in their agency. Yep. They sure knew how te filibuster them lawmen. But their time came when the governor tendered them Californy Rangers into the mix. It were a messy business when them rangers track em down near Panoche Pass San Benito and they got them some frenzied gunfight on their hands which duly slay Murieta an Threefingered Jack. Some a them lawmen account fer some twisted theory a cleavin off Murieta's head and Jack's hand and picklin them in jars a brandy proovin they butchered them hateful outlaws then settin them exhibits on display back in town like some sideshow attraction an makin some pertty dollar on the side.

Creed flicked the dogend of his cigar out on to the prairie floor with dispatch and it dispersed the red embers abroad on its descent. He looked the boy square in the eye. Where ye think them jars er settin now? Here he gave pause. In some pesky San Francisco saloon is where. Purchased by the owner fer behind that there bar te draw in them pilgrims. And them Lugo cousins were found strung up by their heels from a thirtyfoot bristlecone with them throats cut an their eyes gouged outta their skulls.

IT WAS MIDNIGHT and it had just started to rain as they came upon that vast adobe cantonment and the campfires and torches burnished the loam walls in all its form and a sentry stood aloft in the mud turret clinching his carbine to his chest. As they entered the gates a deputation of riders jostled past close to twentyhead summoned to some chartless territory with all their trappings and armament inveterate. The bivouac within was broad in its construction and a cartel of sutlers barrelled their merchandise with wagon sheets to shelter peltries, serapes and poblanos among other wares. The civilians were miscellaneous and the presidio accommodated four companies both cavalry and infantry and it was said the quartermaster depot was outfitted to supply all other garrisons in New Mexico.

As they rode singlefile through the main plaza the rain was falling harder and a few men were hauling scantling and laying them for walkboards across the yard while a pair of bony curs viciously contested the lumber as if it were something inimical. They saw a small eatinghouse near a well sheltered livery and they dismounted and tethered their horses there for the night and Hite employed the farrier to see to his horse since it had thrown a shoe a couple miles back. The boy was dead on his legs and they all made for the eatinghouse haggard and spent and the streets were silent and empty save for the wagons and rain.

The premises within was strewn with debris from its patrons and their revelry of the day and a thin old man was sweeping the floor at the farthest corner of the bar and he looked up and propped the floorbrush against it when they entered and gestured they seat themselves with welcome. He beckoned to a large woman standing gaping at him dolorouswise from the kitchen and he held up eight fingers to signal the order.

Some minutes later she brought out a large salver of sofky and tortillas sufficient for twelvehead and the old man placed a pitcher of mescal on the table and left them to it. After they had eaten the old man left a sizeable spittoon abreast their table and the partisans gave him a few pieces to settle the account. They sojourned that place wordless and somnolent and at length they returned to the livery frayed by the rain where they would camp for the night in the swath. Some of the retinue divest themselves of their britches and the boy swaddled the serapes given him by the proprietor and set himself under a chipwagon on his pallet where he lay awake for hours turning over in his head devices that beleaguer and he listened to the snuffling of the men and horses and the volley of rain cracking on the tin roof as it punctured the trussing aloft.

THE MORNING BROUGHT forth fresh misadventure and after little sleep the boy was rendered unprepared. Creed and his men had sallied out at first light and when the boy rose from his pallet a gold piece toppled from the serapes. The Mexicans were scurrilous in their action as they hove up their boots and consulted their pistols and as they were seeing to their equipage two officers entered through the livery doors. They were young and taut in their bluecoats with the Mexicans half senseless in their address.

The captain requests the presence of you and your company in his quarters, said one of the corporals while scanning the premises. Directly.

La hostia, said Tavo under his breath.

And the men you rode in with last evening? The Mexicans shook their heads. You can leave your possibles here in the livery. Then he turned his head towards the farrier and gestured his chin at the tenants. You'll keep guard of their horses and such? The farrier nodded in accord.

The rain had resigned itself to the blistering sun and the roofs and peel steamed in its vehicle against a cloudless sky. They walked out on to the main plaza and the flooded streets were being pailed by a group of civilians as the sutlers sold their wares from trundlecarts. Some of the townsfolk peered at them from doorways and veiled windows as if in fear of an incursion and more walkboards were in place across the mud to aid movement for the infantry.

They led them through the broad porticos of the empty stores and saloon and passed the eatinghouse where they had suppered the night before then through to a courtyard where the captain's quarters were. Abreast these quarters was a concealed entrance to a manmade tunnel and the boy catalogued this as they ascended the wide stairs of the lodgings and shuffled along to the end of the long corridor to the captain's office.

The corporal who had addressed them in the livery rapped his knuckle at the door before entering and a voice said for them to come in. The captain sat at a desk poring over correspondence and wrote on undistracted. He clenched a small pipe between his teeth puffing the occasional skein and grunted to himself as he scratched away. His regimentals were flawless and he wore a trim Burnside which favoured his features. He was not old.

By and by he gestured they seat themselves. The boy stood. The captain looked up and surveyed the Mexicans then eyed the boy briefly. He laid down his pen then pushed his chair back and rose and made his way around the front of the desk where he perched himself with his arms folded. He paused for a measure looking at the Mexicans. Gentlemen, he said, I feel as though we are acquainted. What are your names? The Mexicans answered and stared down at their boots. I don't recall your names but I never forget a face. Sergeant. Do you know these men?

The sergeant qualified the men for a moment. No, Sir.

The captain nodded and grunted quietly. Ever find yourselves in Socorro, gentlemen? Or better still conscripted to the Second New Mexico Volunteers? The Mexicans gave no answer. Why, this very year, January in fact, we had a mutiny on our hands. And what transpired was a dispute of remuneration. Now, I personally would not condone the likes of mutiny but owing to the volunteers' pay being bridled would naturally warrant a feud of some scale. Wouldn't you agree, gentlemen? His question still earned him no claim. He took the pipe from his mouth and turned his head towards the window where he took several moments deliberating then communed the pipe to his mouth and toked. I was stationed under Colonel Canby against the Confederate forces at Glorieta Pass, and I don't mind saying gentlemen, what an honour it was serving under him. My sergeant here can testify to that since we both witnessed the retreat of the Confederates after the Union's strategic victory.

At this moment the captain rose and walked over to the window and looked out on to the courtyard where a dog was barking, then proceeded with his left arm folded against his back. And what a victory that was. But as you say you are unfamiliar with the workings of a regiment so I will grant you a summary and perhaps an education on the subject. The mutiny of which I have before mentioned was incited by twenty-eight Hispanos of the Second New Mexico Volunteers. And it was Canby's belief that these men were provoked by Confederate spies whom he feared would carry information regarding our troops to the Texans – or worse still join Sibley's command. Of course this did not transpire since those gutless rejects deserted and fled to the mountains. Most of them were later apprehended by a patrol from Fort Craig. I say most, since there was a handful that got away.

The captain here turned to address the Mexicans with a steely eye. This might be familiar to you. The Mexicans remained mute and the captain turned back to face the window. The Colonel left the fort with a little over a thousand volunteers and regulars including batteries and encamped on the Sapello then on to Bernal Springs. Myself and the sergeant were sent on under Major Chivington with four hundred-odd men towards Glorieta Pass where we halted at midnight at Kozlowski's Ranch. Our objective was to capture or defeat a certain force of the enemy stationed in these parts where they had encamped at the western entrance to Apache Canyon. At two in the morning twenty scouts, myself included, were sent ahead five mile to capture four enemy pickets who were apprehended and brought back to camp. This deprived the Confederates forewarning of our presence in the vicinity and lost them our first battle at Apache Canyon. They had of course expected an easy victory since they had the advantage of two sixpounder cannons, but Chivington outmanoeuvred them with superior numbers and deployed troops either side of the canyon at an elevated range. From this vantage point gentlemen, we could fire down on the enemy artillery which had become ineffective in that terrain. Indeed a decisive blow to the Confederate invasion wouldn't you agree?

The captain paused here for a measure and ordered the corporal to serve water to the company while he refilled the bowl of his pipe with tobacco. The boy watched.

On that day of reckoning gentlemen, four hundred and thirty of Chivington's men deployed a rearguard action to the switchbacks of Glorieta up on to the mesa overlooking the enemy ranch. And Chavez, a lieutenant colonel of the New Mexico Volunteers was to deliver the linchpin of this incursion by informing the major news of his scouts. They had located the Confederate supply train at Johnson's Ranch at which Chavez would harry from the rear while nine hundred Union troops deployed over the Santa Fe Trail. One hour they waited before descending the slope then attacked looted and burned seventy supply wagons containing food, ammunition and medical supplies. With the cannon spiked and ammunition exploded nothing remained save the irons of the wagons. Five hundredhead horses and mules were killed or driven off before we returned to Kozlowski's Ranch and with no supplies to sustain Confederate advance they were forced to retreat to Santa Fe and Texas.

Here, the captain wandered over to the sergeant and whispered something to him at which the sergeant promptly left the room. And that, gentlemen, said the captain, is how a victory is claimed. The Mexicans became uneasy now and before long the sergeant returned with three other corporals who then stood sentry at the office door while the captain seated himself behind the desk. He again addressed the Mexicans.

Being Hispanos yourselves, I wonder if you might know of Manuel Chavez? A lieutenant colonel to you. You may have come across him on your jornadas. Well, he is an exemplary, gentlemen, of whom I am sure you could learn a trick or two. And having now spent a little time in your company I feel sure that you are in fact the spineless escapees of which I speak. This final statement set forth a vicious scuffle among all persons present and Campa tried to escape out the window while Tavo harried at the officers flanked at the door, one of which had to incite a bludgeon.

Apprehend these men, Sergeant. Take them to the cárcel. The captain lit his pipe evenly. Get them out of here!

The room had emptied and all but the captain and the boy were left, save the sergeant who therein stood attending. There was silence for a time and the boy looked on while the captain referred briefly to the letters on the desk. Outside there was a gnarled cry from the dog in the courtyard then a harrowed yelp which caused the sergeant to contest from the window.

What is it, Sergeant?

I'm guessing a snake, Sir. That dog's been sniffing at the tunnel entrance again.

The infestation needs to be dealt with, Sergeant. Can't afford losses in the infantry can we? An ireful cur is one thing but the men are indispensable. See that it's handled properly hereafter, Sergeant.

Captain.

The captain bent his head back down to the letters then looked up and qualified the boy. What happened to you son? The boy stood silent. You may speak freely here. You are in very different company now, is he not, Sergeant? The boy stared down at the floor. I assume you were heckled into coming here. And no doubt for a hefty remunerate. Am I right? The boy nodded. Mm. What we're dealing with here is a couple of degenerates. And where did they acquire you son? It's important I know the details.

Near Santa Fe, sir.

Santa Fe aye? Is that where your folks reside?

The boy's eyes became moist as he turned his gaze back to the floor.

I see. Was it indians?

Yes, Sir.

The captain shook his head and seemed made sad by the boy's answer. Well, you need not concern yourself of your safety here. And you're certainly not the sort to fall concomitant to a heathen horde like the men you rode in here with last evening. By God their kind propagate like rabbits let me tell you. I will personally see to it that you are given an outfit, provisions and board.

An outfit, sir?

Why, yes. Consider it a privilege to be instrument to the Union infantry son.

The boy was puzzled by this and cast his eyes away.

Why anyone would think you were offended by the offer. The boy glanced at the sergeant, then to the captain and back down at the floor. How old are you son?

Near thirteen, sir.

A promising age to join our cause for president and country. Why, I was your age when I signed up. What do you say son? Are you willing to spearhead the fight against those heathen cutthroats? To avenge your folk. The captain looked on with a grin. The boy gave a wordless nod. Sergeant, sign this boy up. And take him to the cantina for a little mess. He would benefit from some additional flesh on those bones.

MENNONITE MILE

THE TIMBER HUT was candlelit and sparse within and when he moved from the desk the flames pitched and leaned then righted themselves. That night the wind moaned in the stovepipe while lightning flared in the north and no rain came until firstlight. The breach in the door intruded squally from without and leavened the embers in the firehole to lurch and strain and he bridled the crack with a buffalo pelt his father had slain the year eighteen and ninety. He watched the flame of the candle for a time and the wax pool on to the oak surface and the stern portraits of his forebears looked out from the lumber facade on to that solitary room and as he fixed on their faces he considered what form of reasoning shifted through their minds at the moment of rendering.

Out on that terra damnata before dusk he had stood and qualified the vast ocean from the bluff and the waves drew brutal kerfs of white spume as they rolled inland with impunity and the pumice wind gnawed at the bone and skin like rangy death rodents and the steel sun fused through the cloudsprent sky while tiny sanderlings skittered along the brackish shoreline. A gibbous moon hung high in that void and he knew a storm was coming.

He rose from the desk and laboured toward the door moved the pelt aside with his boot then opened the door. A revolt of wind snuffed the candles out then cuffed him as he stepped outside. He waded out yonder toward the fell and steadied himself against the stone coping took the pail and set it down into the well, hauled it up then took it inside. The only light now within was firelight so he tendered a flame to the candles with a brand from the fire. He took the gourd from the bucket and filled the brass kettle with water then set it firm in the flames. He sat studying the embers. That morning he had buried the corpse of his father out in the scrubland. Took him above two hours to dig that grave and the wind was swelling even then. A lone buzzard hovered aloft watching like some stubborn cloud then dove in for forage as soon as his back was turned. The day before he had fashioned a coffin from remnants of timber, lay his father in his best suit then sealed the lid shut and that same night was spent in morbid wake in the silence of death's presence and he irked to recall some scriptural verse to quiet his mind which had been learned by rote some years before.

Nothing came.

Humble words of eulogy were tendered at the foot of that grave and a grey wolf watched on from a crag aloft while he gathered and set about a formation of stones for a cairn to chronicle the burial. With his father in the earth and the wind howling at the door he felt the outset of loneliness take hold and as he stared into the flames he drew solemn on his tobacco and set his mind at prior days of mirth.

HE WAS SECOND BORN of four and in him a soul prevising to liberate itself. He came into this world amid the heat and grit of alien territory where his folk had settled among Mennonite. Born to colony life. Roots he would drug up in adolescence and leave behind for good. The Missouri River his home. His folk sworn to refuse both social and military service. Forbidden fruit he would later sample.

The gebet dominated the day after he had laboured the fields and livestock and the minister led the congregation on to some deific plain with pious hymn and sacred augury of men now lost, and through his laconic sermon he aimed to attest the meaning and purpose of their lives into sharp focus as they kneeled reverently with bowed head before God. And as the child watched on in question his mind strayed to a world beyond the doctrines of the elders and boundaries of the colony.

The farm was upriver and forty-five mile north a dam and spillway had been built on the James River and it was knowledge of this that taunted the boy. His day commenced in the blazing heat and at nine years of age he was sent to a neighbouring farm to help break the virgin prairie frontier. He rode out on to the brush after communal breakfast and ministered prayer and passed the chapel and school where ancient verse and strange tongue emulated. He stood his horse a while to regard his father and brother grind wheat into flour in that structure of white pestle while the hatches waded and moiled and his mother and sisters waved on from their chores. In the trace his horse threw a shoe and farmer Irwin took time out of his day to teach the boy proper farriering and with the hoofpick the boy cleaned out debris from the underside of the hoof then tested the nails in the shoe before hammering it on. Irwin fit the shoe to the hoof and let Jacob tap the nails into former holes. He showed him the use of the cinchblock to tighten the shoe to hoof and pry the nail with nippers and crook the heads with a clincher and they repeated the process until it had branded finite in his mind.

His day was long in that sultry sun where man and beast were pushed beyond their limits hoeing down with a team of horses and their walkingplows in tow, and his wages were scant and he begrudged turning his laboured cent over to the colony and returning there after his absence. On that day and many following he spent the night at the farm and lay out in the night sky watching the Pleiades arc the empty black void with the moon burning some great white hole of coruscation and earlier he joined the fieldhands in forging some towering bonfire with the midden and they sat and regarded the flames spitting and lurching like some tormented viper with its splinters lofting up into the darkness. They warmed their mess on the embers and Kinter took to regaling a tune on the fiddle while they ate and drank and smoked and Jacob squailed at the pyre with loose stobs and the coyotes related with their yammering. When morning came their heads were bedevilled and sotol bitten yet their day commenced as before and they hove forth on to that parched environ drudging their way through the hours of heat and mud and sweat.

When he rode in one evening after his labour the boy

Jude had preceded him in the stable. He had not seen him on first entering for his mind was fixed on dismounting and uncinching the horse and just as he was about to stand in his stirrup he felt a harsh jerk on the back of his shirt which was ripped in two as he hit the ground. The horse shied and scuffed with the boy's left foot mired still in the stirrup and had the trailing reins snagged about his left arm.

Best you be stayin put in that there dirt, Jude said, else I be kickin you down with my boot.

Jacob lifted his face from the loam and regarded him with animus.

What in hell ye do that for?

Do I gotta have reason?

With me ye has. Dont care who ye pa is.

Jude was the son of the elder Hofer and was burly in frame and manner with a broad scar lashed across his chin which he'd acquired from the buckle of his father's belt for cussing and spitting in his face.

My pa says you aint fit to be part a this here colony on account a you bein stray in the head.

What?

You heard. Stray in the head. That mean somethin aint workin right upstairs.

I know what it mean asshat.

The contempt in his face was malign and berate and he sat up unwound the reins from his arm picked himself up off the floor and brushed down his trousers. He took hold of the reins and tied them to the hitching rail then swung round with his right arm outstretched and whacked Jude's cheekbone hard with his balled fist. Jude dropped to the ground with a thud and he was rolling about like some trammelled pig squealing and yipping with both hands pressed to his face with his knees bent up toward his chest.

You'll pay for that, he said as he rose from the dust and within a split second he had propelled himself forward and hauled his heavy frame at Jacob and they both hit the ground like some weighted gunny of grain. Jacob gasped violently and was winded and he lay there for a few moments watching the dust settle as he drew breath. Jude had rebound off him and was lain face down in the arid mud choking and whooping and by and by Jacob hove up and was lurching toward him then threw himself headlong at Jude's limbs where for a time they slogged and grappled and Jacob pinned him to the floor as he commenced to shove handfuls of dirt into his mouth. A cloud of dust was pensile amid thrashing limbs and malicious yammering and barking as the ruckus commenced and before long Jacob's father entered the stable to separate the two boys from the contention.

What in hell is goin on here?

But Jacob was still trying to get at Jude and it was all Joseph could do to hold his son back for he was slugging about like some halfbroken colt with his face hot and ferric and his gaze morose.

I said whats all this then? Is you two fixin to get yerselves flogged or somethin? Yous know you caint behave in this here manner. Why some curious punishment will incur an you know it.

Please dont be tellin my pa nothin sir. I caint be takin no further beatin.

Now Jude I aint sayin Im goin to them elders just yet but what I is suggestin is that we rectify this here matter right here and now between three of us. Otherwise I be forced to take it to your pa understood? Now whats gone on? Jacob?

He done pull me from my horse soon as I come in here and fore I can even hitch off the saddle then he took to callin me names sir. Said I was stray in the head.

Did he now. An what you got to say bout this here accusation Jude? You done this? You pull him clean off his horse unawares?

Jude was sniffling and bawling by this point and he was stood with one shoe discalced since it had dislodged itself in the fray. Yessir, he said. Aint meanin nothin by it. Thems the truth. I just repeatin what my pa done said is all.

Well Im sure your pa aint meanin for you to set upon no one on their horse now is he? Im thinkin that there's your idea. I right?

Yessir.

Furthermore your pa should know better than to be inventin tall tales bout folk here in the colony. True or not. That done make him no betteren some churlish adolescent himself. What you fixin to say bout that? You think he be settin good example? Christian like?

No sir.

No sir he aint. Now Jude, I seen you apply that there irritation a yours on more than three occasion an Im guessin your pa either aint seen it or he be turnin a blind eye to it an you know it aint right to be tormentin them thats younger an you. Nor any folk for that matter. So what you say we settle this here scrap by yous apologisin to Jacob? But Im wantin some straight leanin oath from you indicatin yous gone halt that there hectorin. Else I be havin words with your pa. Ye hear?

Yessir. Sorry sir.

Not to me damn it. Hims who you been takin issue with. Well go on.

Sorry Jacob.

And.

I swears I wont be provokin no other a no kind from this here day.

Right then. Now y'all shake hands an be done with it.

The boys shook hands but with a measure of loathness on Jacob's part then Jude stood and stared at the ground.

Next time I sees you baitin them there bairn you is fixin to have some mighty reckonin. An not just from me. An I get to feelin you aint much enchanted with the idea a your pa payin his wrath neither. So best you pay heed boy cause I aint the sort to go back on my word. Now you go on then.

Yessir.

And that boy Jude scanned his inordinate gaze across the dirt to seek out his shoe and he slunk forth with the impact of some idle sloth picked up his shoe turned back to regard Joseph shamefaced and cowed then sauntered out into the yard. Jacob was mute and walked over to his horse to uncinch the saddle and as he loosened the girthstraps his torn shirt parted and raw scars were visible in their nefarious state of aggravation. His father measured the roiled facet jarred and uneasy and he took his son by the arm to face him then held him by the shoulders with both hands. Jacob could no more than look him straight in the eye so he stared down at his father's worn shoes.

Who done this to you boy?

He gave no answer.

Look at me son. Who done this?

Jacob stared into the black of his father's eyes and he bore down a whole spate of emotion and it circumscribed about him with such retribution he could not utter a word.

You know you can tell me any damn thing. I aint gone punish you none.

There was a heavy silence. The horse whinnied.

Was it one a them fieldhands at Irwins farm?

The boy nodded it wasn't.

Them lashes look fresh as primed meat son an Im thinkin that there violence can only be inflicted by one other individual. An it aint your kin.

The boy was at essay with himself to preserve his silence then he could feel his eyes filling up and the tears emerged and made a trace down one side of his mud peppered face.

His father qualified the wounds with circumspection and a storm was foraging across his every feature with the ferocity of some nebulous spectre and he dropped down to one knee to address his son with absolute amenity.

Now you dont have to say nothin. You just nod ye hear?

The boy nodded in agreement.

Now Im guessin he give you some coal black warnin not to say nothin. I right?

Jacob nodded.

Judgin by them scars look like some a them aint so fresh as others. How long this here been goin on boy? Weeks?

He nodded no.

Months?

He nodded and began to weep.

That son of a bitch. Now I know clear as shit it were Baurock but you never spoke nothin to me bout who the culprit were ye hear? You aint said a word. An you dont need to of neither. An that alright. I might be slow as a turtle some but what I aint is stupid.

What you gone do Pa? If he find out I done told you he gone kill me.

No. You aint told me nothin son. You never utter his name. Dont you worry none. I gone see to it he caint set on his haunches for week.

Joseph rose from his knee and set out across the yard with asperity branded athwart his face and he charged towards the house in a fit of mania and tore through the chicken coop like some malefic cyclone and the fowl strew their plumage and evicted their stations in a throe of panic as he commenced forth toward the adobe hut and Jacob was hollering after him like some goading drover beset by an impending crag and he could no more stop him than any man can the unruly tide. Jacob's mother was now stood in the doorway regarding the commotion with question and she was calling out to attain reason while her offspring convoked and glared in bewilderment yet no account was cited and deaf to it all Joseph took up the rifle and shucked it back and the spent shells discharged to the ground then he levered in a fresh round and sallied out toward the hearth of Baurock propulsive in enterprise. By this point the colony citizens were eluded by the logic of the business and were trailing behind him like he was the Hamelin gambit himself and they were alarmed by the sight of the firearm since any such munitions were prohibited and usurped due to settlement rule.

He approached the portico at the front of the property and hove up the steps to the door and with the butt of the rifle forced entry without so much as a knock and as he cocked the rifle Baurock was stood rigid and aghast scripture in hand and Joseph measured him feralwise with his gaze and he launched forth charging Baurock rearward into a corner and Baurock in his paltry state stepped back and had his spine pressed to the wall then recoiled his tall frame to the floorboards his hands uplifted to fend off the revenant before him. What in God's name has possessed you to this fiendish state? Baurock said in his temporal air of grievance. Am I not brethren to you? Tell me instantly what it is I have done in offense. For God is my witness I've done naught to smite the Joseph Stahl.

Joseph glared baleful at the minister and sweat was beading at his forehead and a motley of acolyte faces peered in through the windows without as they awaited some inimical explication. He aimed the barrel of the rifle at Baurock's head and exhaled deeply through his nose and qualified him with halberd eye then said, I gone ask you one time to bring that there quirt a yours you so attach to so as all folk here can survey the piece for emselves.

Baurock was mute.

Joseph raised the rifle and fired up into the scantling and the explosion clove sherds of wood which fell upon the boards like pinnate and the crowd jounced and gasped with harrowed faces then he deployed the rifle back at Baurock's head.

You git, he said, else I gone shoot somethin you caint be without.

SAMUEL CRUITE

HE IS BORN the year eighteen and forty-two behind a tavern in a dark street where rodents and mangy curs scratch and forage the dank corners. Where senseless brawls take place with fist or broken glass and inept fornication be it day, night, anted or filched. Mother scarcely fourteen and innocent of the crimes attended her some eight months prior where someplace between Contention and Benson a gang of outlaws applied themselves to her with mindless violence. Now ignorant to which of the culprits' deed had altered her predicament, she screams her final breath giving birth to the boy as the Hunter stove, who would in turn carry away her soul into that hollow void. Yet he would take his first of sultry air in the sullied dirt and afterbirth of the woman he would never know.

When they found him he was still as stone and dead so they thought until he finally remit a sigh. His tiny spiderlike limbs folded like a Slipjoint. That pious woman who came upon them searched the dead girl's body to identify her finding all she possessed was a sealed letter and gold pocketwatch. It was by irregular means his name came to him taken from the addressee of said letter, knowing not how to signify the person there written be it brother, father, sweetheart or the like. Yet Samuel Cruite was the name he bore and many a solitary migrant would come to know him. He is neither for nor against the world he entered and could put his skilled hand to many a sullen trade. At twelve he is taken on to work the cable ferry on a tributary of the Columbia River where his folk run a supply store miles from any neighbouring town, and its patrons are varied in kind – drovers herders settlers thieves bounty hunters and Paiute – and seldom did they pass without incident.

THE TRADINGPOST was nestled in the sod by the river and a deep wood of spruce and oak stretched beyond with miles of plain superseding it. A trail of oblique smoke was rising from the chase and clearly visible to the vagrants journeying the traces. Hissing in the wind were the tall trees shedding their russet leaves that lay like skin upon the river, shifting docile like some murmuration. Now a man of nineteen, Cruite could work the ferry blindfold and that day he hauled his return while the store's dog commenced its usual craze of skittering to and fro the bank in the long river grass, contesting the landing of the vehicle it couldn't get at. A posse of seven rode in as he came ashore and he watched them hitch down stiffly one by one and tether their horses at the hitchingrail. One of the men had an eyepatch at his left eye and a scar rightside of his mouth as if a blade had ripped right through it. He wore a torn oilcloth slicker which looked like it had seen better days and a queer plughat of black felt upon his head. Four of the men hailed up to the tradingpost door while the other two kept with the horses and the man aforementioned sat smoking. Cruite tethered the dog to a small hitchrail which stood aside from the horses by the river, and the dog was growling and baring its teeth at the strangers yonder before Cruite commenced rearside into the store.

Within was a strong smell of coffee and timber and a small fire burned in the hearth, and the stock of merchandise was various to the left where stood a small rail of used apparel with a shelf of folded blankets overhead. From the scantling hung a miscellany of hides and pelts, with a passel of tobacco, dried peppers and a peculiar garni of herbs. At a table in the corner three of the men sat hunkered over their sofky and the fourth sauntered about the place without expression. As Cruite entered through the kitchen at the rear where his folk laboured the fourth man hailed up at the counter and rapped his knuckle sharply on the surface.

Caint a man get a sup a water out here? he said.

The proprietor gave a nod at Cruite then he took up his post at the counter under his father's charge. He chins a nod at the location of the bucket and the man followed him to where it stood.

This here fresh water aint it? Cos I aint drinkin no rancid sup none if some rodent done gone bout its business side it.

The three men chuckled from across the room.

Yessir, said Cruite.

Yessir what?

Proprietor done haul it up from the well just fore you ride in.

Well that's right fine.

He took up the gourd and dipped it into the bucket with his eye fixed on Cruite then took it to his mouth and drank. The dog was baying some outside and the man eyed him sideways to qualify his bearing and though Cruite was afraid for the dog outside, he showed little by way of it to the man.

Reckon I'll take some a that mess ye got outback. Water done give me a appetite.

They stood surveying each other.

Well go on boy. Where you at? Dont jus stand there gawkin.

One of the men called out from the table. Leave him be, Nelson. He aint worth nothin.

Scoot goddammit! then he flapped his glove idly at him.

He headed back into the kitchen and doled him out a hearty portion, yet all the while the dog was yelping and snarling without. And it crossed his mind to defile the mess some but he let the thought just come and go. He brought out the serving to him and he was now seated at the table and as he turned to leave his bidding Nelson gripped hold of his wrist to halt his progress.

Well thanky kindly son.

He consulted him with a malign look and Cruite stared him out stubbornwise in return. That there dog a yers is jus fine. You leave him be now ye hear.

He watched him move his right hand to his holster and his forefinger was tapping steadily at the grip. Nelson glared at him and sucked his teeth.

Aint nothin more hopeless than a man without a gun, he said. Nor scary neither.

He tried to pull his arm loose but Nelson's grip was rigid

like a ligature. There was a commotion gaining outside and the dog was yelping hard and woundedly so Cruite started toward the door. Nelson drew his pistol and cocked the hammer. Now you hold on there son. I dont rightly recall I give you leave. Make no sense none in you strugglin neither cos that aint gone make life none the easier for ye. Ned jus playin some out yonder is all, an it aint advisable for you to go disturbin a man in his progress. Expect yer pa done told you that.

He watched Cruite shift his eyes to the pistol held steady in his hand. I seen you regard this here piece a mine. Caint deny it. You want familiarise yerself with it?

The other three men at the table slowly consulted their pistols and targeted a look of reprisal at Cruite, but Cruite stood his ground solemn and stalwart.

Whats yer name boy?

Cruite. Samuel Cruite.

Well, Cruite, some men are rightly or wrongly at odds with hisself, an Ned jus such a man. He contest ever livin creature that walk this earth aside them that service him ye foller. Other month, he done shoot a sidewinder clean in half some two hundred yard from a ridge. From my recollecting, that there sun was right in his line a vision. That aint all. He done beat a man senseless for conversin with him uninvited. Way his mind ponder the like, he can sniff out meanness from lowliest a creatures. Me on other hand I dont waste no time on the weighing. I jus shoot damn creature cold. Rightly man or beast. Make no odds to me. Now, what you say you git on with yer business an permit Ned hims amusement, an we all jus sit nice an respectable like the gentlemen we are.

Cruite yanked his arm free. Im goin on out there fore that friend a yours gone do that dog some damage.

The chairs scraped back along the pine floor and the three other men drew and cocked their pistols fast then they all stood deadlocked waiting for someone to move. The dog was yammering a whole spate of distress out in the yard and the horses were rearing and squealing and jerking at the trailing reins at the rail. There was a shot fired and Cruite started for the door. Out in the dust yard he saw the man Ned aiming his .45 at the dog and that man had black vengeance in his eyes and from what he could figure a shot had been fired mindlessly into the air. Ned seemed as fixed as any man with a grudge to kill the first thing that moved in his eyeline and the dog was trembling and quiet as the firmament. The man with the eyepatch rose slowly to his feet, took his .38 from the holster thumbed the hammer back and aimed fast at his partisan.

You shoot that dog Ned and I'll fuckin open up your head.

Ned's eyes were stark and livid and had the bearing of someone in a crazed predicament like he was grappling with voices within, or as if he'd forsworn some augural oath to a merciless spectral fiend. Beads of sweat were forming at his brow and his eyes were filling to burst but the remorse he felt was not for the thinking of the deed but for the knowing not how to avoid it. The proprietor edged from the rear of the store with his old carbine at his shoulder and he gave warning to the crazed man to relinquish his weapon and go quietly on his way. Nothing moved.

Cruite communicated a nod for his pa to move out of Ned's range so he lowered the rifle and slowly backed up behind the store, and looking upon that scene was as if some volatile Ginn had swept through with its thousand tongues and transformed every element and corporeal to ore. The man Ned was weighing his next gambit while tears streaked his face and the hand that gripped the .45 was laden and trembling like he'd been holding it for an age. I aint goin back, he yelled. Caint suffer that there confined cantonment again. Ye hear me Floyd. I aint. Dont you make me.

Well you dont got to.

But I aint doin it.

I hear you.

If he'd a mind to, I reckon a man can damn hang by his heels for weeks than suffer them voices or seein them contorted apparitions fore his rancid eye. Caint go back, Floyd.

I dont see that you would.

You dont know shit Floyd. Nor neither y'all. You try spendin time side this here stray head a mine or in that portion a black hell back in Taos with them attendants, then y'all can damn apply yer reckonin.

He was waving and flapping his gun about with no mind as he spoke then pointed it at each man present in turn, starting with Floyd. You. I'll bet them boys a yers would contest none to ridin me back to New Mexico click of a damn Colt Dragoon. Yep. An they be drinkin they brains out to mark damn occasion jus fer hell of it.

That aint true now.

An you, Nelson. You be laughin in yer boots they got me strung up like some hobbled mount in that godforsaken hole.

Now, Ned. You know I do nothin a sort.

You just shut yer piehole.

He hissed at him and strings of nasal mucus were hanging from his lip and he wiped it clean with his shirt sleeve then he was babbling and wheezing like some half mad hermit too long in solitude. Boot wearer only know where it pinch, he rasped.

What you say Ned?

Nothin.

He dropped to the dirt and sat rocking back and forth humming some plaintive riddle he'd heard back at that primitive purgatory of a keep for those of his kind and he was stroking his Colt Walker like it was plated in gold.

You want me to shine that there piece a yours how you like it? Floyd said, with his .38 still aimed fast at Ned, but the halfwit paid him no heed and he commenced to finger the Colt in his hand. Then he whispered. Had me that same twisted portents last night, Floyd.

That aint no portents son. Just some bad dream.

Ye know the one. Where I seen that poor kid I shoot in that mine while back. Well he jus keep comin at me an tellin me everthin gone be jus fine, then he start ballin an his tears aint natural like us folk, they black like ink an he reach to take my hand an I go to take it but then everthin go dark like I gone blind or somethin, an I is feelin about in some fevered panic not knowin where I was at. Then I hear some vicious cur growlin in the blackness an it drawin closer but I caint see it none an I got nothin to fend it off with but my bare hands.

He drew his pistol and aimed straight at the dog.

Jus like this one.

Dont you fuckin do it boy. Thats my final warnin.

Why d'you suppose a wretch like me been dealt this hand? God's choosin ye think fer me to suffer fool's torment? Reckon I done somethin awful bad to warrant such a punishment.

Dont rightly know son. But we all got grievance, one way or other. Now, you put away your pistol an we can be on our way.

On our way where? I aint goin to Taos, he screamed.

We headin toward Texas. You recall?

Texas?

That's right. We done talk about it last night. Aint we men.

No one spoke.

We gone see them dancin girls again? An that green eyed peach of a whore?

Whatever you want Ned. We can drink some at that dramhouse, jus come away now.

You tryin to trick me you son of a bitch.

Ned. Throw your fuckin gun to the dirt you hear.

Turmoil was stark upon Ned's face and he was hitting his head with his balled fist and moaning like some injured animal.

It done plague me somethin cruel that malignant spirit. I got shoot that damn dog then that fiend'll leave me be. Dont y'all see it make sense? I gone do it.

He rose up from the dirt aimed and fired at the dog but hit the ground before it. Another shot followed and drove straight through the back of Ned's head and out through his left eye.

HE IS OLDER NOW and with that quarter century comes wisdom and a man can choose his path be it in the agency of destruction or progress, and he weighs the sense and reason of it all and those small minds of man that seek trappings that draw in citizenry which lead them like sheep to barren cliffs then headlong to the valley floor. And he has made his peace with God and man like someone who has seen darkness in all its guises and in the workings of his mind where man is tested he sharpens objectivity as time would bone palings. He sees portents like other men would opportunity clearing the trail ahead of what's to come and in that unknown future he commences staidlike gathering shrewdness of unwritten rule.

His folk have long passed on and he has never yet seen a burning sun set behind the rim of a vast body of water deep and fierce in its wake, nor the great workings of ships upon it or majestic vessels of old that harrow through latitudes of oceans and perilous storms. And out there beyond the tradingpost the scalloped canyons and huge basalt turrets that stand virtuous as appointed bishops, nor the endless swales of grass on the prairie with antelope wheeling or stampeding buffalo, and in him now is an appetite burgeoning to qualify that which exists far beyond any border imaginable and he ponders it often among the meagre minutes of his perennial laboured day.

TO THE EAST, sourceless lightning flashed and a deep rumble followed shortly after. The wind was picking up and spitting detritus from the spruce grove onto the dust yard and the coyote laboured off the terrain with their howling while the horses shifted and stamped in the livery. A solitary buzzard was carried steep and flightless in the arid heat in strange postures of motile fugue. Two men stole in from the traces and they were stooped over in their saddles swathed in ragged slickers with neckerchiefs at their mouths to fend off grit and their hats tilted low over their eyes. The third horse trailing behind carried an embalmed body slumped corpulent across the saddle. They dismounted and recruited their horses into the livery with the clank of their gear ensuing.

Inside the tradingpost in a dark corner sat a Paiute at a table smoking a calumet reading a wanted sign tacked to the boards. It was a dark portrayal of two outlaws named Tom Floyd and Jim Nelson who were known Indian scouts in the territory and it was told their reputation preceded them as far south as Fort Summer. Cruite qualified the two men riding in as he towelled at some glasses then he poured himself a whiskey and one for the Paiute. We got company, he said. The wind harried without and groaned through a section of the chase while Cruite stoked the fire in the hearth. The door swung open and the men hobbled in like a couple of castaways from some alien terrain and their eyes were bloodshot and redrimmed with hourless sleep and they slunk forth to the nearest table and sat down. One of the men regarded the Paiute on the other side of the room and spat. Storms comin, he said, and glared. Cruite eyed the men from the hearth and recognised them instantly then rose and dusted off his hands.

What'll it be gentlemen?

Whiskey, said one. He removed his hat and placed it on the table in front of him then fingered the eyepatch at his left eye. Better make that the bottle and two glasses barkeep.

The other man turned his head and squinted then measured Cruite the whole time it took for him to oversee the order. He approached the table with the tray of drinks and put the whiskey and glasses on the surface then looked at the men.

I'll be takin your pieces gents while you're in this here store.

The men looked at each other then unholstered their pistols and lay them on the tray Cruite was holding.

I'll have me a passel a that bacca you got yonder, said the other as he stared fast and hard at Cruite.

Can I get you men some hot mess outback? Got hardtack to go with it. Might fill your boots if y'all got a ways to go through the night.

Reckon I'll have me some a that, said Floyd.

Best give me a portion a that too. I aint had nothin since sunup.

Cruite settled the pistols behind the counter and went into the kitchen and doled out two portions then put the hardtack on a plate of unfired clay. He put the mess on a tray and took it through to the counter then unhooked a passel of tobacco. He attended the food to the men and tucked the empty tray under his left arm then commenced to pitch a couple of boles on the embers.

Speakin a which, said Floyd, we aim to sleep out yonder with them horses if you'll permit? Caint see as that storm gone quit fore daybreak. Aint no peach of a night for ridin that for sure.

Got no quarrel with that mister, just long as you can curb ye smokin out in the barn. Cost you dollar a piece for the night.

Nelson was shovelling the sofky into his mouth and all the while he was surveying the Paiute with a deviant eye.

If you dont mind me askin, said Cruite, what you aim to do with that there comrade a yours? Might unsettle them horses some.

Well, said Nelson picking his teeth, we most likely gone bury him out in that there grove a trees somewheres.

I wouldn't recommend it. That grove harbours wolves and bear an the like. Be no time fore them beasts sniff out a fresh corpse in the ground.

Do I knows you mister? Nelson regarded him asquint with both eyes. Been sittin here tryin an failin I might add to recollect where I seen that mug a yers. You done time in Santa Fe?

No I aint mister. Point of fact it was right here in this here store.

Nelson frowned. Then his face lent turn to acknowledgement. Well if it aint Samuel Cruite. I know I knowed ye someplace. This here all ye got to show fer twenty some years? Man go crazy haltin out same place hims whole life. Rather shoot myself in the foot.

Aint that the truth mister. Dont aim to die here. Reckon you fellers taken in some mileage.

That we have, said Floyd looking over at the Paiute. Who's your friend in the corner?

That there's Milton.

Milton?

The Paiute sat unmoved blowing plumes out of fissures like some great Aztec mould.

Fact of matter is I never known his Paiute name.

Paiute ha?

Some years back he fell upon some dyin pastor comin up the switchbacks at Wolf Creek, an that pastor dealt him some irregular request to trade a piece of literature all way from England for a smoke. Fair trade for a dyin man. So they did just that an he read him a few stanzas from them pages an the pastor died smokin the pipe an Milton walk away with copy of Paradise Lost. He was so taken with the content therein, he adopt hisself the author's name. I wager he could recite whats chronicled entire, but he hindered some on account of him bein without his tongue. He carry that book everwhere he go so as to convey his name to strangers.

Well aint that the brittle shits, said Nelson.

The room fell silent and they each eyed the other with misgiving. The Paiute didn't move an eyeball. You gents be welcome to put that shovel to good use. It just out yonder.

That's a peach of an idea. Where you suggest we be putting old Gus to rest then if not the grove? Im guessin he be none too pleased his remains become carrion for beasts an such.

There's a patch a land behind the barn suitable for the task, but you best get to work soon afore storm hit an it get too dark to see your damn hand in front a you. You folk go on an eat while I see to them horses then I'll be rootin out them shovels.

Go easy with that there bay mare mister. She a pinch frisky.

He commenced forth out into the dry storm toward the livery and it was stirring up merry hell with the barn door pummelling against the scantling like it was contesting its station. The horses within were stamping and roaring and were far off being easily settled and it was a while before they could be provisioned and sated with the wind harrying and rousing like some escapee varmint. The rank odour of the corpse was prevalent and seeping something foul through the hessian serape and he jostled it with his foot to measure the weight of the man invalidate and decaying within. It was plain to see he was a bulk of a man that would need no less than two men to vehicle to its interment.

In the store some extemporary deed was commencing and the partisans were eyeing Milton with nothing less than guile. You smell that? said Nelson. Smell like somethin died.

They guffawed hard as they rose from the table and sallied forth toward the counter. Floyd sought out their pistols while Nelson surveyed the wares for an implement of his devising. That son of a bitch done shucked our pieces, said Floyd. Fuckin jackass. Must be some damn shells stored up round here somewheres.

Nelson attained a sixty-foot lasso which was hanging from some iron hooks, unsnarled it from where he stood then hurled one end over the crosspiece. He fashioned a loop at the other and all the while he was conveying an aslant grin toward the Paiute. Floyd reloaded their pistols and chucked one at Nelson. They reholstered and he regarded the Paiute with his black eye and stood like some querent before a chantry. Don't you worry none, he said. We aint gone shoot you. Not yet anyways.

They proceeded to cackle pernicious in manner while Nelson fashioned something resembling a pulley and the execution of this grievous manoeuvre gave the Paiute no pause as to the ruse doubtless intended for his demise. He just sat solemn in demeanour as if to qualify the embers of a fire.

Aint you gone grunt nor move or nothin? said Nelson to the man before them. I seen more action in a damn crag or tombstone.

The Paiute turned his head, looked him in the eye, blinked then resumed his posture. Well this gone make it hell of a lot easier for us if you aint gone fight none. Damn sight more amenable than pissin straight after a bladder full. Aint that right, Floyd?

Nelson proceeded to hook the readymade loop over the Paiute's head and as he commenced to gibbet Milton pulled a Bowie swiftlike from his left boot and stabbed him in the chest. Floyd drew his pistol and shot the Paiute in the leg and he keeled over and dropped to the floor with his hands cupped to stanch the arterial blood spurting acute in every direction.

You fuckin redskin. I was savin the damn shootin till we had you hoist up in that there noose. Oh but don't you be thinkin I aint gone lynch that sorry ass a yours none. You gone suffer some demise you caint even imagine for bushwhackin this here partner a mine. It gone be a hangin fit for a lowlife son of a whore Gentile as you rightly is. Fact, you gone be beggin for damn retribution to halt desperatelike I swear it.

Floyd yanked the rope tight about his neck and proceeded to drag the Paiute across the floor to a chair to have him stand on and with a definition untamed he said: You'll pardon me for not conversin with ye prior but there aint gone be no counsel sought for your black ass. Not today. Not ever. The day of reckonin has come just as it had for them countless souls I done kill in the name a justice or of that which is writ. Never can true reconcilement grow where wounds of deadly hate have pierced so deep, he recited, and Milton looked upon him in defined horror as his hector echoed the article itself that was etched within his memory, and he feared that which may have blinded him or any man that has made an occupation of revenge his idol, yet he didn't struggle.

Get up on that fuckin chair fore I dispatch a bullet through your eye. And the Paiute did so without protest. Now it gone be less than no time fore I incite that heathen soul a yours to hell an I take that which is mine a your pitiful scalp then I gone hack them limbs a yours to disjecta membra an cast them about for carrion ye hear.

Floyd hauled the rope with action beyond all reprieve then tied it to a lintel and jolted the chair out from underneath him and the Paiute Milton hung pendant and choking with his feet jostling like some thwarted Medusa and that scene entire was akin to an Attic tragedy to any spectator or witness to behold. A shot came from without and its inimical terminus clove through the spine of the outlaw incensed and a great vomit of blood exited his mouth as he turned and fired his weapon at its genesis. With his father's old carbine at his shoulder, Samuel Cruite stood austere in the dark and he charged forth with a bullet in his left shoulder and his reprisal came like death itself would come at dead of night; silent and wholly unforeseen. He shucked the rifle and consulted the man before him in a spate of blood and confusion then shot him clean through the head before he aimed and fired at the rope fixed about the crosspiece and Milton fell free to the ground clawing at the ligature about his throat. And that night they buried the three corpses in the grove and no mention of that happening was ever again spoken, neither did they exact said reward.

THE MAN WHO

HE LAY FLAT on his belly on the ground cocked rifle in hand with the forestock resting upon his fist, his face against the cheekpiece. He reckoned the course of the wind and reckoned against the glare of the sun abreast the foresight and waited. He had a clear shot of the beast but measured the exact moment to fire. It was immobile entire but for the shift of its eyes that blinked. Its widespread antlers arcuated regal. He inhaled long, held the rifle fast and barely touched off the piece. The shot ploughed into the emptiness and the smoke ambled away. It was faultless. The shell pierced its rump rightside but didn't falter just scampered off into the hemlock. He followed the blood trail through a deep forest which led him to a creek where the trail was lost, crossed it and picked up a faint trace again on the other side. They traversed low along the valley wall where several waterfalls nested in a thin forest of larch and the redness of the morning sun hit the trees as if by some artificial histrionic article, stained and flush against the jagged upland. They came to lichen-covered granite boulders colossal in mass whose view from which could scope the dramatic ridge of Cutthroat Peak and the north cascades with its snowfall deposits of winter. The bloodflow of the beast was effected on climbing the switchbacks which appeared to slow the animal some and he could hear its wailing bugle herald the rocks as they climbed altitude. From a ridge his keen eye took in the vast terrain below undulated wide with huckleberry and dark heather across vast meadows and he spotted the stag on a bluff not yards away where its aim entire was to lay panting in the agony of its wound. He approached the beast slowly, its head lifted with its monarchical crown splay and treelike its breath abating and for a moment he looked into the eyes of the creature whose dark pools reflected the figure of the man before it and tiny perfect suns and in that instant a facile admission was exchanged between man and beast as if they had together regressed to the very core of the earth's genesis and entered a void remote and mineral. Clemency dwelt there and he weighed the deed and how best to proceed knowing wholly the chief outcome and remorse lay heavy as he cocked the piece and fired and watched the animal expire to the ground.

That night he made camp some distance from the creature he had slain and coyote and wolf packs were general in that terrain and they foraged the flesh of the corpse where it lay. He watched the sun decline behind the craggy spires and before dark he surveyed the little blue pool of Cutthroat Lake in the valley below. In the night he heard the echoed clatter of small hooves upon the gravel shelf of skittish mountain goats and the haunting throttle of the bobcat that harboured the wooded draw and the night wore an empty black maw aglow with a sea of stars nameless to the eye that perceived them. When morning broke the skylarks chittered their creed while he decamped from that eastern slope and sallied down the switchbacks toward the valley. At noon he nestled in a hollow of a bluff where he could see a train of Mexicans ten or twelvesome wagons loaded with wares and they made their camp by a creek and scattered their pallets and hessian store of corn and flour then corralled up to commence their cooking. He ventured down to that selfsame creek to water his animal and snare a fish or two for his supper and a woman was there halfnaked pumicing a host of linens and the like in the shade of the white heat of noon. She spoke to him in a tongue strange to his ear and he communicated he had no comprehending of it but it hindered her flow none, then in a curious parody she sought his attendance to eat with her and the company which he accepted with an obliging nod.

There was food enough for fiftyhead and he sat among thirty men, women and their kin and they ate charred tortillas and beans while the halfnaked woman doled out second helpings to he who sojourned their train. He regarded this small citizenry gathered about the fire hunched over their repast with faces sated with glee and a group of boys stoked the fire to such a height its grey smoke could be seen abroad ten miles. He learned from a frail old man with pidgin language that the sutlers were headed for Fort Steilacoom to sell wares to the soldiers and he'd be welcome to join them on their jornadas if he so chose, and he measured the man as he examined and tooled the tiny mechanisms of a gold pocketwatch which he later took apart piece by piece then reassembled it just for the musing of it.

Within the impromptu corral were a medley of cattle, sheep, goats and pigs and the horses were being groomed and saddled by the same group of boys, and they ran barefoot in the dust with the livestock and halfbroken nags while the women washed the unfired clay and utensils by the creek. The men by the fire parleyed and by their expressions he surmised they shared tall tales and fables of marauders in that quarter for their eyes were each of two beset with fear or brim with laughter and it regaled him though he understood not a word. As the day wore on their revelry was swelled by music and dancing and a lively chase ensued among the children and several dogs and two or three young goats were slaughtered then roasted on spits for their evening vittle but he would depart their company long before. They sent him on his way with a parcel of dry meat and pinole and filled his canteen with several measures of mescal and they motioned him farewell with their bright kerchiefs in hand as he ascended the same switchbacks of the morning.

He made a dry camp atop a shaled bench where he could see clearly the small figures of the citizenry with whom he had leisured and he saw a column of twentyhead horses riding in from the east whereon their laggard trail entered the corral of the Mexicans. From his field of vision the discourse between the two bands appeared motionless and after a long silence the men dismounted and hitched their horses in the corral. These men were invited to share the fire and food and as they took leave of the horses it was plain to see they were Indians, for some were halfnaked with their black hair to their shoulders while others were wardrobed in strange attire of jackets and pieces of cavalry uniforms or headgear of eaglefeathers and lace finery with their faces daubed grotesque, yet this fabled menagerie gave no rumour of hostility. The halfnaked woman cut portions of meat from the spit and shared it equally among the natives and the company entire sat about the fire of buffalo chips smoking civilly in the crimson dusk. From that rocky promontory he surveyed the scene with watchful eye and felt the mescal harry his vision and he dozed in and out like some nocturnal bird and his horse gave the occasional nicker. He resumed his watch of the Gentiles below and saw them pass the pipe among the circle then they each rose and shook hands with the migrants every man woman and child. He watched them mount their ponies at the rear of the corral and start out toward the east from where they stole and in the distance there was a great snarl of dust heading toward them of a herd of fifty ponies or more. At that instant the natives-twenty turned their horses and joined ranks with the stampede and you could hear the pounding of the hooves as they came full upon the flanks of the camp and a horror of screeching and howling of hellish tongue drove forth with their arrows as they swung Herculean, lances in hand. The sutlers were fleeing aimlessly in terror and the horses reared and lurched like some mad equine herd condemned to a curse demonic and the livestock breached the corral and dispersed into the smoke while the Mexicans sought refuge under the wagons. The gaudy argonauts were bearing down upon them with their yammering and squalid reckonings and commenced to pull the hidden out from underneath the carts and man and beast were scrambling and flailing as the nags of war trampled the fallen as they speared the helpless through limb and torso and the savages pitched from their mounts with unnatural ease with a batch of arrows clenched at their teeth. Everywhere there were mangled corpses and haunting groans from the dying and a nightmare of faces clubbing and spearing, their knives held aloft as they stripped the dead of their clothes seizing clumps of hair to clove scalps from their skulls and they were violating living and dead alike chopping heads and limbs and holding handfuls of entrails and trophies of bloody wigs. Now advancing the murk wheeled the horses of the dead through the smoke and dust and trampling the death ground underfoot with demented white eyes and denuded teeth some incised with arrowshafts or lanced through their flanks and the warriors oblique rescinded the pan toward the curve of the earth in a pandemonium of manic discord as the scarlet sun fell behind that frayed waste.

THAT NIGHT IN HIS sleep he entered a fevered darkness whereon a strange blighted wasteland lay before him and against the backdrop of a brittle grey sky stood upright as bishops a mob of stag shod in pitch Saltillo blankets that bore bloodred insignia as arcane as their spoken tongue. This trinity erect conceded their truth upon his ear and although recondite in its vehicle he understood it as clear as his own, and they weren't apostate in their supposings but cautionary of the direction of humanity and what he could comprehend of the ordered parable would declare a great famine unto the known collective soul, consuming itself by ignorance and greed and a war was coming that would wipe out entire civilisations. So vivid was this night delirium that on waking he felt that selfsame trinity of stag hunched giant over him like a circle of primordial stones.

With morning came a fresh parody of queerness. He

rolled away his pallet and decamped the bench and traversed a forest of colossal red cedars from where their towering limbs could be heard the monotone call of a nuthatch conversing with a solitary junco. He scanned the peaks against the cloudless sky where very high in the emptiness was an eagle broad and motile, its kek muted in the unfixed altitude. He passed seasonal waterfalls wherein a colony of beavers combed the wash and puzzled a weir of their own making, and two elk stood tall and postured surveying the grove and whatever harboured there within. He then sallied down the switchbacks and through a succession of small creeks where he halted to water his horse. He bathed there and rinsed out his flask, refilled it and walked on.

Their way led them to a steep trace of coniferous trees and a wide spread of various phlox and as they descended he could see the outline of something humanlike tied to a tree. He felt for the rifle under the fender, shouldered the piece and cocked it then approached the object stealthwise leaving his horse a way up the trace. The man before him had his limbs splayed and roped out to neighbouring trees and was all but wardrobed in his union suit with his boots flung several feet from where he stood. With the muzzle of the rifle he prodded at the man's chest where hung his head and a mass of black hair, his chin pressed against his breastplate.

Hey mister.

The man groaned in response but did not move.

Mister. You conscious?

He remit another groan.

What in hell you doin out in these parts in nothin but your underwears?

Caint feel my damn legs.

His speech was slurred and he was trying to lift his head.

That'll be on account a you bein roped up to some tree. How long you been trussed up like this anyways? Must a been overnight cause I done pass these parts yesterday mornin an you sure as hell werent here then.

Must a been afore dark. Caint rightly say.

What happen here? You recall?

All I know is I was settin up a dry camp there in yonder trees an some son of a bitch done took to cloutin me from behind an steelin off with my damn horse.

Dont you remember nothin else?

Well.

You see who done this to ye?

Guess I was fallin in an out cause I got some mighty strange images a them folk in my perceivins. Less I done fabricate them lunatics outta some provocation of the injury itself.

He fell mute for several moments and flopped his head forward.

Mister.

Say what?

You aint right mister. Havin some trouble keepin your eyes open. Whats your name? You reckon you can recall that?

Mose.

Mose what?

Just Mose. It aint nothin.

What aint?

My damn boots is all.

You aint makin no sense, Mose. I gone cut you from this here rope so you best be ready to catch yer fall now. Alright.

He took his knife from the inside of his boot and

proceeded to cut away at the rope at his ankles. Now. Put your feet together mister out in front a you so you can support your weight against this here tree for when I cut your arms loose.

I apologise.

What in hell for? Aint your doin. Less you done tie yourself in this here predicament. But I dont see hows you would none.

He cut the last of the rope and Mose pitched sideways and hit the ground like a dead weight.

Woh now. Lets get you sat upright.

He lay his rifle to the ground and rebooted his knife then lifted him up from underneath his arms and dragged him and propped him against the tree.

Thanks mister. You seen my boots anywheres?

His eyes darted about the phlox. I'll go fetch em.

He picked up the rifle and wandered over to where they lay.

Whats your name mister?

Gilchrist. John Gilchrist. Not that youll remember it in your present humour. Dont expect ye to neither.

Gilchrist. What sort a names that?

Forebears from Scotland. So Im told. Aint never been there myself.

Well, Gilchrist. Thems was craziern some degenerate theatrics.

What was damn it?

Them that did this an stole my horse.

You describe em any?

Well. Them was just boys. Eighteen or so I reckon.

Injins?

Nope. Mexican. Id sure as hell be dead if they were. One a them was wearin some strange lace pantaloons over hims breeches and a blue bonnet bowed under his chin. The other. Least I think it were other cause he look the selfsame crazy idiot as that other there feller. Him had some bridal veil on his head all bloodied and torn some, an a pigeontail coat over his attire an both thems eyes were wildlookin as a scavenging grey wolf.

Twins maybe. Where you suppose they come from?

Dont rightly know.

There was a train a Mexicans passin through yesterday aways up the pass. Could be them boys was travellin with them sutlers an broke off fore they made camp.

You see where them sutlers went?

Injins came upon them. Killed ever last one a em.

All of em? Thems children among em?

Yep.

You seen it?

I did. It were some violence like I never seen. Queerest thing was, they parleyed with em all friendly like, an they was eatin an smoking together for a time fore they shook hands an mounted up. Then I could see a great horde a them ridin in from the east. Fifty of em I reckon an they merge into some hideous stampede an with no provocation at all they was hackin an murderin like it were some natural occurrence to em, an I keep my person well hid outta sight while I witness them remorseless reckonins. Like the wrath a some unordained god. An they ride out just as quick as they ride in leavin a battleground a dismembered corpses strewn across the pan.

Christ almighty. Them poor souls.

Somethin I aint never gone forget. That were some terrifyin ordeal to behold.

They gone?

Who?

Redskins.

They long gone mister.

You suppose thems comin back?

Aint likely. They destroy just about everthin in sight that you could rightly.

Mose started shivering and it was hard to determine whether it was fear or the cold that grieved him. Gilchrist looked at him. You set yourself here a while so I can go fetch a blanket an my horse.

Mose just stared back. He returned with the horse and handed him a blanket and a canteen of water and watched as he darted his eyes about the trees.

Dont you worry none. We'll be on our ways soon.

What you aim to do?

Aim to get ye back your damn horse.

How you suppose we do that? Thems most likely over border by now.

Well we gone try. You see which way they went?

Back out direction I come.

Which is?

Ways you was headin I guess.

Alright. You think you can raise yourself up on your feet?

I can try.

He handed the canteen back to Gilchrist and put his arm about his shoulders. They hove up and walked slowly toward the horse. Gilchrist took his foot to the stirrup and hitched him up then mounted the horse himself and rode on.

You hold on now cause I caint catch ye none you so much as fall.

Mose rested himself against him and started lurching to the right so Gilchrist stood the horse and unhooked the rope from the pommel and tied it about the two of them to secure him in the saddle.

They rode for some time through deep woodland where the traces snaked to the right then curved back on itself and out along the esker of a lake, and all through that forest it was quiet save for a species of hawk that seemed to mirror their progress. When the traces opened out onto the river they could hear shore larks and pipits talking and from a nearby bluff a solitary cougar reconnoitred the region below and the blue skyline out to the west. They made camp on the bank where Gilchrist hooked a couple of trout for their vittles, then they mounted up and headed north along the shoreline. They reached a shallow pass through the river and waded through to the other side onto a tongue of land whereon a hand crafted skiff was moored and some distance south was the wreckage of a flatbed wagon capsized on its axles with remnants of chattels scattered about the trail up ahead of them. The men looked at each other in question and rode on. They traversed this cut for a way and within their scope they could see an object moving crablike at what seemed no speed at all and the sun recoiled off it like small glinting stars, and as they drew nearer they saw two men lugging a brass bedframe through the grove which they surmised had been salvaged from the river they had just passed. When they caught up, the two men had stripped themselves naked and settled their damp attire about the bedframe to dry in the sun. They had made a small fire in a sinkhole and shaped a clothesline whereon hung their undergarments and they were sat on their haunches warming their hands as they puffed signals of smoke from their pipes.

Afternoon, said Gilchrist. The two men looked up at him without expression. Yall in some mighty strange fix there. You got a ways to go with that thing?

Whats it to you mister?

Well. Nothin. Like as not you gone need some help is all.

You think it funny?

No sir, I dont. Seen your wagon back there in the river. Could maybe try haulin it out for ye if that be your choosin.

An what alls your strategy for that mister? Damn horse bolted soon as we set foot on land an a couple a wildlookin fellers pound right on through the water like it were hot coals an chase after it. Most likely catched it too.

Were thems Mexican? said Mose.

They was.

On horseback?

Yep.

Thats my damn horse they got there.

Well. Theys likely got both our horses now.

Likely they have, said Gilchrist. You want help with that there wagon yonder or not? Take it or leave it. Makes no odds to me.

One of the men spat and the other kept to smoking with his eyes aslant.

Dont need none a your charity mister. Damn strategy's our own.

Now hold there Tighe, said the other, lets not be too hasty turnin away a man's charity. Im pretty tired some an we got a ways to go yet fore we reach the camp. In truth Im mighty disenchanted by the whole idea of haulin this here contraption halfway across the territory. Well hell, I could do with that wagon some if this gentleman's offerin his horse to salvage it. What you say Tighe?

Well alright. Got to admit my back is givin me somethin evil.

Happy to oblige, said Gilchrist. We'll head on back there then. Reckon two of us can hitch it upface an my horse can do the rest. Yall best stay put less we be needin another pair a hands. I'll come fetch ye if I do.

Right kind a you sir.

Names Gilchrist.

Pleased to meet ye.

An who might I be addressin?

Chet. An this heres Tighe.

I be Mose.

You fellers knowed each other?

We acquainted ourselves this mornin. Found Mose tethered in some peculiar fashion to some trees. Thats where we be goin now. Aim to get him his horse back.

Well. That alls your business mister. Rather it be you if Im honest.

That it is. You might want think about puttin yer clothes back on case some other folk done pass through here. Just sayin is all.

Obliged to ye mister.

Try not to smoke yourselves to death while we gone.

Gilchrist turned his horse south and they restepped the selfsame prints in the trace back to the river. Neither of them spoke. When they reached the bank, Gilchrist hitched his horse to a tree and they commenced to study how it was they would upturn the wagon in the current while knee deep in water, then they waded through the shale floor of the river and took to the exposed structure of the thing and hauled it one man either side to its wheels. No effort seemed to remedy it and in their progress a halfnaked child stood gawking at them from where the skiff was moored and he hollered in excitement when they had it upright. Gilchrist fetched his horse and tended it to the vehicle, hitched it to the framework with rope and Mose led the horse forward while Gilchrist pushed the flatbed from the rear and manoeuvred it through the unsettled shale to land.

The two sorry pilgrims were exactly as they first found them on their return and it took some heeding for Gilchrist to hold his tongue as he wheeled the vehicle abreast the bedframe.

You fellers look right comfortable, he said. What alls a man got to do to incite you to movement? We gone done the scheme of the thing for ye, now only right yall get off yer behinds an get that there article a yours secure on the wagon.

We was waitin for our damn clothes to dry, said Chet.

Well they must be right about now. Prefer to get ye to wherever it is you want go fore it get dark, if its all the same with you folk.

Aint you in some hurry mister.

Ye think? Reckon I need to if we gone catch them pair a wayward Mexicans. We already a passel a mile behind.

He and Mose sat the horse waiting for the two pilgrims to dress themselves and attend the bedframe and those fools skittered about like some domesticated fowl with its head lopped off going in neither one direction nor the other. It was a good half hour before they took to the road and the four of them were hunkered over on the buckboard packed like some sullied merchandise enroute to a vaquero market. The pass took them through a deep snowcapped arroyo where the lake narrowed and expanded among varied forms of woodland and up ahead was a posse of four riders circling something unclear to the eye and they each had snared the article with their lariats and were tormenting it and flailing rocks with such violence as if some mindless witch stoning. As they drew nearer to the band they could perceive the thing itself was a great grizzly bear, colossal in its mass of black fur wheezing and roaring and baring its bladelike claws and teeth in a spasm of uncontrollable agitation.

What in hell we got here? said Gilchrist. Take these here reins would ye Mose.

What you aim to do?

Them got that there beast trussed up for a lynchin and I sure aint gone permit nothin of the kind while I is livin an breathin. That sorry beast got no hope in hell.

I would I was them. He some vicious lookin animal.

Is you crazy? said Chet. You got no damn sense or nothin interferin with the likes a them. Not to mention that fuckin griz. You aim to get us all killed?

You fellers climb in the back there an I'll deal with them militants.

Where you suppose we all gone fit with this here hunk a furniture?

You figure it out. Just make yourselves scarce an them like as not wont be fixin to agent no blood bath.

I dont like it. Not one little bit, said Chet. Caint we turn back?

Shut yer pecker, said Mose. You best do like he says.

Gilchrist took the reins and gave the horse its head till it halted at a distance from the site. The four horses circling the animal were wild with fear with their nostrils splay and their necks braced as they shied and screamed as if bedevilled by some foul visitant, and the bear was gasping and growling and thrashing its limbs about the rope while the dragoons yowled and guffawed in a senseless spate of mirth. One of the recruits eyed Gilchrist and handed his lariat to a confederate then led his horse over to where they halted. He reined up and stopped then addressed him directly. Can we help yous gentlemen? he said, measuring the four men in the wagon.

Nope. We just passin through.

Well yous can go exercise that curiosity a yours someplace else. Aint nothin to see here mister.

Gilchrist looked through the man at the tormented creature and his confederates in their ripe hysteria then qualified the soldier before him. That some feat apprehendin that there beast yonder. What yall aim to do with it?

Well sir, yes it is but that aint none a your concern. So best you be movin along now. Like I said. Aint nothin to see here.

He made a shooing motion with the back of his hand.

See now that dont sit right with me soldier.

Oh it dont?

Thats what I said.

An exactly what is it you dont accord? Not that its any a yer goddamn business. The stoning? Or the lynchin?

None of it. Them practises a yours is savage.

Savage? You dont comprehend the meanin of the word mister. Savage is them redskins tearin up the damn territory.

I seen it. They done murder my brother. Took his damn scalp for a fuckin keepsake.

And you surmise that what yall effectuatin right here aint in the vicinity a them redskins crimes?

Its just some dumb animal.

And hows it that beast got lesser right to be here than us folk? You reckon that what God intended?

You done tellin me where its at with ye preachin?

Aint right is what Im sayin.

Well fuck you mister. I aint gone listen. Them just empty words that dont mean shit.

Let me ask you somethin. Would you be treatin your horse in that same manner?

I might. It rile me up some.

Then you dont deserve that there horse. Im seldom mistaken in the character of a man and the way I see it you sure as hell dont deserve that there uniform on your back neither.

The recruit spat and lowered his hand to his pistol slowly. That a warnin?

I reckon. Best you fellers pay heed and quit maimin that animal.

Or what. What exactly you proposin to do about it pilgrim if we dont?

You think I be tellin you my strategy son?

The soldier sucked his teeth. Well aint you some tough dog. Now, I be givin yall one last chance to go on about ye business. Or you gone be right familiar with some damn lead in yer skull.

That so.

Just you test me mister.

Gilchrist drew his .38 so fast and fired that the recruit scarcely had time to draw and with a quick succession of three shots with the heel of his hand pierced the belly of each of the recruits behind him and they lurched from their mounts and hit the ground while being trampled underfoot in the exodus of the bolting horses. The bear skittered its eyes about nervously with the rope about its neck and it was yanking at it so hard it almost uprooted the tree whereon it was tethered.

Well shit, said Mose. Aint you some dead gun.

Christ almighty, said Tighe. Where in hell you learn how to shoot?

Need to free that there griz, said Gilchrist. You fellers stay put.

What you gone do?

I aim to cut that creature free.

You is one crazy son of a bitch, said Chet. That there griz gone come at us.

Well I aint gone just leave it there.

He took up the reins and led the horse and wagon a couple hundred yards up the trace then untethered his horse from the scantling. He mounted up and tapped the horse with the reins then motioned it forward gently with the stirrup. When he approached the animal it stood still entire and stared, for if it had any reprisal left in it it did not show it, just panted and looked him plain in the eye. There was several inches of rope divide between the bear's head and the limb of the tree and from some yards back Gilchrist qualified the distance. The bear's demeanour remained calm as if it'd know his mind and ultimate design and as he spoke to the animal he eased his hand to his boot and unsheathed the knife. Both horse and beast were still and he took aim and drove the blade at the rope and it pelted through the air and sliced it clean from the limb liberating the beast from its scrag. The blade landed edge down in the dirt and for a moment the bear measured the mounted man and grunted as it tottered toward him as if to attack then it bent its great neck to the ground and stove its jaw into the leg of one of the trampled dead and drug the bloodied corpse off into the trees leaving an arterial soaked track of waste behind it.

THE SUN DECLINED in that cobalt sky behind the inkblack mountains, jagged against the vault like the spine of some gigantic primeval fossil and they made camp and ate dried meat and hardtack with coffee round a towering fire while they each of them studied the flames in silence. A lone wolf howled from some faroff crag in the darkness and they could hear the flow of water driving downstream from a nearby creek and they saw the winking light from a distant fire about a mile off of other travellers without aim or terminus. In the morning dark they crested the mountains where at first light they could see for miles across a green vista of trees and rock and the river snaking through the valley, and they came upon the dying embers of the fire they had seen not hours before when night had enshadowed the earth. They made sorties down the switchbacks and followed the trace to the flats of the river whereon they watered and fed the horse and at noon when the sun was high they passed a pair of bucks rutting on a hillock, their racks meshed and clattering like some nigh thunderclap.

Their way led them along a great walled bluff wherein lay structured ricks of bones of every device, man beast and bird, pumice white and primitive like heralds or cautionary foretokens and thereafter the man Tighe jabbered to himself words incoherent for within him spoke of incidents past that brewed fear and horror and the like.

What in hells he squakin about? said Gilchrist. You make sense of it Chet?

Nope. He have occasion to spout shit once in a while and I never knowed what in hell he communicatin. I just let him rant on when he need.

I seen them face bones before, said Tighe. Thems to ward off folk.

Ward off from what?

Injins. I aint goin no further.

If that's so, said Gilchrist, our hides best stick together. We got more chance survivin in formation than we does disbandin, so aint nobody goin nowhere ye hear?

Aint goins what I said.

You step off that cart Tighe and your ass is good as dead.

Mighty ripe spot for a ambush, said Mose.

Gilchrist surveyed the mesa above to the east then to the west. I reckon. Yall best keep your damn heads. Dont make no sense bein beset with them jitters.

A few extra pistols be right favourable about now.

Faint dry tracks of horses crossed the trace they came upon, with one set heading north and one northwest. Then they saw it. From a high branch hung two naked men head down and pierced through their ankles. The skin of their torso clove through from sternum to stomach with their entrails jutting from their prior quarters and their heads scalped to the bone still dripping a mire of blood in the dirt below them and their hands were bound at their spine and their skulls bore great holes where eyes once sat. Strewn about the ground were varied articles of attire, a bonnet of blue, lace pantaloons, bridal veil, pigeontail coat.

Oh my God, said Mose. Thems the selfsame Mexicans done stole my horse.

The men stared unsettled about the scene.

I reckon both them horses is long gone, said Chet.

At that instant an arrow fell from the sky and burrowed into Gilchrist's leg to the fletching and he was hollering to the men to take cover as the three hurdled from the wagon. A rattle of shafts fell aslant from the walled canyon and there were eight, nine of them all afoot save one mounted upon an overo mustang, and he jostled a great lance aloft with his face painted red howling out queer stoneage rogations to a deaf void and Gilchrist fell upon his elbows and cocked and levelled the rifle while launching his pistol at Mose. The rifle bucked and a pall of smoke hung static in the dry air and he reloaded the chamber and aimed upon the wounded man lurching from his horse and his shot dispatched the warrior over the bluff and he fell to his demise with a hollow thud. What followed was a discharge of gunfire and arrowshafts hurtling through that gloomy purgatory of dust and smoke alike and a din of agony yielding from the mouths of both ally and foe and they each at the point of dying saw truth in the mindless violence wherein they had long partook and of the world undiscerning of the portents of man and war and its endless millennia preceding it.

Out of that waste rose one soul injured and defeated and he lurched and limped rifle in hand as he looked upon that desolate battleground, the brass bedframe idle in the wagon, his horse dead the dismembered and arrowbit confederates face down in the dirt in horrible attitudes of death. He came upon a dark hidden cavity and rested there and slept for he knew not how long and it was dark before he woke again. He consulted the shaft in his leg and slept once more. When he awoke a second time it was first light and a great figure of a man was bent over him shifting an article of smoke about his wound and as he came to he perceived this man was a native of some anonymous tribe and he wore the hide of an animal on his back his black hair to his shoulders. He had lacerated scars about his neck as if he'd been lynched at some interval and escaped it.

What are you? said Gilchrist. Shoshone?

Paiute.

What in hell you doin out here? You lost.

Travellin through.

You alone.

I am. You need to sleep if you want that wound to heal.

I been sleepin. God knows how long.

He regarded the Paiute and saw he had a benevolence about him and he watched him as he performed a ream of Neolithic rituals at his feet. The Paiute took from his apparel a pipe that he proceeded to scratch out with some flint then he smoked it at the mouth of the cave. My name's Milton, he said. You must sleep little white man. He will need strength for much mile ahead.

FRAGMENTS

TWO A.M. They rise from the recliners in silence and qualify the striking fullness of the moon for several minutes, with its retinue of ordered stars arcing the dark empty mouth beyond. They descend the steps below deck where all is still. They are motionless at his door. Their eyes engaged. They enter the room and stand facing one another. For a moment they do nothing. Her tentative hand then touches his chest. The million cells that comprise his skin. He touches her mouth with his thumb. Utters one word. Habibi. They hear nothing outside of themselves and time transcends them. Their mouths meet and in his arousal he touches her soft skin. Her naval. Pubis. He exhales a groan. A sequestered cave. Her breath quickens. They have nowhere else to go but with the current and they are consumed by it, like a god absorbs the sun. There is a divine presence as they taste flesh and saliva, then sinew coils and the intensity writhes displacing who they once were to an impassable space. His euphoria leaves impressions upon her skin like a carving on stone and before they expire they know neither of them can revert to what came before. They are no longer sightless, nor in darkness. An alignment shifts and their apogee is endless. The world around them is extinguished.

FOUR A.M. The motion of the dahabiya moderates their silence with the gentle ripples of the unsettled water. They are transfixed. His cheek rests against her naval. His right arm about her naked limbs. The tips of his fingers move along her thigh. His breath abates. They exist in a sphere of their own making. No one can enter. Its landscape is far beyond the trappings of this world. There is neither commerce nor treaty. Decadence nor war. It's their own private wilderness and they abandon themselves to it. She extends her fingers like tree roots through his hair the way her father used to when she was a child, when she would wake from some disordered dream or from the tapping of some errant branch on the windowpane. They share childhood histories. Memories embedded and long forgot.

What gives you joy? she asks. This moment, he answers. The composition of it. He kisses the promontory of her ribcage. Your skin. It has a truth. A knowledge. There's no demarcation between yours and mine. She smiles. What else? He looks up and is suddenly conscious of the pre-dawn twilight. The sea, he says. Art in all its form. But above all, words. Words give me purpose. Yes, she says, I see that now. And you? he asks. Trees. I like to stand anonymous among great armies of trees. To breathe with them. Listen to their ambiguous language. And the sea. She pauses to kiss him. My work. She then takes him into her life of antiquities. Certain places where she has felt an affinity with the posthumous lives of those she excavates.

She leads him to a place not far from the Step Pyramid of Djoser, where until recent years it lay undiscovered for four millennia. It is the tomb of a royal official. A well-preserved rock-cut tomb-chapel with beautifully painted reliefs, sculptures and inscriptions. She extends his hand to one of fifty adorned statues of Wahtye and guides it along the stone bicep, down the forearm to the shendyt. She rests his fingers on the foot of the priest as if to bless it. Together they read the blue inscriptions alongside him on the walls. She tells him of the skeletal analysis of Wahtye and his family resting there who had, they propose, fallen victim to malaria. These could represent the earliest known cases of the disease.

They exit the tomb and he takes her four hundred kilometres north of Khartoum where an assignment had taken him in recent months. They enter the ancient Kushite kingdom of Nubia where a complex of sacred temples were built for their deity, Amun. Where kings would have entered the Holy of Holies to fulfil ordination. He takes her hand and walks her up the stone path that leads to the sandstone mesa of Jebel Barkal, where pallid swifts and rock buntings nest. When they climb the hundred-metre plateau they are met by panoramic views of the vast landscape of Karima, the Nile and scattered temple ruins. He describes the view in detail. On the horizon are the pyramids of the black pharaohs, which appear to jut out of the ground like a convoy of ebony teeth, jagged against the endless desert vista and searing coral sun. And within the sacred mountain is a labyrinth. He brushes her hand along the carved wall painted chambers of the Temple of Mut where blue and argil composites of nature are daubed. Its ruins of Hathor columns stand at the foot of the mesa, and near a large bend of the river are remnants of the Temple of Amun. He walks her through these ruins where solitary ram sculptures sit and, although the kings of this lost civilisation are gone and their inventions now relics, the proximity of the divine resides. Four millennia of transient souls have wandered this vicinity.

They are back in the cabin of the dahabiya, inert on the bed. Entangled limbs. The calming chant of the cicadas is general, along with the neutral swell of the river and the call of little grebe. They are silent for a long time in their secret wilderness. He takes her arm and kisses the wound left by her former lover. Nothing can hinder you now, he says as he catches a falling tear from her cheek. What follows are the beginnings of sexual movement.

AT BREAKFAST not hours later they find their fellow passengers have already departed for Kom Ombo so they remain behind for the rest of the day. No sleep has come to either of them and neither will it until nightfall. Their day will consist of words of poets and historians long since forgot together with the intimacy that now governs their every moment. They settle themselves among great scholars of men who question everything. All rhetoric of existence. Their beliefs. Their assumptions. The arias of Mozart weave in and out of their discourse like a guest at a feast. Night precedes them before they are ready to untangle themselves form carnal language and the time collectively spent invokes a need in them as an arid plant receives rain. He watches her movement throughout the day. How she holds a book or assumes a demure frown. He surveys the contours of her back when they bathe, every aspect of her torso. The curves of her womanly form, lithe and sensual. How she greets the spray of water upon her neck and twists her long dark hair like twine. But she too studies his cast as if to investigate something freshly unearthed. Reads it like some inscrutable text, her fingertips scanning braille. The eye receives every detail of their anatomy and for him it is as if he is retaining a map to memory, a snapshot to draw on at a later date so as to commit it to the page, or sketch from memory. When they lie in each other's arms they watch the light change in the room as dusk descends and the reflections of the water on the walls, just as civilisations would have before Caesar, Alexander or Christianity. The river. A spine whose vertebrae stretches over six and a half thousand kilometres feeding life to eleven countries. He is suddenly dwarfed by this knowledge.

THEY ARE SITTING on the balcony adjoining his room watching the wildlife move on the fertile shoreline. There is no moon or stars visible and the nuance that twilight is giving off is enough to decipher certain objects clearly. The slow pull of the dahabiya has an almost sedative effect on them as they listen to the drone of different insects. They are nestled within their own secure fortress which they've consciously erected to veto the world outside of it. Lightning flashes across the night sky and they watch as it transmits intermittent disorder like a dispatch of Morse code. They hear the soft tap of single drops of rain hit the river, their skin, the table, the wine in the flutes, then the drops steadily increase and drown the lone candle flame that has acted as a beacon in their secrecy. Their retreat from the world. They stand

and receive the rain like children alien to it, laughing, and their attention is entirely unbroken reading every sensation the beads of water emit as they crawl down a cheek, a limb, hairs on their arms, a vertebra, slipping down the spine to be absorbed by the manufactured fabric against their skin. They consume every element of the storm. Ingest its language. Its errorless prose. Its furious composition. He tastes the rain on her lips, swallows it as if to quench a thirst. He consumes the body of water collating around her mouth. He unclothes her and watches the rain search her anatomy as if its sole purpose were to galvanise. They are naked in the storm.

HE CONTEMPLATES the stunning contrast of the deep blue tone of the river against the nuance of high rocks, cataracts and sand dunes flanking the banks. There is an abundance of green palm trees along the fertile shoreline with an overwhelming welter of feluccas and other sailing vessels that navigate north and south of Aswan. The pale pre-dawn twilight gives this primitive composition an almost transcendental aspect. It holds his attention for a measurable time yet he is unaware himself of the time that has lapsed until prayer mantras emerge from a passing minaret. Minutes earlier he had gazed at the imposing beauty of the pylons and colonnades of Isis Temple on the island of Agilika, Philae. He glances into the room where she sleeps. He feels a tenderness towards her that only comes during complete resignation to a lover, an adoration of every cell. He studies each variation of movement on her face that occurs during sleep. A shifting eyebrow, a small gesture at the corner of her mouth. This contentment he feels is unknown to him and it invokes a peace he was certain did not exist, or at least not for him. He had only witnessed it between his mother and father; their admiration and devotion to one another. He had believed it inaccessible. Unconquerable. Gifted to the few. He rises and walks towards the bed and places the notebook on the table as he enters the room. He sits by her sleeping body and watches the progression of her breathing, her cheek away from him on the pillow. He is aware of a deepness in his sleep due to her presence in his life. The comfort he feels when he is in her arms before he plummets into nothingness. She reminds him of a certain solace through childhood. When he was ill or unable to sleep, his mother would ease his discomfort and put her hand on his small infant back, circling her palm in a restful motion. He wants her to receive this tenderness, so he puts his hand where the rain had fallen two hours earlier. He connects with her skin. Seizing intimacy through touch. He rests his hand there and feels the dull pulse through his fingertips. His desire for this moment to never cease capsizes and within his consciousness he makes an effort to let it go. To practise nonattachment. To consider the emotion attached to the object as being the source rather than the object itself. For him there was no ownership. No possessing. Not with her. There was complete equanimity residing between them.

She stirs from her sleep and feels his hand rested on her spine. She smiles and turns her head towards him. He brushes the hair from her face and places it on the pillow behind her. The blue shade of dawn envelops them and the geography of the room. He kisses her shoulder. Come to bed then, she says.

GINEIH

ON THIS DAY he had consciously chosen to walk in the opposite direction of Karnak. His route took him north-east on Kornish Al Nile, which was amply tree-lined and lending him a clear view of the Nile to his left. Without having any firm direction in mind he turned right on to Mahbad Al Karnak, where he could see Luxor Temple up ahead. He noticed a small park area on his right and a café within its grounds so he took another right where its entrance could be found just yards ahead. It was a Bedouin tent-style café, in a sort of courtyard where tables and chairs were laid out, with large plant pots housing small evergreen trees. As he entered, there was a strong smell of coffee and cardamom on the air and, barely underlying, the subtle odour of kif. The staccato sound of a tabla came from somewhere adjacent, tapping methodical patterns above the transient cartage. Some men were seated on chairs, others on portions of reed matting on the floor. Most of them were plain-clothed but others wore linen thobes or burouses with either turbans or chechias on their heads, which Kit thought lent the scene uniformity.

He ordered a coffee and cream and sat at a small table in the shade with a spectacular view of the temple. His thoughts took an inward turn. His state of mind was remediable and he thought of Katherine; nothing of substance, more an abstract thought of relative value. Then a very brief fear spoke; he listened and acknowledged it was fear of change. Fear of an end. He shelved it and the idea elated him. Then it occurred to him that rather than resist any imminent change he would make an effort to ease the tension between them by allowing the transition to occur naturally in the passage of time. And should Katherine be the one to fuel it, he would become flexible and simply submit to her will, for he saw no purpose in denying her happiness.

But for him it was more the object of time itself that bothered him. He was now the age his father had been when he had disappeared and this gave him the stark observation of how fleeting time is. He was conscious of their having made a near fatal error in assuming time was non-existent from one year to the next. Neither of them ever really achieving anything of value.

He watched the horse and carriages pass by and the people became amorphous patterns of colour as he let his mind wander aimlessly while drinking his coffee. Normally coffee would accelerate his pulse to an irregular degree but here he noticed, rather than stimulate, it had had an adverse effect to an almost dulling result, and he wondered whether the coffee had been infused with kif but discounted the idea straight off.

As he was sitting there, a young thin man wearing a shabby thobe sauntered in and went directly to the coffee bar where he began conversing with the owner. He took out an Egyptian banknote from deep within his robe and while holding it out in his hand began a sort of mild protest as he became more and more animated. The owner appeared sedate and unmoved by him and just nodded and shooed him away, so the man plunged the note back into the recesses of his robe and started off, looking suitably forlorn. The customers seated on the floor seemed mildly troubled by the event and talked amongst themselves in low tones. At that moment, the man made eye contact with Kit and started walking towards him with a direct glower. As he drew nearer, the glower dropped into a benevolent friendly guise and he at once began speaking to Kit in English.

Excuse me, sir, he said politely. I notice you were entertained by the dispute I have with the owner.

Not knowing which direction to steer the dialogue, Kit resorted to politeness, particularly as he found the man oddly direct. No, not really, he answered. I think you'll find the attention to the matter was pretty universal.

Universal, sir?

Yes, everyone in the garden here.

Ah, everyone, he said nodding in coherence. Well, let me explain to you why I was upset with this gentleman.

You really don't need to explain yourself to me, replied Kit plainly. Whatever has gone on between you and the owner is none of my business.

But I want to explain, said the man persistently, and perhaps you can help.

Kit just looked at him with no expression to interpret.

I was in here for coffee, he began, about one hour ago and I pay for my coffee with two hundred gineih. This banknote, you understand, was the only money I carry as I not like to carry too much on me. The man then dove his hands into the pockets of his robe and pulled each of them inside out to reveal empty pockets, save for the note he had disputed with earlier. And, as you see, he said referring to his pockets, I have no wallet.

Kit started to feel uncomfortable with the direction this was leading and sighed a little impatiently. Now, said the man evasively, I am sure you know, as you have purchase a coffee yourself that I pay no more than twenty gineih for espresso. Do you agree?

Kit gave no answer.

By my calculation I should have been given one hundred eighty in change from two hundred note. Yes?

Then here the man waited expectantly for an answer from Kit, at which he gave an impassive reply: That sounds right.

Okay, said the man, placing his right hand on Kit's shoulder, which irritated Kit immeasurably. By this time, everyone in the garden had fallen silent, as if to anticipate the next move. The man continued: Let me show you the gineih this man give me, and he gestured at the owner furiously then held the banknote for Kit to examine. What this gineih read? he asked abruptly.

One hundred, answered Kit a little nettled now.

Exactly! said the man defensively. Then I am owed eighty.

Kit was starting to lose composure and was anxious to hurry things along so he could be left alone and return to his coffee, so in a mild state of intolerance he said: Look, how is it you think I can help?

I explain, said the man vaguely. This man, the owner, refuse to give me my change and he say that I give him exact money when I pay for the coffee, which I know is a lie! And now he accuse me of trying to cheat him with my story, which I not do! This terrible for me because now I not have enough money to buy medicine for my sick child and I not know what to do. So, you understand my difficulty, sir? The man now appeared very distraught and continued to stress to Kit how expensive medicine can be and how he was struggling to find regular work, and by this stage Kit was beginning to feel sorry for the man and thought perhaps he might have misinterpreted his behaviour, so he responded in the only way he knew best to resolve the situation quickly.

Would it help you, said Kit sympathetically, if I compensated your losses?

Losses? asked the man.

Yes. You say you are owed eighty gineih from the owner?

Yes, eighty.

Then allow me to give you what you have lost. It makes no odds to me.

At this, the man's face brightened considerably, and he extended his hand in gratitude. Thank you, thank you, exclaimed the man with excitement. You very kind. Shukran! Shukran! and he was bowing with great enthusiasm and shaking Kit's hand vigorously. Although Kit was flattered by the man's display of appreciation, he felt for some reason simultaneously disquieted by it. Something in his intuition warned him, but despite this he lent it no stock and ignored it. Kit then stood up to fish in his trouser pockets for the small gelt of notes he knew to be there, and as he unfolded the roll to count the sum conceded upon, the man snatched the banknotes from his hand and bolted out the café at high speed.

STALEMATE

Dedicated to Shaun Evans, E. M.
i.m. David Cornwell

1

ON THAT uniformly dull and wet August morning at D Branch, an intelligence product had descended upon the desk of Charles Rutherford, marked 'RX' (Rutherford exclusive), which had been sent down from the Director General for his urgent attention. Having taken a brief look at its contents, he bellowed out to his secretary in the adjoining room, who then entered the office promptly. Penny was a small, bookish woman in tweed, with mousy features and spectacles recently promoted from the typing pool.

'Get me Creagh-West, sharpish!' Rutherford demanded.

All that could be done was to politely answer 'Sir', being that Penny found him invariably intimidating.

'And Penny. Get me a coffee. Black. I want no disturbances during our call, do you hear?'

Moments later the call was put through.

'Morning Rutherford,' came a voice from the receiving end. 'Questions?'

'Indeed, Sir. Where the hell did you dig this one up from? Something of an anachronism.'

'Fifteen years old to be precise. And as you mention it, your chap Rodchenko stumbled across it in Registry. It appears to have been conveniently buried there for some time.'

'How the devil does a high-priority product lose its way so competently?'

'With ease, evidently, the way those clowns are running things. Incidentally, I'll be ordering an overhaul of that entire department. Bunch of torpid individuals down there. Sordidly below the salt. Too many loose ends Ruthers. Need to up our game. Get things shipshape.'

Rutherford conceded. 'And meanwhile, Sir?'

'Meanwhile, I want your best men on the job and a score of people down the pipe. Get Menzies on it. I understand he was integral to its success at Eastcote in the day. Produced some solid tracking throughout the entire operation. If anyone can shed some light, it's him.'

Rutherford sat in a sort of mute unease for some time post-conversation, assessing the endless ramifications and disputable autonomy of the Service. After scrutinising the file, he instructed Penny to allocate Menzies, who would most likely be found rattling around the premises somewhere; and while she was at it, she was to ensure Rodchenko tagged along also.

•

RUTHERFORD SUMMONED Menzies and Rodchenko in with an arbitrary tone and, on entering, they found him standing at the window, regimental in stance, hands clasped firmly behind him. Without turning to face them, he continued to glare out on to the street below, then uttered, 'On my desk, gentlemen, is an intelligence product familiar to you both.' After a lengthy pause he looked round at Menzies and added tersely, 'Well, pick it up man!' which Menzies did, full tilt, and he began to assess its contents in silence.

Guy Menzies was a tall and lean fellow with dark patrician features; something of a codebreaker, which he had unwittingly fallen into straight from Oxford. His father was a don at Cambridge, also a cryptographer, and had joined the legion at Bletchley during the war; and this was quite possibly the only thing that they had in common. Having lost his mother during the Blitz, Menzies was henceforth packed off to Sherborne School for the duration.

'Well?' questioned Rutherford impatiently. 'Ringing any bells?'

'Yes, Sir,' blundered Menzies. 'Operation Vesna. My second encryption assignment for GCHQ. Major operation at the time.'

'Mm, well, Rodchenko chanced upon it in Registry not days ago, which is how it has come to arrive at my desk.'

Suspicion hung heavy in the air as Menzies scanned the documents solemnly. 'But this was archived, Sir. Closed case.'

'Yes, well I want it reopened. It's come from on high. Wants all loose ends knotted. Understood?'

Rodchenko, being a diffident man, found the whole

posture of things far out of his depth and stood mute like a remiss schoolboy waiting to be scolded by the headmaster.

'Describe to me, Oleg, exactly how you came across this file,' the chief instructed. 'It's all right man, I'm not hauling you over the coals. I just want facts.'

Looking sheepishly at his superior, Rodchenko began to explain, in his mild Russian accent, that his orders were to reorganise the filing system chronologically as well as alphabetically, and being that he was just one of many officers on the task, he was personally assigned K–M. 'It wasn't until I reached L that I came across it, Sir. The first thing that caught my eye was emboldened text quoting "High Priority". On observing it had been misfiled, I then raise query with section head who immediately notify the Director General. Its contents are completely unknown to me, Sir.'

On hearing this guiltless confession, Rutherford exhaled deeply, nodding his assurance to Rodchenko, while Menzies stood in a sort of lucid restraint. 'Before we make this privy to other ears, I require a laconic narrative from you, Menzies, if only to bring Rodchenko up to speed. Omit nothing. I understand you'll be dredging up past hurts but I need first-hand knowledge of the operation.'

Menzies affirmed respectfully, 'Understood, Sir.'

As Rutherford seated himself behind the desk, he barked, 'For God's sake men, do sit down! We're here for the long haul.' They did so. 'I'm giving you high category clearance on this, Rodchenko. You've proved yourself competent.'

'Thank you, Sir,' came the nervous response.

Menzies returned the file to its original state on the desk, before recalling to memory the course of events, which he vouchsafed succinctly. 'Shortly after having been recruited by GCHQ to the decryption team at Eastcote Buildings, I, among many others, was assigned the task of decrypting the highly sensitive material of Operation Vesna, a subdivision of a monumental operation by rights. In fact, it would be apt for me to fill you in on the principal operation first, due to its importance. Vesna was a secondary product put in play some years later. The National Security Agency had aided the principal operation's inception to decrypt activities of a Soviet network in British Intelligence. The encoded transmissions that had been gathered began to surface, but at torturous speed. The decodes were problematic, revealing mere fragments of words initially, but over weeks of labour those fragments finally exposed how widespread the Soviet networks had embedded into the Secret Service globally.'

At this point of the brief, the phone rang, which Rutherford answered with no small degree of agitation. 'What is it?' he said abruptly. 'Well can't you get someone else on it? I'm in a briefing.' Long pause. 'Menzies and Rodchenko. Mm … Well …' This relay went on periodically and for a time, with the occasional deep syllable heard from the telephone's earpiece, then Rutherford snapped, 'And he has clearance, has he?' Yet another long pause. 'Bona fides? Gone through all the right channels?' More audible syllables. 'Right, send him up in about an hour. No, I'll deal with him mono y mono.'

The conversation terminated.

'Creagh-West,' Rutherford said. 'Bee in his bonnet about a fellow comrade of yours.' This statement was aimed directly at Rodchenko, who looked as startled as a deer caught in headlights.

'Sir?'

'Koshkin, Sergei. Former Soviet Red Army compatriot?

Defected around the same period?' to which Rodchenko silently nodded his acknowledgement.

Then Menzies chimed in, 'Koshkin?'

'He's one of our sleepers. Rather invaluable photographer for Scotland Yard, matter of fact. Creagh-West thinks the chap might have an asset or two up his sleeve. Could be chicken feed but might be worth the dalliance.' Lighting his cigar, Rutherford then urged Menzies to continue his brief, at which Guy picked up the thread instantly.

'At that time, Soviet Intelligence was at an advantage due to the use of the one-time-pad system, which was virtually impenetrable; and while this was going on at Eastcote, both MI5 and MI6 magnified their search for Soviet spies involved in other branches, such as counter-intelligence and liaison units. Countless Whitehall civil servants were given the third degree but were never told why they were subject to accusation. At least twenty had their employment terminated, several of which were big guns during the Second World War. Dozens were transferred to mundane duties with lowest category security clearance. The vacated desks lay fallow and those who were accountable were assigned to some godforsaken outpost of the Government.'

During Menzies' narrative, Penny had brought in a pot of tea on a tray, which was devoured in an instant; but her presence put paid to the general flow of things, causing a minor bout of paranoia on Menzies' part. Rutherford, having clocked this, prompted him to 'go on' after Penny had at last left the room.

'At this stage of the operation,' Menzies continued, 'the NSA had acquired over twelve thousand highly skilled cryptographers, and up-to-the-minute decoding machines to excavate all Soviet messages located to pinpoint the moles. This was a necessary exercise, for many of the intercepted messages hadn't been properly decrypted from the get-go.'

Rutherford interrupted, 'For Rodchenko's benefit, what or who was the linchpin to the whole operation?'

'A Russian Intelligence officer who wanted to defect. He approached the British Consulate stating he had vital information relating to a Soviet spy ring operating at the very core of our government.'

'Yes, yes,' said the chief portentously. 'I believe we're all familiar with the two guilty parties of the Foreign Office who were mercifully burned. Bunch of pliable archetypal reprobates.'

A cloud of tobacco smoke now drenched the air and the silence in the room was equally as suffocating. On digesting this information, Rodchenko began to feel increasingly ill at ease, yet sat as still as stone. Menzies, on the other hand, registered Oleg nettle marginally, but continued to make his enquiry to the chief on whether he should proceed with his brief.

'By all means do,' retorted Rutherford, standing as if on ceremony, then walking towards the window, returning to the original stance he had assumed from their first entering the room. Menzies rather carefully set things back in motion.

'I shall from this point on refer to the Russian Intelligence officer in question as D. SIS had stationed a team somewhere on the Bosphorus to monitor wireless transmissions, and not days after D had approached the British Consulate, a spate of coded messages rallied between the Soviet Embassy and Moscow alluding to D's disappearance. In response, an agent was sent out to locate D for immediate exfiltration, but D had vanished. A week had lapsed and there was still no sign of him, so the then imminent defection was aborted and the assigned agent returned to London. Days later, intelligence had reached us of an unscheduled landing in the capital's airport of a Soviet military craft. The concealed identity of a person was transported by stretcher on to the aircraft. D had been marked for certain death.'

'And that put an end to the entire operation?' challenged Rutherford.

'Well, Sir, we, I mean the Eastcote lot, assumed the net had closed in on the informants after the two from the Foreign Office had been blown. Several years on, Vesna was set in motion to continue the hunt for active Soviet spies who might have substituted the two exposed from the Foreign Office. Little intelligence was decoded, revealing nothing of consequence, so a section officer put the kibosh on the case and other operations took priority.'

'Yes, well, be that as it may, this file has been deliberately planted on the QT and I want the bastard found, do you hear?'

Menzies agreed with expedience as he stood to take his leave.

'I understand Rodchenko has experience in the province of cryptography,' added the chief, 'is that correct?' to which Oleg affirmed mutely. 'That being the case, I need you, Menzies, to front the cipher room and Rodchenko will be your second. Naturally, there'll be an outfit down the pipe skilled in areas of decoding as well as the usual birdwatchers in the field. Probably get Mercer in on the team. In face of the undertaking you have ahead of you, I feel certain it can be achieved. You're nothing if not resilient, and I'm allotting no timescale. Oh, and I want no great acts of derring-do, is that understood? Tradecraft rules only. Best use Dryden's as a dead-letter drop. Now, get on chaps. I've got that other brief lined up.'

2

THAT SAME EVENING, Menzies decided to divert his usual route home by way of Curzon Street, where he could drop in on a former colleague and chum. The premises in question was a reputable bookstore, but also renowned to a certain breed for backstairs machinations. Its proprietor, George Dryden, was a tall, sharply tailored man with a shrewd intellect and charming looks. His father, who had prematurely bequeathed his legacy to his son, expired suddenly after a game of indoor croquet in his club at Whitehall Place. Dryden senior had had it in mind to contrive a game in the billiards room under the influence of several hours' indulgence. With no particular aversion to club rules, he was on this occasion set to celebrate his birthday largely. It had been reported by several club members that said gentleman had run riot through the establishment with his right trouser leg rolled above the knee, his left shoe absconded, his right stuffed into his left jacket pocket, and his pipe clutched firmly between his teeth. These concluding actions resulted in him calling it a day, at the objection and inconvenience of the institution.

Thereafter, on obtaining his new station, George took instant measures to render the premises a sorely needed facelift. It was a large space, plush and well outfitted with both new and rare titles for the dedicated bibliophile. At the far-left corner of the store stood a spiral staircase, which gave access to a small library for those quiet unions between reader and potential investment. Among the many nooks and corners of the building was a private room to regale book readings, signings and the like, of which Dryden oversaw the smooth running with ease. On resigning from the Service at a ripe age, he had found himself contented with his lot, and acquiring residence of the apartments above, was a consummate bachelor, footloose and fancy free with the regular flow of clandestine schemes, completely undetected by the regular Joe.

It was now after hours and a deluge was running its course outside while Dryden fixed himself a large scotch. As was very often the case in these quiet times, he lit himself an ample pipe to chew on while reviewing the daily accounts. On making a rather down-at-the-heel stroll towards the desk – glass in hand – the din of the brass doorbell indicated entrance of an individual. Dryden turned slowly, ingesting a liberal draft, and articulated, 'Hullo Menzies, you leper. What brings you to this neighbourhood? Been a while.'

Menzies returned wearily, 'Dryden. How goes it?' Closing the door behind him, he removed his hat then impudently shook himself down with the action of a wet dog.

'Could you not,' countered Dryden ironically, accompanied by the raising of an eyebrow and a smirk. 'The merchandise.' Then, raising his glass in the general direction of the door, he said, 'Care for one, Guy?'

'Thanks. Don't mind if I do.'

'What can I get you?'

'Scotch would do nicely. Better make it a large one.'

Dryden poured a double measure into a somewhat costly tumbler, and on handing it over playfully he enquired, 'How's your little Red defector coming along? Ironed out all the wrinkles, have we?'

'Rodchenko?'

'That's the fellow.'

'Reliable product, matter of fact. Worth the investment.

Never strays from the path. He'll be on the rota, so you'll no doubt be rubbing shoulders at some stage.'

'Good,' intoned Dryden blandly. 'Difficult to know how they'll pan out. Code of the guild and all that.'

Menzies concurred quietly, while taking a swig. 'White as snow, far as I can tell. Rutherford seems satisfied. Giving him the benefit of the doubt.'

'Have you been on leave? Or have I missed something?'

'Short sabbatical. Time owing. Thought I would indulge in a little nectar at the vineyard with Father. Half-cut most of the time. Him, not me. Bloody hot too.'

'France, isn't it?'

Menzies nodded. 'South. Reckon the old man will retire out there. Spend the evening of his life bending the elbow and obsessing over chess.'

Dryden chuckled. 'Not a bad way to go. Can't be doing with all this damned fog and inclemency. Bloody sham. Top-up?'

'Please, George. Mind if I smoke?'

'Go ahead. Use the ashtray on the desk. No remnants if you please.'

Now easing into a state of collective idleness, the conversation steered towards the delicate subject of a mutual colleague, Alan Soames. Treading carefully, Menzies tested the water with menial enquiry, as one would, since he had lost track while he had been away. The response landed as expected.

'Now there's a question,' answered Dryden, with unrestrained concern. 'At a loss what to do with the man. His binges aren't dwindling, and he'll find himself out on his ear if he's not careful. Creagh-West is far more forgiving than

Ruthers. I mean to say, one can't just turn up to a briefing half-inebriated … as was sadly the case the other evening. It's getting out of hand.'

'Can't someone gently put him in check? Bend his ear a little?'

'God knows I've tried. His family aren't any help either. Pious lot. Get on their soapboxes. Lack diplomacy … know what I mean?'

'Quite. You came up together didn't you? From Eton?'

'Mm,' replied Dryden, as he refilled his pipe. 'Rowdy bunch in those days, but nothing was ever bent out of shape. Just kids, you know. Innocence. Of course, once we had entered the lofty halls of Cambridge, the vices sprung up, but they were never an issue. Soames always liked a tipple, but we all did.'

There was a long hiatus.

'It will all go ball of chalk, Guy. Mark my words.'

'Surely not, George? He'll get on top of it. Rap on the knuckles should do the trick.'

'Well, I don't know, I really don't. Took him home after the club the other week. Caused a bit of a scene with one of the other members. Christ knows what the disagreement was about. It was all very vague.' Dryden took a prolonged draw on his pipe before he continued, while Menzies watched the tobacco blister in the bowl. 'Got him home all right, eventually, but his flat was a bloody mess. Looked like he had been burgled. Have you seen his place?' Dryden discounted any response. 'So, put him to bed as was, and tidied up a bit for him. Left him clutching his hat. Out for the count.'

3

LATE THAT particular Sunday morning in September, the two comrades Koshkin and Rodchenko met for their routine game of chess off Little Russell Street, in the Upper Vestry House of St George's Church. Entered upon via the rear, the assigned space was light and generous in size with the essential devices intact, including a small adjoining kitchen for communal use.

By rule of thumb, the conversation that took place between the two men was held in Russian, concealing any sensitive subject matter to that of the perceptive ear. This was achieved sporadically and with little noise, and having manoeuvred their five opening moves of defence, Koshkin shoehorned the initial syllables of their approaching transmission. 'I have some proofs that might prove invaluable.'

Finding the opportune moment during the din of the clock timer being clicked around the room, Rodchenko would at length put in his reply. 'Are you carrying them?'

Koshkin would delay his reply until at least two moves had played out between them.

(W) Knight to F1, Knight takes Rook. (B) Queen to A5. (W) Bishop to G5. (B) Pawn to D5. Then his response: 'No. Safety deposit box.'

Rodchenko then lit a cigarette, offering the pack to his opponent, and before starting towards the kitchen, he uttered, 'Accessible?' On leaving the table he walked cautiously, registering any wandering or quietly judging eyes, and while waiting for the kettle to boil he gazed out of the window, watching the passers-by setting about their day with the untarnished knowledge of the hazardous province he now found himself in.

Settling back into the game after placing the drinks he had prepared on the table, he at once realised he had failed to take his move prior to his trip to the kitchen, leaving Koshkin to ruminate his play. (W) Bishop to F6 was played. Koshkin, after a long pause, moved (B) Rook to G8, and simultaneously answered the earlier question in the affirmative. At this juncture, their concentration intensified, for the game was heating up, yet all the while Rodchenko thought of little else but the unspoken topic of the proofs held in his friend's possession. Determined to prise out of him an unabridged account, it was suggested they chew it over at the Museum Tavern, not yards from the club. This was instantly agreed on after Rodchenko had checkmated the King with his Rook.

Not a word was spoken between them as they walked from A to B, but in his mind, Koshkin was mapping out in detail the relevant events that would be communicated. Any noticeable disparity that existed between the compatriots was their height, Rodchenko being short, Koshkin its antithesis. Their respective and analogous merits laid claim to an inexhaustible loyalty, which their current cause demanded of them. Neither faltered from their path, and anything that might chance to fall foul of it was immediately discounted. Having both served in the Soviet Red Army during the war, they knew precisely what it was to be not only a soldier but how to commit themselves to an ideology worth giving their lives for. In the face of the Cold War, however, this would rattle their somewhat resolute allegiance, toppling them off their fickle perch and into an alien territory.

The public house, where they were to spend the remainder of the day, was heaving but would serve as an ideal environment for their purpose. On entering, they allocated a recently vacated booth at the far end of the establishment, neatly tucked away from the hordes, and ordered some food. As before, their communion was held in their mother tongue, which did not commence until their order had arrived, by which time Rodchenko was beyond eager to proceed. Koshkin began.

'Shortly after I had defected ten years ago, I was approached by a fellow émigré who was also a colleague at Scotland Yard. "Sergei," he says, "what would you say to earning a little tax-free cash on the side for a rudimentary job … all expenses paid?" I was of course dubious, but I was struggling at the time and I was in dire need. You know how it is, my friend? So, I asked him to expand on the details before I considered committing to it. He then explained that the assignment was to track and photograph someone of importance, which would take place in Prague that coming weekend. "Someone of importance?" I asked. "Who might that be?" So, my colleague, Slavsky, then assures me there was nothing underhand in play, but I was to discreetly acquire said photos at a specific time and place.' Koshkin then took pause to light a cigarette mid-mouthful, as if to calm his nerves, then continued. 'So, in return I said I required further information of this assignment and needed to know the full extent of what I was getting myself into.'

Rodchenko's eyes widened at this point, since he sensed the distress in his friend as fear descended over his face.

'It was nothing risky, he told me, provided I wasn't seen. "Jesus!" I said, then who in God's name was I to photograph? I was getting a little hot under the collar by this stage, so I demanded that if he didn't make things clear, I would walk away from the offer altogether.'

There was now a strained pause hanging as Rodchenko glared at his friend with anticipation. Koshkin took several drawn-out drags on his cigarette before bringing himself to continue. 'Eventually, after tugging back and forth, Slavsky came clean. The actual assignment was to photograph a Soviet handler who was to meet his courier for a handover. The rendezvous was due to take place at St Vitus Cathedral, Sunday morning at six, and my objective would be to obtain photographs of the asset outside the rendezvous from the roof of an adjacent building.'

Koshkin stopped to drain a double shot of vodka, while Rodchenko sat mute with considerable unease. 'I told Slavsky I wanted nothing to do with it; that I was an honest man trying to make ends meet … but he dangled a very large carrot, to which I shamefully yielded. It was a substantial sum, Oleg. I couldn't afford to turn it down. I was in arrears with rent and could barely scrape the barrel for food.' A remorseful silence supervened. '"It's an easy job," says Slavsky, to sweeten the pill. "Act the tourist for the weekend. See the sights … get a free lunch. Obtain the proofs and you're out, job done." So, it was finally agreed. Slavsky handed over the assignment details, along with the plane tickets and a cash payment that same day; and the weekend soon came round.

'I flew out on the Saturday, settled into the hotel, which was walking distance from the rendezvous, then sat out the interim. I stayed awake the entire night as I was feeling pretty edgy, and I wandered the cobblestone backstreets leading down to the canal, moving in and out of coffee shops to pass the time. I needed to assess the roof of the building from where I was to work, to ensure my concealment was conclusive. I returned to the hotel for dinner, trying far too hard to appear inconspicuous, which I doubtless failed. I arrived at my vantage point two hours early to prepare my equipment in good stead. From 5.30 a.m. I was counting down the seconds in a severe sweat and ascending heart rate, waiting for the sunrise.

'The seconds dragged on and there wasn't a soul wandering the Old Town Square, until … there he was. Two minutes to six. He obscured himself behind one of the two Gothic pillars, which stood at the Mosaic of the Last Judgement. A minute later, the courier appeared. Tall figure, wearing a long trench coat. I was able to snap a couple of photos of them individually before the courier joined his handler behind the pillars. I waited for what seemed an age before they reappeared, which they did eventually. They surfaced separately and I was beginning to panic that I wouldn't have the opportunity to capture them together, but a window presented itself and the courier turned back, offering a clear portrait shot of them together at close range.'

A second round of drinks were ordered and their discarded meals were shuffled off, giving the impression that they too would be quietly escorted out, making room for the successive patron. But they were in for the duration, adopting their plight as if guards at the gate and creating a sort of invisible barrier to deter unwanted trespassers.

Koshkin resumed. 'After allowing ample time for them to disappear from view, I packed away my camera and accessories and made my way back to the hotel. I had the chilling feeling I was being followed. Being that there was no one about, I dodged into a tobacconist for cover, procrastinating for as long as possible and until the streets began to fill. It was nothing. Whoever it was, they soon gave up the ghost.'

Koshkin was now displaying signs of irritability, shifting about his seat with transparent tension, and Rodchenko registered the colour drain rapidly from his face. 'When I returned to England that Sunday evening, I developed the film in my makeshift darkroom and locked away every shred of evidence until they were to be collected. I resumed work Monday to find that Slavsky was absent, which was not unusual for him; except he was absent the following day, and the following, and the next ten days until word reached the Yard of a body found on the Embankment. Superintendent Fenhill had identified the body and there had been clear signs of a struggle imprinted on Slavsky's neck. Foul play was evident. Asphyxiation by drowning was the pathologist's verdict.'

'Christ Sergei!' came the first syllables uttered from Rodchenko's mouth. 'What did you do with the film?'

'What could I do? I was terrified they would come to find me. Once I could think straight, I made the decision to move house. Rentals are easy to obtain, and as I was in a better position financially, I paid everything up front and moved the same day. The evidence has been sitting in my safety deposit locker at Scotland Yard these ten years, and no one has come to claim it.'

'But why are you telling me this now? After ten years, Sergei!'

'Because MI6 have requested my assistance in an operation. A dead operation. One I know to implicate the Russian spy.'

'What makes you think it's him? There are countless Russian spies floating about.'

'I know this because Slavsky left me a handwritten letter at the Yard. It disclosed one word. YURI.'

4

THE FORMER marital home of Saul Mercer lay bare to its remorseful existence in the form of an empty shell, which could also be said of the marriage that had resided within its four walls. This consequence had occurred quite unexpectedly on returning home from an operation located in Lisbon to a bleakly vacated property. He knew instinctively the marriage was nearing its close, owing to the three joyless years of exertion made on his part, and the lack on her part, yet that misery she had gained through the exercise was imputed entirely on him. He had failed, in her eyes, to extinguish or fulfil her needs as a husband, a lover or even a companion since his commitment to the Service outranked all else. Saul, on several occasions, admitted to this fact whenever she felt the need to exploit it as a means of ammunition, which she discharged regularly with contempt. In all honesty, he had felt a mild commiseration towards the whole affair, and even a sense of relief that the marriage had expired on her terms; for in this process, he had been saved of any further abusive adjectives, which would have doubtless been thrown about the vicinity to no great end.

After the event in question, Saul's wife had failed to provide him with any forwarding address, therefore granting him sole ownership of the connubial property, which naturally strengthened his resolve to sell up immediately. Through these measures, he obtained an impeccable apartment on Markham Square, SW3. A spacious open-plan property, offering one bedroom and the essential reception rooms, accompanied with clinically up-to-date appliances. This was a suitable situation for him, for Saul had a more natural bent for solitude and did not express a constant desire for company – as did his wife; neither did he need endless entertaining or toilsome gatherings to fill a void that could not be quenched. He simply never possessed one. He was an entirely whole and forthright human being. A man of stature and integrity, of whom now, having the coop hightailed, could commit himself to his field unreservedly.

The morning of 7 September would prove an absorbing one, which was a welcome change to the menial enterprises forerunning it, and as Mercer sat poring over some mundanity in his ten by twelve office, the phone rang, which was an oddity in itself. The call was from Rutherford, summoning him up to his office to 'chew the fat' over some resurfaced case on which he had recently received memorandum. Its content was far more extensive than the chief had let on, as he was soon to discover.

Equipped with his quota cup of coffee of the day, Mercer politely wished Penny a good morning then entered the chief's office in succession. Rutherford was sat silently engaged in a phone call, which was an unusual occurrence, with the back of his chair presented and him staring out of the window puffing heavily on a cigar. On hearing Mercer's entrance, he swivelled the chair round and motioned an abrasive nod towards the vacant chairs, then promptly rounded off the call, in which he appeared so shamelessly unengaged.

'Ah, Mercer. Take a pew.' Saul toed the line directly. 'Hope I haven't prised you away from any pressing matters? I know how methodically you like to run things.'

'Not at all, Sir. All pretty paltry if I'm honest. Received the memorandum. Shall we mull over the details?'

Rutherford rose and walked towards his personal safe,

which he unlocked carefully, then pulled a large, hefty folder from the cabinet drawer and plonked it heavy-handedly on the desk. 'No doubt you're familiar with this intelligence product?' He did not mention it by name; he simply left it for Mercer's scrutiny.

'Yes, Sir. I believe you would be hard-pressed to find a Service officer who isn't. No slight intended Sir, but what's its relevance to the Vesna case?'

'By association,' returned Rutherford. 'In fact, Vesna supersedes it chronologically by some years, but I don't expect you to know that since I've only recently been made privy to its existence myself.'

Mercer's ears pricked up at this snippet of information. He then waited patiently for his superior to propound.

'Had Menzies and Rodchenko in here yesterday. It appears Guy had substantial experience on both operations while at GCHQ. By the looks of it, he delivered some solid tracking throughout the entire operation, as you'll see. Hell of a lot of wireless traffic to thumb through. You know, he practically usurped the entire brief yesterday, but I'll give him his due, he was very thorough in achieving a succinct account for Rodchenko's benefit. Incidentally, it was Oleg who unearthed Vesna in Registry, purely by accident of course. Christ knows how long it's been sitting down there!'

After allowing a meaningless pause to take its course, Mercer piped in. 'What is it you require of me, Sir?'

'Yes, quite right. Digressing. I want you to review this product. Familiarise yourself. That's your first port of call. See if you can't sift out further intelligence on other possible undesirables. Check all telephone recorded transmissions. Survey them with a fine-tooth comb. Menzies is leading the decoding team, which will be decrypting every grubby little activity of Soviet communications. Rodchenko has shown his mettle so I've given him high security clearance to work under Menzies.'

Still standing, assertive and ex officio, Rutherford now gave way to a short pause while he opened the cedarwood cigar box sitting on the desk. Placing one of the cigars between his teeth, he picked up the box and offered it to Mercer, which he politely declined. 'Once you've got through that lot, you can investigate Vesna. You'll find its scale greatly diminished, since according to Menzies the operation was pretty futile. Barely got off the ground. Quietly forgotten. Rather conveniently for the bugger who planted it in Registry, wouldn't you say?' After Rutherford let off a furious minute or so, he continued relatively equably with his brief. 'Confer with Menzies regularly. I want you on the same page, Saul, so update each other on every tiny detail you've surfaced.'

'Of course, Sir. Will Soames be an additional?'

'Not bloody likely! The man's a liability. Can't have him muddying the waters, not on my watch. Which brings me to the other matter.' But before Rutherford advanced on this subject, he took long determined strides towards the door, opened it, then growled an order at Penny to whip up a couple of coffees, which she was to achieve on the double. Returning to the desk, he sat down and finally lit the cigar that was wedged between his teeth. He continued: 'But before I get ahead of myself, I must first bring you up to date on our promising émigrés.'

'Émigrés, Sir?'

'I now refer to Koshkin, Sergei. Defected about ten years ago. Former Red Army. Turned the same period as

Rodchenko. Not one of us. Took a more deviated route than his fellow compatriot. Forensic photographer for Scotland Yard.' Mercer listened with charge and astuteness. 'He's recently approached us, stating he has some documented proof of a Soviet handler and his courier, which was apparently obtained soon after his defection.'

'What sort of documentation?'

'I assume photographic, but he didn't amplify … at least not to me. Could have scant value but worth pursuing, don't you think?'

'Quite, Sir. A possible link to the buried case perhaps?'

'Christ, anything's possible. Anyway, thought you could stand as his point of contact. Nothing set in concrete yet, but any exchange of materials could run through Dryden's.'

'Where's he holding the documentation?'

'That he didn't divulge. Rather prickly about it if I'm honest. Mind you, poor chap's probably unfamiliar with backstairs dealings, not to mention the long-standing possession of the stuff. No doubt he's desperate to get them off his hands.' Rutherford then handed Mercer a written scrap containing Koshkin's contact details, while inhaling a prolonged draw on his cigar, at which point Penny entered the room with the order of coffees. 'Get on to him soon as, Mercer. With any luck it has significant value. At any rate, he's on the payroll, and actually, thinking about it, use a safe house for the exchange. Russell Square. He might find that a more convivial arrangement.'

A hiatus supervened and Rutherford quickly adopted the manner of an old pedagogue. 'Now,' he said scornfully, 'Soames. Short mention should be made of recent events, which have regrettably enforced my current resolve on pushing forward. Firstly, I've given him two weeks' leave to hammer out the cause of his personal difficulties. Secondly, as much as I detest having to take such measures, I think it a necessary evil. Alas, no alternative, Saul. Need to watch his movements. Keep an eye. Can't be doing with an unequable sot. Turning up at meetings half-cut. Could become an epidemic. Might have to refer him to the psychiatrist if it continues. Hope it doesn't come to that quite frankly, but rules are rules.'

A heavy lull was now prominent in the room and Mercer felt the burden of its gravity. 'I'm sorry to hear that, Sir. He's a good officer.'

'Can you do it though, Saul? Pushing your boundaries somewhat, I know. Need someone trustworthy, you see.'

Mercer felt as though the form of his integrity had been put in traction, and he genuinely struggled with the idea of being birdwatcher to a friend and colleague. Being ordered to watch a Soviet hood was one thing, but in Mercer's mind it didn't alter the principle of the thing. The imposition itself required a temporary bulwark by way of self-preservation. A necessary armour. He then answered accordingly, 'Of course, Sir. I'll tail him loosely.'

'Just focus on his movements. See if we can't get to the bottom of it all. Appreciate your grit, Mercer.'

5

IF IT HAD NOT been for Alan Soames' carousing and its disastrous results, he would never have found himself sitting in the interview room at Scotland Yard. This predicament did not only compromise his dignity but also his long-standing tenure with the Secret Service, whereat he would doubtless be subject to ridicule. A sobering prospect was before him, and as he sat in the deafening solitude of the cold room, he measured his pitiful conduct with damning reproach; it was an abrasive wake-up call and one that could not be diminished by any stretch.

Its consequences were irrevocable, but deep within Soames' mind he had almost wanted it to happen; he felt an incessant need to create chaos and had a loathing towards the illusion of a fair democracy. Within his contemplation he remembered even as a child he had longed to escape the limiting dogma of the faith he had been inherently born into, one that would hinder his very evolution. That same dogma would abandon him, exile him and brand him a pariah. These were the thoughts that occupied his mind while he solemnly prepared for the melee ahead, and during those moments he grappled with guilt and the truth of who he truly was. He was a paradox; a person whom few understood.

Though Soames was slight in build, he was robust and of medium height. His features were puckish, and a mass of dark hair graced his head. His eyes were astute and direct and were never averse to confrontation. During his extensive education he had often been pegged a near idiot, when in fact quite the opposite was true, which only became evident as an undergraduate.

After what seemed like an eternity, Detective Fenhill finally entered the interview room. It was twenty past four in the morning and a ruckus could be heard from a group of thugs, which travelled from one of the adjoining rooms beyond the interview room door. The din dissipated marginally after Fenhill had taken a seat. He placed an unopened packet of cigarettes on the table, along with a box of matches and two cups of coffee. He then introduced himself politely, but Soames sensed an element of terseness in his voice. The preliminaries were over, and the interview began.

'Am I addressing Peter Fawkes?' Fenhill enquired.

Out of the dozen identities Soames had been given under his tenure at MI6, Fawkes, he decided, would be used in this instance. Soames nodded, which seemed to suffice since the interview was not being recorded at that point. He then motioned towards the cigarettes on the table and added, 'Do you mind?'

'Go right ahead,' came the reply, and he did so. Fenhill then allowed a little time before he delivered his next question. 'I assume, now compos mentis, that you understand why you're here?' Soames made no reply; he simply glared at his interlocutor and exhaled a long stream of smoke.

'A few hours ago, you were physically removed from the premises of the Savile Club on Mayfair. Can you remember why that occurred, Mr Fawkes?'

Again, no answer was submitted.

'Let me refresh your memory. According to the manager of the club, several attempts had been made to remind you of certain club ethos and since you were overstretching those rules, due to excessive drinking, your removal from said club was “de rigueur”, as the gentleman put it. Is this sounding familiar to you at all?’

Soames made no effort to respond to the questions being thrown his way; he merely smoked equably with controlled aloofness.

‘Then let’s see whether this jogs your memory, shall we? On reviewing several statements made by club members, one account states that you had “refrained from using the men’s room and proceeded to urinate on the upper landing of the principal staircase in full view of several other club members”. Another reported that you had caused extensive damage to the club’s bar, whereat several fixtures, windows and oddments of furniture were destroyed. Are any of these events dislodging anything from that skull of yours, Mr Fawkes?’

At this stage of the interview, Soames was even less compliant and reinforced his training in matters of interrogation. He was determined to offer as little information as was mundanely possible.

‘Now, I don’t know about you,’ Fenhill went on, ‘but if I see a chap behaving like this, my first thought is that the person is clearly unhappy. Dissatisfied with his lot. There’s an underlying impulse, a darker source driving that person … cause and effect, if you will. A much deeper reason behind the expressed behaviour. Or perhaps the person in question has something missing … but I’m sure I can make an informed guess.’

‘How spectacularly self-evident,’ replied Soames with scathing sarcasm.

‘There’s no need for rudeness, Mr Fawkes. I’m merely trying to establish the cause of your little outburst.’

'Well, you're clearly stumbling about in the dark, Detective, however perceptive you think you might be.'

'Popular at school were we, sir?'

Soames pitched him a perfunctory look.

'Hit a nerve, have I? Well, no doubt you'll be putty in my hands in due course.'

Soames took another cigarette from the packet and placed it between his lips while he wrapped his oversized trench coat around his sinewy body. He lit the cigarette then glanced briefly at his watch.

'Holding you up, are we Mr Fawkes? I do understand this is all a frightful bore but the sooner you cooperate the better. That's generally how these things work. Now, let's move beyond the frivolities, shall we? I'm sure you're familiar with how the law tends to work. More often than not there are repercussions to such violations … despite how minor that infraction might be. Unfortunately for you, the Savile Club wish to press charges in recompense for the damage you've inflicted on the property.'

There was a glance exchanged between them that created a long coarse silence, followed by a rather punctual interruption from an officer opening the interview room door. Fenhill motioned the officer to speak.

'Pardon the intrusion, Sir. Telephone for you.'

'Do excuse me, Mr Fawkes.' Fenhill took his leave.

During the detective's absence, for some reason unknown to Soames, a memory popped into his head of a particular incident that had occurred at Eton; a memory he had long since forgotten of when up to their usual tomfoolery between lessons, he and Dryden had locked poor Bertie Hanbury in the downstairs broom cupboard. Bertie was a regular candidate for humiliation being that he had the unfortunate impediment of a stutter. He was also a little plump and it took the two of them to carry him to his lengthy confinement, where he was eventually found quite by accident by the caretaker. Soames chuckled to himself on recalling their finding him passed out or asleep (they could not tell) where they had left him – and how they had threatened a bed drench for a whole week if he imputed the culprits' names. Explanation should be made of the popularity of the bed drench. This was achieved by filling a shoebox or any large airtight object with water and pouring it at any given hour over the sleeping recipient.

A sudden cloud overshadowed Soames' temporary amusement as he felt himself yearning for that cheerful Eden when life was simpler and far less methodised. His eyes welled slightly as he stared at the interview room table and tugged away on the dog-end through to its filter. His thoughts then switched to the detective with whom he had to endure the half-baked notions of an amateur in matters of the psyche. He had, in fact, reminded Soames of some bumbling politician who had the resources to spew an inexhaustible idiom of empty words, but whose endowment intellectually was somewhat slender.

Minutes later, Detective Fenhill re-entered the room. 'It appears luck is on your side, Mr Fawkes. Or is it Soames? Just spoke to your superior. Mr Rutherford? Proper sergeant major. Expect you have to watch your Ps and Qs with that one.'

In the acknowledgement that 6 were now involved, Soames felt a pang of dread swallow in his conscience. He knew instantly that a hauling over the coals would be

Rutherford's initial line, which would predictably conform to pattern but was unavoidable, nonetheless.

Fenhill continued. 'Now, as these circumstances are … shall we say, unusual, I would like to remind you of the severity of your recent actions. Your behaviour last evening at the Savile will have doubtless attracted public comment, and I suggest you make efforts to preclude any further embarrassment. As your superior, Rutherford seems to have ample clout. I'm assuming you're of government tenure and therefore out of deep waters for the time being. However, I strongly advise that you do not strengthen the hands of the press by repeating any recent exercises. You'll forfeit, Mr Fawkes. Like trout to the fly.'

'Thank you for that inciteful analogy, Detective. Once again your choice of platitudes is remarkably patent.'

'Now listen here you jumped-up little squirt; if you do find yourself returning to these premises again, for whatever reason that might be, there'll be no special treatment extended to you … I don't care who you are! Understood, Mr Fawkes?'

Fenhill then started towards the door, and as he flung it open, he barked at the nearest officer within earshot. 'Someone get him out of here. Anyone? He can bloody well wait for his committee out front!'

6

THAT COMMITTEE came in the shape of Saul Mercer, whose orders were to deliver Soames directly to headquarters without delay. When Mercer entered the station, Soames was sat dozing with his coat tightly wrapped around him, legs outstretched, feet crossed, his chin resting on his chest and a forelock dangling over a portion of his face. As Mercer examined him quietly, his immediate thought was of an incident when his young nephew had got himself lost in a department store in Tunbridge Wells. An employee had discovered the boy hiding under a large table display of trainsets and model aircraft, where he had been sobbing at length. When they were eventually reunited, the boy was found asleep, but his tear-stained face was stark evidence of the torture that had burned within. This was how Soames appeared to Mercer. Lost and tormented. Careful not to alarm Soames, he spoke his name quietly.

'Christ!' blurted Soames, and as he looked up at Mercer, he said, 'Oh, it's you. I wondered who they might send.'

'Sorry to disappoint old chap. Got to take you in I'm afraid.'

'Oh good, a rollicking from Ruthers. What joy.'

Mercer took Soames' arm by way of helping him to his feet, but Soames shook him off with irritation. 'I'm not a bloody cripple!' he shouted, while attracting the attention of everyone in the vicinity.

An officer called out from the far end of the room, 'Everything all right, sir?'

'Yes, quite all right, thank you,' answered Mercer politely. 'Bit worse for wear it would seem,' and the officer acknowledged with a nod.

As they walked out the rear entrance of the Yard, Mercer tried to hail a taxi and Soames sermonised in an accusing tone: 'So, it was you, was it? Who called it in?' Mercer did not answer, he just focused on flagging down a cab. 'There's no point denying it. And I don't appreciate being tailed either.'

'I wasn't following you; I was merely—'

'I'm not a complete idiot, Saul! Who put you up to it? Rutherford?'

'As a matter of fact, yes, it was.'

'What are you playing at?'

'They were orders! Do you think I took pleasure in it? You can't imagine how demeaning it is having to tail a chum.'

'Actually, I can.'

'Oh? Done a little menial observance work on your pals have we?'

'Never mind.'

A taxi pulled up and Mercer gave his instruction to the driver while Soames climbed in. There was a long awkward silence as Soames lit himself a cigarette and stared out of the window, not looking at anything of interest.

Mercer broke the silence. 'What's going on with you Alan? All gone a bit ball of chalk recently. Want to talk? Can I help in any way?'

'I'm beyond all that now.'

Mercer was careful not to push things but tried to appease him in his uniquely sentinel manner. When they arrived at headquarters, the reception committee was less than cordial. Everything seemed to momentarily come to a halt as Mercer led Soames through the deadened offices filled with statue-like figures and quietly judging eyes. Even the air was stultifying, but Mercer did his best to avoid eye contact, except for those of Rutherford, who was waiting for their arrival.

'It's not a bloody parade!' Rutherford bellowed. 'I'm sure you've all got better things to be doing. Get back to work … the lot of you!'

The three of them entered Rutherford's office in an almost funereal mood and Soames made a beeline for the nearest chair. 'Excuse me for not standing to attention but I've not had a wink all night,' he said.

Rutherford peered over his half-lens specs and began to deprecate with vigour. 'Christ, Soames, you're not on leave two minutes and you've already got yourself into some godawful mess!'

Soames ignored the slur. 'It's bloody arctic in here! What's come of the heating, Ruthers?'

'Might I remind you that I'm your superior, or had you forgotten that small detail?'

'No, Sir,' Soames answered curtly.

'Right. Let's get down to the nuts and bolts, shall we?'

Rutherford closed the office door and motioned Mercer to sit down. His manner continued to be of a no-nonsense military tone and Soames was unreceptive to it all.

'Your exploits of last evening have called into question your tenure with 6 and a demotion could be on the cards if you reject the terms being offered.'

'Demotion?'

'Just shut up, Soames, and hear me out! I've had to pull out all the stops on your behalf … so listen up. Now, the Savile are naturally wanting to press charges for the mischief caused on the premises, but Creagh-West thinks we can wangle that little hiccup with MI6 settling the claim by pleading emotional instability. Or a breakdown brought on by stress … something of the ilk.'

'That's absurd!' countered Soames.

'Is it? I would call your showing up to briefings half-cut pretty absurd, wouldn't you? My God man, it's been going on for weeks and we've turned a blind eye for long enough. Too damned lenient if you ask me. Hell, Soames, you're a good officer but these episodes have tarnished your cunning and ability to spotlight what's at hand.'

Mercer felt, until that moment, rather like a rejected piece of furniture but thought it appropriate to now pipe in. 'We want to help you, Alan.'

Soames took immediate offence to this remark. 'I don't need any help. What I need is a bloody holiday for Christ's sake!'

'And you'll get one!' shouted Rutherford. 'One the length of a permanent suspension if you play your cards right!'

The tension in the room was intolerable. Rutherford was still standing, and he sauntered over to the desk to fetch a cigar. As he lit it, he reasoned off the incensed bout of irritation.

Soames paid scant notice to Rutherford's rebuke and casually lit himself a cigarette. 'For the sake of brevity, can we not just crack on with the terms?' he said.

'Oh, I hadn't realised you had somewhere to be,' answered Rutherford with acrimony, 'only, we do have rather pressing matters to attend to … like your bloody head on the block! Now, since you've failed to do anything spectacular in the past few months, aside from rustle up a sodding lawsuit, I suggest you drop the armoury of witticisms and espy the gravity of your current standing.'

Another unpleasant pause ensued.

Rutherford became marginally neutral from this point and continued. 'I've spoken with Gladstone, and since he's assigned to handling sensitive cases such as these, you'll be put under his charge.'

'Dr Rupert Gladstone?'

'That's correct. Why? Do we have qualms?'

'Well, yes I do, matter of fact. I wasn't aware I was being referred.'

'I was getting to that. You'll be hospitalised forthwith. In fact, Gladstone is on his way up as we speak. He'll take you to your flat to gather your gear for the long haul. I'm afraid a psychiatrist is an essential part of the terms, Alan. We need to get to the bottom of your episodes. He'll put you right.'

Soames was pinned in a tight corner and knew he had to concede without dispute, otherwise his fixed tenure would fall duly on its arse.

Rutherford resumed calmly. 'Once we have some cogent evidence of your recovery, then we might be in a position to discuss placing you down the pipe in our current leading operation.'

'Which is?'

'Vesna. But until then, those are the terms, Alan … take it or leave it.'

This statement ruffled Soames' feathers somewhat, but his options were grossly limited and he was forced to concede collectedly.

'We'll handle the paperwork later,' added Rutherford. 'So, if you don't mind, I have some pressing business to discuss with Mercer. You can wait for Gladstone in Penny's office.'

Soames shuffled out of the room with his tail between

his legs and the debriefing began between Rutherford and Mercer. They were both now seated, and the chief produced two tumblers from the desk drawer, filling them amply with a shot of whisky.

'Think we've earned these, eh, Mercer. Mud in your eye. What an utter travesty.' He took a large swig from the glass. 'What have you got for me Saul? Aside from the obvious.'

'Well, from the start of the surveillance he was on a slippery slope. Tailed him to his local convenience store—'

'On foot?'

'Car, Sir, where he purchased a couple of inebriants and five packets of cigarettes. He then took me on a wild goose chase. Tried to shake me off around Green Park area where his car broke down. He left the car on double yellows and flagged a taxi down, which took him to Dryden's on Curzon Street. He was there a good couple of hours. There was some sort of book signing going on, so by the time he left he was already pretty pickled.'

'Did he leave alone?'

'Yes, Sir. Walked to the Savile from there. I followed him on foot. He disappeared into some public toilets for a while, but eventually emerged and made his way to the club. The rest is history, Sir.'

'Right. Did you manage to get in on the brouhaha? Witness any events prior to his being chucked off the premises?'

'I did, Sir. Made a note of his mishaps … damages, that sort of thing. When it all kicked off I entered the premises to witness it first-hand but stayed out of sight. All pretty unremarkable as far as I could see; the club staircase notwithstanding.'

'Mm … right. What's he up to, the bugger? Something not sitting right.' There was a long silence where Rutherford took a deep inhale and squinted with blatant reproof. As he exhaled, he enjoined, 'I want him under surveillance, good and proper this time … for when he's released from hospital. Get his flat tapped tonight, soon as he's out of the way. And Mercer? Break ranks from here on. Go it alone.'

7

MERCER HAD telephoned Scotland Yard earlier that day to arrange the preliminaries with Sergei Koshkin, who had been out on an assignment related to a theft. On receiving the message, Koshkin returned the call promptly from a phone box near the Yard. By and large, the plan was for the documentation in Koshkin's possession to exchange hands at eight o'clock that same evening at the safe house on Russell Square. Their safety signal would be two full bottles of milk, which were to be left on the doorstep. The countersignal was three bell rings and the delivery of said milk appointed at the meet and greet. The fallback would involve, on Koshkin's insistence, his comrade Oleg Rodchenko, should things take an unavoidable turn. He suggested he leave communication of some form for Rodchenko to collect at a dead-letter drop, which Mercer instructed should be left at Dryden's on Curzon Street. This was finally agreed on by both parties with Mercer's confident assurance of its success.

That evening at his flat in Wood Green, Koshkin made the essential preparations for the exchange but first took a light supper of bread and kolbasa with a strong black coffee. Laid out on the kitchen table, aside from the tableware and its accompanying food items, were a roll of cellophane, a box of food bags, a small piece of fabric, needle and thread and some scissors. His first objective was to wrap one single negative proof into layers of cellophane and, having used a knife to prise open the heel of his left shoe, he took the proof from inside and began the procedure. This he concluded while smoking a cigarette. He encased the proof hermetically then sealed it within a food bag, folding it as many times as possible without damaging its contents. After threading the needle, he stitched the plastic contrivance into the piece of fabric. The end product was then placed inside his shoe under the innersole of his left foot. From the kitchen drawer, he cut some twine of nylon fishing wire, which was fastened to a small fishhook, then placed it into the right inside pocket of his jacket.

His usual route to Russell Square would have been direct from the nearest underground station but Koshkin did not on this occasion conform to pattern. Instead, he changed at Holborn for Tottenham Court Road, where he then walked as the crow flies to the British Museum. As he entered the gates, a plague of pigeons was scattered on the pavement leading up to the museum steps – feasting on some discarded remnants. He paid no heed to the crowds and made straight for the shop, where he purchased a single postcard displaying the exterior of the building, along with a small packet of envelopes. The receipt he pocketed. These items were then taken to the café, where he seated himself in a quiet corner of the room. He tore the postcard in half, placing each half into separate envelopes – one addressed to Rodchenko, the other to an address in Lisbon. On completing this procedure, he noticed two dubious-looking men standing at the café entrance, who immediately averted their eyes when Koshkin looked over in their direction. One of the men feigned to read the newspaper he was holding, the other glanced swiftly at his watch.

Before heading to the nearest post office, Koshkin used the men's room; chiefly to observe whether the two men would follow. They did so. On leaving the lavatory, he found them standing some twenty feet away, and they continued to tail his every movement thereafter. Koshkin purchased a signed-for service at the post office for the envelope addressed to Lisbon, and on this instance, he burned and discarded the receipt. The presence of the two men aroused grave anxiety within Koshkin's mind as he made tracks for Dryden's bookshop. He made several backward glances in a failed attempt to allay his immediate fears as he began to perspire.

Now standing outside the bookshop on Curzon Street, Koshkin observed that there were a handful of female customers in conversation with a gentleman – who he assumed was the proprietor. He entered the shop and exchanged glances with said gentleman while closing the door behind him. With a measure of apprehension, he furthered his step into the store while simultaneously permitting said customers their leave.

Dryden looked at Koshkin quizzically. 'Can I help you?' he enquired with charm.

'You are the proprietor, yes?'

'I am, indeed, sir. George Dryden, how do you do. And how may I be of help?'

'I would like to leave item for Rodchenko. Oleg Rodchenko. I was instructed by Mr Mercer. He say you are intermediary for ... certain correspondence. Correct?'

'Right you are, old chap. If you wish, I could deposit said item into his safety deposit box for you.' This did not appear a desirable option, for Koshkin wanted absolute assurance of its delivery. 'Or better still, you might prefer to deposit the item yourself?'

In contrast to Dryden's complaisance, Koshkin's manner appeared fraught and uneasy but the reply he gave was civil. 'Please. Where I deposit?'

'By all means. The deposit boxes are situated in the room to my left here. You'll need locker D9 for Mister Rodchenko … Mister?'

Without providing his name, Koshkin answered, 'Thank you,' rather tensely.

The deposit was made and Koshkin left the store promptly, thanking Dryden on his way out. Dryden, on the other hand, wished him a good day and was left feeling inanely baffled by the whole encounter.

Back on the street, Koshkin found the watchers loitering one block up, at which point he headed east towards Russell Square. There was a couple of hours spare before the rendezvous, so he led his pursuers on a merry dance by way of a rather dislocated route through the byways.

•

WHILE THIS WAS in play, Mercer prepped things an hour ahead of schedule. The curtains had been drawn, the property sufficiently lit and the safety signal strategically set on cue. The safe house itself was a large, sparse flat situated on the fifth floor of Bloomsbury Mansions, with views of Russell Park. An ungodly row was in motion as Mercer climbed the five storeys back up to the flat; it seemed to be travelling from the second floor. On hearing the din of this senseless altercation, it reminded Mercer of his own single and morbid experience of married life – a life that he was fully prepared to forgo post hoc. When he reached the fifth floor, the quarrel abruptly stopped, followed by an enraged slamming of a door and the quick succession of feet running down the stairs. He peered briefly over the bannisters, but the person had already exited the building, with the ensuing screech of a car's rear wheels that echoed as it jeered off up the road.

Now nearing eight o'clock, the net was closing in on Koshkin as he entered Russell Park. The acuteness of his situation had accrued gravitas as his anxiety escalated out of control. The sweat was now falling from his face and he was hyperventilating, so he sat and rested briefly on the nearest bench, checking regularly over his shoulder for his pursuers. Naturally, they fell in with his every move, ensuring their location was cunningly set at ample distance. A woman was sprinting towards Koshkin with a dog, which alarmed him initially, but by way of deterrent, if only for the sake of his watchers, he called out to her and asked her for the time.

'Two minutes to eight,' she replied as she jogged sportively on the spot, but as she went to take her leave, Koshkin noticed a third man entering the south end of the park. Koshkin's instinct urged him to keep the woman talking while the two watchers hovered at their location. The third man walked briskly in the direction of the two men and Koshkin knew that the woman and her dog were now the redundant pieces on the board. A nod of exchange was subtly prompted between the three men as the woman started off, then the third man walked directly past her with his head down, situating himself at Koshkin's rear. The woman and her dog vanished.

•

MERCER PACED WITH agitation up and down the room. The time was now almost 8.30 p.m. All manner of thoughts floundered in his head as he questioned over and over whether Koshkin had taken down the correct address. He telephoned the Yard to determine when Koshkin might have left but was informed that he had left the Yard earlier than usual, ostensibly concerning a personal matter. Mercer then inspected the street below from a front-facing window overlooking the park. He drew back the curtain carefully but there was no one in sight. He poured himself a large whisky and decided to allow a two-hour lapse before shutting up shop and addressing Koshkin's whereabouts.

•

IT WAS NOW 9.10 p.m. and Mercer had briefly dozed off in the armchair, which was often the case after a libation. He was suddenly woken by a woman's scream, which came from somewhere outside the premises. He shot towards the window and scrutinised the area but could see nothing of significance, so he switched off all the lights in the room to improve his range of view. There was a small crowd of people gathered in a corner of the park with a random set of individuals being drawn slowly to the spot, like fish to a bait. Mercer followed suit and hotfooted it down the five flights of stairs. When he reached the crowd, a man was lying face down on the ground with the back of his skull blown out.

8

THE SITUATION IN the park was in dire need of the attention of the authorities, and before things could spiral out of shape, Mercer hightailed it to the nearest phone box and called Scotland Yard. He then telephoned D Branch to relay the tragedy to Rutherford, who instructed him on several points.

'This matter is for the police, Saul … do you hear? We can't get involved at this stage.'

'No, Sir. Of course.'

'However, in face of those orders, I would like you to remain on site … be a fly on the wall while they mop up. Check for any compromising items on the body. I'm sure I don't need to remind you to get as much data as you can: materials, witnesses, that sort of thing. Just get it down. Rid the area before the Yard turns up. Sorry to foist this on you, Mercer. Thing is … well you're there and—'

'I'm on it, Sir.'

At that, Mercer darted back to the scene of the crime and took immediate action to make scarce the growing numbers surrounding the body. No witnesses could be established, aside from the woman who found the body, and Mercer advised her to remain on site until the police arrived, as she would need to provide them with a statement. Mercer took full advantage of the situation before the authorities homed in by examining the body punctiliously. The first thing that appeared odd to him was that there was no wallet on Koshkin's person. Had it been taken by his assassin? Or was it a deliberate act on Koshkin's part? A thorough search of his flat would be a necessary step at a later stage. The materials found on his person were a pouch of rolling tobacco and papers, a box of matches, a receipt with today's date from the British Museum and a small penknife. In his trouser pockets were some small change amounting to three pounds and seventeen pence, an underground ticket and a set of keys.

Due to the imbecile actions and curiosity of the public and their trampling under foot, the odyssey of the malefactors was practically stamped out and failed to yield any positive benefit in Mercer's investigation. As for the witness, she offered more than was originally conceived, for she had seen the victim alive earlier that evening while walking her dog. A statement of monumental value was vouchsafed. She had described to Mercer a detailed and well-stocked account of her entrance and subsequent exit of the park, beginning with her first encounter.

'The victim,' she began, 'was sitting in somewhat disarray on that bench over there.' She pointed to its location, offering Mercer a clear picture of the scene. 'I was sprinting towards him, as I invariably do through the park, to give Toby a good run. The man appeared jittery, if not a little spooked, and there were two men standing in the trees over in that direction.' Once again, she motioned the position at where the men had stood. 'Something felt odd about it,' she continued.

'In what way odd?' enquired Mercer earnestly.

'Couldn't put my finger on it at the time, but on recalling it to memory, I had the distinct feeling the man was being watched, but something felt disjointed to me.'

'Can you describe the two men?'

'Yes. They were both tall and lean and wore trench coats and trilby hats, which obscured their faces slightly. Their features were sharp … or at least what I could see of them. Foreign perhaps.'

'You said that something felt disjointed,' probed Mercer gently. 'Please go on with your statement.'

'Well, as I approached the man on the bench, he called out to me and asked me for the time, which I gave to him promptly.'

'Can you recall what the time was?'

'It was two minutes to eight. His accent was Russian, I think, if that's of any use? Then something rather strange happened. As I was about to move on, he started talking to me again, only this time his attention was drawn to the south entrance of the park where a third man of similar bearing to the other two had entered the park. This unnerved the victim considerably, so out of charity I continued talking to him. It was awkward and strained and all the while he just kept looking over at the third man, who by this stage was heading straight for the other two men.'

'Are you able to describe him? The third man?'

'I couldn't see his face. He too wore a hat.'

'Was anything exchanged between them?'

'No. Not that I could see. The third man just walked briskly past me with his head down as I started off towards the exit; almost as if he was walking back on himself. When I left the park, the victim was still sitting on the same bench as when I had first entered the park.'

'And there were no other bystanders in the park?' Mercer enquired with marked sobriety.

'No, none. The park is often empty at that particular time of my run.' She paused. 'Are you police?' she appealed uncomfortably.

'I'm afraid not. He was a colleague.'

The blare of the emergency services interrupted their commune and Mercer thanked the woman for her thorough and perceptive statement. A small body of ambulance crew and police officers arrived expeditiously to the site, and on seeing the grim state of the murdered victim, one of the police officers almost passed out, while the detective investigating the case stepped resolutely forward.

'Mr Mercer?' he said candidly, as he held out his hand. 'Detective Fenhill.' A handshake followed between them. 'I received a phone call from your superior, Mr Rutherford. He requested rather strongly that your presence might prove helpful to the investigation.'

'Ah, right,' returned Mercer. 'Well, if you don't mind my hanging around. It could be beneficial to both parties.'

'Not at all, sir. Mr Rutherford and I are becoming pretty well acquainted of late.'

'Oh?' replied Mercer somewhat muddled.

'Yes. I expect the chap in question is something of a colleague. A regular misfit. Caused a bit of a set-to at a certain club recently.'

'Ah, yes.' Mercer added nothing further to his statement.

'Now, what do we have here?' incited Fenhill as he approached the body. 'Poor blighter … Constable Clarke?' he yelled. 'Go and rustle up the forensic photographer, would you? I think he's with the ambulance crew.' Then with deep commiseration, he added, 'Bloody shame.' He glanced down at the body. 'What loathsome trap did you entangle yourself in, Koshkin? A morbid end for such an honourable chap. Damn good at his job too. Never veered off the beaten track.' He chuckled to himself, as if to suddenly realise he was at fault. 'Evidently that's quite contrary to the testament we have before us. Outflanked good and proper.'

Fenhill and Mercer exchanged glances, then with little warning, Fenhill proceeded with the investigation precipitously as if nothing had transpired or any morsel of compassion had been shed. 'Right, men, let's get the area cordoned off. Better seal off the perimeter and block all entrances to the park. We don't want some Jonah wandering in off the street disturbing the balance.'

Mercer saw fit to chime in. 'We have one witness, Detective. She's waiting to give a full account. She has vested a pretty coal-and-ice statement. I took the liberty since my rendezvous with the deceased was set to take place nearby. Hope I wasn't overstepping the mark.'

'Not at all, sir. You did the necessary.' Glancing again at the annihilation of the bullet wound, Fenhill's face clouded over and he appeared entirely lost in thought. Then he broke the silence: 'Anyone come forward with regard to hearing a gunshot?'

'I'm afraid not,' replied Mercer ruefully. 'I made meticulous enquiries of the surge of bystanders prior to your arrival. A silencer perhaps? That's an informed guess but it would make sense, would it not?'

'Indeed. Just strikes me as odd is all.' Fenhill was stricken once again in a momentary lapse, but after a short interval he returned to the present. 'He's the second Russian expat to be murdered under suspicious circumstances,' he added.

Mercer remained completely silent, offering Fenhill the appropriate spell to vouchsafe the subsequent intelligence, which he did freely.

'He was a responsible functionary. A friend and colleague

of Koshkin. Can't really discuss the case, as I'm sure you understand, but Chief Superintendent Hamilton had rather a soft spot for the two émigrés. Damned awful case. Ten years or so now.'

'Are you inferring it could be linked?'

'It's certainly possible. The case was never solved. Call it a hunch.'

Police Constable Clarke interrupted their dialogue by requesting Fenhill's assistance with the witness, for it appeared she was anxious to press on with her statement. As he started off in the direction of the witness, Fenhill turned back to Mercer and muttered, 'Respecting that case we were just discussing, the name was Slavsky,' and he gave a nod of approval before he strode off.

The apparent absence of the press could have been the result of only one conclusion: Rutherford had released a D-notice well ahead of the game. This was in fact the long and short of it, as Mercer discovered on his return to D Branch. There, he offered Rutherford an accurate compendium of the train of events leading up to and ensuing the murder, including his conversation with both the witness and Fenhill. Mercer propounded his conviction that the two cases of Koshkin and Slavsky were linked, so he began to put into effect the unravelling of the essential threads.

9

COLLECTION WAS MADE of the first component of Koshkin's final transmission the very next morning, which Rodchenko delivered directly to Mercer's office. Koshkin had taken the liberty of opening the envelope left to him before returning to D Branch and was equally as puzzled as Mercer on surveying it. One half of a postcard of the museum with no inscription on its reverse. To whom had Koshkin vested the other half? After glancing at each other with mild mystification, Mercer stated that there had been a receipt on Koshkin's person from the British Museum dated yesterday at three minutes past five, to which he duly added that it would be prudent to search Koshkin's flat for any corresponding evidence.

This was therefore the line they took that September morning, where they did not demur their journey to the property in Wood Green. On their way they skimmed over the idea of Koshkin having planted significant evidence within the museum somewhere, but in Mercer's mind he needed some concrete proof to eliminate and measure all the facts.

On their arrival at Koshkin's flat, Mercer took surreptitious measures on gaining access to the property while Rodchenko stood sentinel on the first-floor landing. A neighbour opened her door marginally with slight apprehension, peering out through the chink with meddling eyes and commented that her neighbour was not home. Mercer expressed his gratitude humbly and waited for her to return behind the closed door. She did not. She went on to say that she had heard a terrific commotion the previous evening, coming from within the apartment, and that she had seen two men leaving the property shortly after eleven o'clock.

Once again, Mercer thanked the woman for her observations and she skulked back into her quarters evasively. No small wonder as they entered the flat that they found a complete overhaul of the premises. An extensive ferreting had indeed taken place, which suggested to Mercer's responsive perception that whatever they had been looking for had not been found.

Mercer and Rodchenko began their inspection in the kitchen, where they found a medley of curious objects on the breakfast table. Aside from the sullied tableware and cutlery there were a pair of scissors, a roll of cellophane, a box of food bags and a needle and thread. Mercer examined the objects with intent, which at length brought him to the conclusion that Koshkin had made deliberate concealment of something of importance; an object that demanded a resolute embalming for complete preservation. He had clearly gone to great lengths to encase the item thoroughly, leaving breadcrumbs behind for the enquirer. It was all conjecture, but on theorising the accumulated facts, Mercer believed that the trove would be discovered at the museum.

Rodchenko continued his search in the kitchen and sitting room, while Mercer moved on to the bedroom, where furniture and oddments had been scattered vigorously across the room, curtains pulled off their railings and pictures destroyed recklessly, all with pointless cause. Mercer's attempt to appropriate further evidence was in vain as he rummaged through the deceased's belongings, until the threadbare carpet over by the window caught his eye. He prised away the corner by the skirting and found a letter of correspondence with a postage stamp of Lisbon franked on the envelope. Its contents were encrypted so he pocketed it for later scrutiny. Rodchenko had found an address book with irregular scribblings of several addresses in code, with the remainder lettered in the usual manner.

Their investigation had shot its bolt and Mercer instructed Rodchenko to head back to D Branch where he should further his work under Menzies. Mercer, on the other hand, made off for the British Museum to make good of his theorems of hidden commodities in unattainable places. On his journey via the underground he began to eliminate scrupulously Koshkin's reasoning for conducting such a concealment. He questioned the method, the motive and its possible destination. It had to be hidden somewhere obscure but obvious enough for the cunning of an intelligence operative. He finally concluded that the item may have been immersed in water for safekeeping, so his first port of call was the lavatories.

The receipt found in Koshkin's pocket indicated that he had purchased two items from the museum shop, so Mercer began his search on the ground level, since the shop was located near the lavatories. On entering the men's room, he began by assessing the urinals, running his fingers along each side to determine any sharp edges or oddities. There was nothing. A man entered, so Mercer shifted his search into the first cubicle. He checked down behind the toilet bowl and on the floor. Nothing. The cistern was fixed high up on the wall at eye level, so he waited for the man to leave before lifting the cistern lid cover to check inside. Nothing. He moved on to the next cubicle, where he repeated the same exercise thoroughly; and then the next and the next, until he was at the final cubicle.

This time when Mercer lifted the cistern cover something dropped to the ground. He picked it up and studied it for a while, until he realised it was a knotted piece of nylon fishing line. He ran his hands along the rim of the cistern, where something smarted his fingers. There was a small hook, which he unfastened, but there was nothing attached to it except a tiny fragment of material. Someone had evidently got to it before him, which rankled with him considerably. His search had been in vain.

•

BACK AT D BRANCH, Mercer began to decode the letter franked Lisbon that he had obtained from Koshkin's flat. It was a Beale cipher so relatively easy to decrypt since he had extensive experience with substitution ciphers. It took him a little under an hour before the numbers computed anything remotely coherent. The sequence finally read: ITEMS RECEIVED STOP SEND COUNTERSIGNAL STOP VITAL FOR REQUISITION STOP. There was no signatory. Who was Koshkin's contact in Lisbon? Evidently someone with principled moral fibre. Someone whom Koshkin trusted implicitly.

Mercer then recalled the conversation he had had with Detective Fenhill – Chief Superintendent Hamilton had rather a soft spot for the two émigrés. Hamilton. It was a long shot but he might be able to shed some light on the matter. Mercer picked up the telephone and dialled Scotland Yard, which brought him directly through to the switchboard.

'Good afternoon,' Mercer said efficiently. 'Chief Superintendent Hamilton please.'

The female voice on the receiving end said, somewhat apologetically, 'Hamilton? I'm afraid he's no longer tenured at Scotland Yard, sir.'

'Oh? Where might I find him? Is he stationed elsewhere?'

'No, sir. He retired three years ago.' This comment was not furthered.

'Right. In that case, might I speak with Detective Fenhill?'

'Of course, sir. Who shall I say is calling?'

'Mercer.'

'Trying the extension now, sir,' and he was instantly connected.

'Fenhill,' came the rather abrupt voice.

'Afternoon, Fenhill. Mercer here from D Branch.'

'Ah, Mr Mercer, sir. To what do I owe the honour?'

'Hamilton. You mentioned him briefly last evening. Are you in a position to divulge the location of his whereabouts? I understand he's retired, is that correct?'

'Indeed he is, sir. I believe he can be found somewhere in Europe. As I recall, he and his wife emigrated three years ago. A proper send-up for his retirement. Now that's a soirée I'm not likely to forget.'

'Europe. Any idea where, exactly?'

'Erm … Portugal, I believe. Living it royally. Lucky bugger.'

'Portugal. Not Lisbon by any chance?'

'Couldn't say for certain, sir, but I believe so.'

'Thank you, Fenhill. Much obliged.' There was a short pause before Mercer continued. 'While I have you on the line, could you give me a rough estimation as to when you'll be releasing Koshkin's possessions at the Yard? I need to do a little ferreting.'

'Well, sir, they're being held as evidence for the time being. You're familiar with procedure I presume? At a guess, they're not likely to be released until the investigation has been resolved. That being said, you would be welcome to come and inspect his belongings if you wish. They can't leave the premises, you understand.'

'That's very obliging, Fenhill. When would be convenient?'

'Now is as good a time as any. Does that suit?'

'It does indeed. Give me an hour or so.'

Hamilton. Lisbon. Koshkin's address book. Mercer referred to it immediately. H. One address encoded. Again, its method was a Beale cipher. He transcribed the address and phone number then locked both the encoded letter and address book in his personal safe.

10

THE TEAM OF cryptographers were rallying their efforts at D Branch in the hope of discovering one minor piece of shrapnel from the Vesna case. Menzies and his unit had spent weeks up until that point in their deliberations, which had failed to yield any positive benefit thus far. A vast majority of the intercepts accumulated at the inception of the case were encrypted using the one-time pad, therefore making it inordinately more difficult to decrypt. The primary objective was to plough through every Soviet message that had transpired between the British and Soviet embassies throughout Europe at that time to espy any clues to a mole's identity.

They were readily equipped with up-to-the-minute decoding machines, which had formulated much faster results. The current intercept Menzies was disentangling had finally revealed something of currency. The telegram stated that a certain informer continued to be 'invaluable', which was a step in the right direction, but who he or she was, was still very much a mystery, so Menzies deepened his search with grave incentive.

•

MERCER ARRIVED at Scotland Yard just within the hour. On arrival he found Fenhill dealing with a member of the public at the helpdesk. Mercer waited resignedly until the detective addressed him and they shook hands.

'Much appreciated, Fenhill. I'm a little stumped but nothing a minor exposé wouldn't remedy.'

'Understood, sir. Sometimes all that's needed is some oiling of the spokes.'

Mercer smirked and Fenhill led them down a long dark corridor past the custody suite and into the evidence room, which was entered upon via a set of keys. A female constable was stationed in the room overseeing the display of evidence. She looked up slowly with large, questioning, brown eyes. She was tall and slender with a pleasing smile and she directed her gaze towards Mercer the moment he entered the room.

'Police Constable White,' began Fenhill. 'Jolly good. Everything in order?'

'Yes, Sir,' she replied competently.

'Right, excellent. Mr Mercer is here to inspect the contents of Koshkin's locker. See to it he has full access to his belongings.'

'Yes, Sir. Right over here, Sir.' She directed them to the table in the left-hand corner of the room.

'All right if I leave you to it, Mercer?' I have a little urgent business to attend to,' said Fenhill.

'Of course,' Mercer replied genially. 'Many thanks.'

'Privilege, sir. Police Constable White will see you out … and I hope it's of use to you.'

The contents of Koshkin's locker consisted of a clean white shirt from British Home Stores, a hand towel, some miscellaneous camera equipment, a small black pocket notebook and pencil, and a large white padded envelope. Mercer requested permission before he emptied the contents on to the table, which PC White obliged him without reserve. Several photographs were found within, along with one single negative proof, which had been cut away at the frame with what appeared to be a sharp-edged instrument. He held it up to the light to examine the image more closely but could only make out two miniscule figures standing side by side in front of what looked like a cathedral. Their faces were not clear but the corresponding developed photographs revealed one of the figures clearly. The other half of the picture had been deliberately discarded and there was no sign of it among the other photographs.

On observing all the images in the collection, it became clear to Mercer that the subject matter on which Koshkin had focused his attention was on one man distinctly. Of whom, was the question. And to what end? A tall man of stocky build and striking features. A person completely unfamiliar to Mercer. Sergei Koshkin had only divulged to Rutherford that he was in possession of documented proofs of what he claimed were a Soviet case officer and his courier but he had failed to impart any names. This would have been disclosed later at the safe house, and the fact that Mercer had been on the edge of something pivotal had incensed him a great deal, but he now had a possible lead in Hamilton.

Mercer recorded to memory each item present in the envelope and stored it in mind for later retrieval. He would now concentrate his labours on unearthing what was necessary to make good of the case.

•

SOON AFTER Mercer returned to D Branch, Menzies paid him a visit to offer an update on his progress. He stood at the doorway, knocking gently on the doorframe, then waited for Mercer to acknowledge his presence before entering.

'Saul, do you have a moment?'

'Of course, Guy. How can I help? Making progress, are we?'

'In actual fact, we are. Just wanted to bring you up to date,' then Menzies placed a set of documents on Mercer's desk and referred to them frequently as he spoke. 'As you can see in this intercept here, which was decrypted this morning, the telegram reports that a certain informer continues to be "invaluable". No sign of a codename or alias yet but I've just this moment discovered a second clue from a different intercept, which refers to a second party, "our ally, Poli", stated here,' which he pointed to. 'If preliminary sallies continue as is, then we'll have substantial evidence in no time.'

'This is excellent progress, Guy. Good work. And no other intercepts relating to Poli or the second party?'

'Not as yet, but a connection does need to be made between both distinctions and employees.'

'Keep digging, Guy. We're finally making headway. Meanwhile, I'll carry out a search on "Poli" through the archived telephone conversations related to the case. It's possible that something may turn up there.'

There was a solemn pause.

'Awful news about Koshkin,' said Menzies. 'I never met the fellow, but Rutherford seemed to think he was quite an asset.'

'Yes, dreadful circumstances. I wouldn't wish that on anyone. I didn't get to meet him either. All set to, of course, but the poor bugger never showed up. We were on the edge of something there, Guy. Damned shame. We'll just have to go the extra mile … take it on the chin for the time being.'

'Quite,' replied Menzies with resolution.

'Rodchenko appears to have taken it badly. Scarcely got two words out of the fellow this morning. How does he seem to you, Guy? You're probably more attune since he's under your feet all day.'

'He's pretty cut-up in truth. They were comrades-in-arms, Saul. Like brothers … or at least that's the impression I got.'

'Devastating.' Mercer stared at the transmissions on his desk while deep in thought, then something occurred to him, and he added, rather curiously, 'Do you think Koshkin might have disclosed any intelligence to Rodchenko about the documentation he was prepared to offer us?'

'Well, it's possible, I suppose,' replied Menzies with optimism.

'What I mean to say is, how he came to have them in his possession in the first place. What measures he took. Names. That sort of thing. Perhaps we could gently press him.'

'It's worth a shot. Want me to send him down, Saul?'

'If you wouldn't mind. Could be meagre pickings, but then again …'

•

RODCHENKO WAS standing at Mercer's door in no time but was a little apprehensive in manner. He knocked and entered.

'You called for me, Sir?' he said with a small measure of consternation.

'Ah, Rodchenko. Thanks for coming so promptly. Please, take a seat.' So as not to alarm him, Mercer felt that he had to tread carefully and he ventured as far from the techniques of interrogation as was duly possible. 'I hope you don't mind my pressing you a little on the subject of Koshkin, since I understand he was a good friend and comrade.'

Rodchenko demurred slightly but Mercer took that more for discomfort and grief than anything else. Oleg shook his head silently.

'You knew him some years, I understand?' Mercer asked.

'Yes, Sir,' Rodchenko replied nervously. 'We serve in Red Army together. He was exceptional man. Entirely principled.'

Mercer nodded sympathetically. 'I'm sorry. You must have taken it hard.'

Rodchenko responded ruefully as he gazed down at his hands folded in his lap.

'It's probably a little left field,' continued Mercer, 'but might I ask, did Koshkin disclose any intelligence to your good self regarding the documentation he was about to vouchsafe? It would help in our enquiries immensely.'

Mercer detected reticence in Rodchenko, which he handled carefully, then went on: 'The proof he was about to give us was of photographic substance, of a Soviet handler and his courier. That much we know. No identity had yet been given. Neither had he been given the opportunity to entrust to us the means by which he had come by the evidence first-hand. If you have even the smallest piece of information you could offer us, it would help further our steps towards discovering who murdered him.'

Rodchenko conceded with an obligatory nod and began his disclosure. 'Well, Sir, a few weeks ago we meet for our routine chess game. Club on Little Russell Street, and it was there that Sergei begin to tell me of the sensitive materials he had in his possession.'

Mercer listened with intent and took notes.

'It wasn't until afterwards that he describe events leading up to attainment of evidence. The job, he said, occurred shortly after his defection, roughly ten years ago.'

'The job?' enquired Mercer gently.

'Yes. He was approached by colleague at Scotland Yard. Slavsky, I think.'

The name heralded a recollection in Mercer's mind. He's the second Russian expat to be murdered under suspicious circumstances, Fenhill had said.

'Go on,' Mercer said with incitement.

'This job, Slavsky say to Sergei, an all-expenses-paid trip to Prague. Weekend trip. What you British call busman's holiday. The objective was for Sergei to take photograph of two men, covertly. One Soviet handler, the other his courier. Their rendezvous take place that Sunday morning at four o'clock at cathedral in Old Town Square, which Sergei achieve successful. But he know nothing of who assigned job to Slavsky or anything relating to spies in transit … he just carried out job for money, that was all.' At this point, distress clouded over Rodchenko's face, almost as if he was about to lose control, but he gathered himself together stolidly and Mercer urged him to go on.

'When Sergei return to England, Slavsky arrange to make collection of film and photographs but he never show up. Ten days or maybe more, then Slavsky body wash up on Embankment. Sergei was terrified.'

'Christ!' interjected Mercer, then asked a question to which he already knew the answer. 'Foul play?'

'Yes, strangled and drowned, Sir.'

'And what of the materials?'

'Sergei say he keep them in locker at Scotland Yard all these years.'

'Any names? Did he give you any names?' This Mercer enquired with stimulus.

'He give me one name. Yuri. Slavsky leave note for Sergei at the Yard. A final attempt to impute enemy.'

11

A FEW WEEKS HAD passed for Alan Soames, during which he had found himself duly under the medical supervision of Dr Rupert Gladstone in a plush clinic somewhere on Harley Street. Soames' existence there afforded him several simple luxuries, none of which included alcohol. He was, however, permitted cigarettes, which he was to smoke in the garden and were rarely permitted during assessments, but Soames had managed to contrive persuasion.

The premises was exorbitantly furnished with its clinical white walls and surfaces, solid oak flooring and vast stone staircases, which would have been the delight of any schoolboy's imaginings to launch himself down their bannisters. This was something Soames had contemplated often during his lengthy residency. He did not conform easily to routine. This was something he had struggled with on a day-to-day basis.

An extensive library was provided for the patients who had come and gone over the years, to which few of them vested any measure of respect. To the dismay of one of the psychiatrists, one incident had been recorded where a former patient had decided to accumulate the entire collection of Agatha Christie novels during their stay and perform a ceremonial burning of them in one of the bathrooms on the third floor. Consequently, the fire alarm had been triggered, causing an exodus from the premises into the garden during a hideous downpour.

Soames, on the other hand, was an avid reader and bestowed more respect for books than he did perhaps for his own car. He owned several first editions, one of which had been signed by Waugh himself at a soirée one year at Dryden's. A paperback copy of the same title honoured the shelves of the clinic's library, so Soames had pilfered it for the duration. However, it gave him little respite from the memories that haunted him and the inescapable quagmire in which he now found himself hostage. A scrape that could not be conveyed to anyone, not even his friend and doctor, Rupert Gladstone.

On this autumn day, the sun was trying its level best to burst through the angry widespread cloud cover, which finally dispersed by the end of the day. Dr Gladstone suggested they conduct Soames' consultation in the garden. Being sensitive in nature, Rupert Gladstone was the ideal candidate to offer both professional and conciliatory counsel to that of Soames' sensibilities and current condition, for they had been friends since boyhood. Gladstone had pleasant features and was of medium build, but there was something very polished about him that indicated an element of the aristocracy, which of course he was not. He had in fact come from a middle-class family of no distinction and had put in the graft to make something of himself in his field.

They selected a bench in a quiet corner of the garden, where they soft-pedalled their way into the consultation and Soames started on a chain of cigarettes.

'How are we doing today, Alan?' began Gladstone earnestly.

'How do you think we're doing?' Soames answered with a mild scoff. 'I haven't had a drink in weeks and I'm treated like some pitiful stray animal. The food is atrocious and the only thing that's even remotely tolerable is the present company, and that's pushing it.' Soames chuckled ironically, as did Gladstone.

'Aside from the menial complaints, I think you're making good progress, Alan.'

'Well, it's like a bloody farce here, so it's difficult not to benefit from some measure of amusement.'

Gladstone allowed a short interval, long enough for Soames to settle in his own time, then he pressed gently: 'You briefly mentioned the other day that you were feeling the pressures of the job. Is that still the case, Alan?'

Soames took a lengthy toke on his cigarette while he thought broadly on the question, and as he exhaled, he said candidly, 'In truth, I want out. Don't think I can stomach it for much longer. It's a ghastly business. Endless drawbacks and, quite frankly, it's a downright hazardous existence. I'm in deep, Gladstone, and I'm at a loss as to how to corkscrew my way out.'

'I'm sorry, Alan. Truly, I am. Surely a resignation is a sensible remedy?'

'It's not as easy as that, Rupert. You know that. Too many pesky cords to cut. I'm entangled good and proper. My exploits at the club were a sorry attempt to force their hand for dismissal.'

'Perhaps you're not trying hard enough.' This was blatantly said in jest, but Soames took it for validation, and Gladstone could see his brain ticking away, concocting some violation for his escape route. 'In all seriousness, Alan, I think you ought to give your tenure another shot. You're a damn good operative and I honestly believe you would miss the game. You would be lost.'

'Yes, and what is the game precisely, Rupert? Putting my life on the line for a bunch of consummate actors who are, quite honestly, stabbing about in the dark!' Soames gave Gladstone a hard stare, which unnerved him considerably.

'Look, I'm sorry, Alan,' Gladstone returned lamentably. 'It's a godawful situation to be in. I do understand … I do. I just can't help thinking that there must be another solution. A demotion? Desk work?'

'Christ, I would go barmy. Rabid even. Have a proper basket case on your hands. No. Desk work would be agonisingly obtund and I'm already pretty numb, thank you very much.'

'In what way numb, Alan?'

There was a deafening pause and Soames extinguished the cigarette, only to light another as a demurral. 'I feel nothing, Rupert. I'm devoid of emotion. I've lost sight of who I am. My relationships are inane mindless pursuits and end in disaster. All the women in my life seem to do is complain that I'm never home, and when I am they harp on about my not being "present emotionally" or some absurd nonsense they've fabricated to legitimise an end. It's a bloody mess. I'm just going through the motions … like some damned battery bunny.'

Gladstone was silent, and as he listened to his friend reveal intimate thoughts of despair, he analysed the long chain of components that now embodied the person sitting before him: the religious fanatics constituting something resembling a family; their somewhat skewed political assertions of a democracy and an Empire that simply did not exist; a father who had little time for him; a mother too self-absorbed to even notice him; and siblings who neither understood him nor wished to. The obtuseness of the upper class, he thought. No small wonder Soames lacked the vigour to see things through or to go above and beyond the call of duty. He had nothing driving him, no incentive, and most appallingly of all he had never known love. These, in Gladstone's mind, comprised a debauched and tragic set of components, and he would strive to use every ounce of his professional ingenuity and counsel to help Soames to weather the storm.

'Do you know?' continued Soames after an interval, 'I've only ever loved one person my entire life … but they're far out of reach.' He stopped for a moment, pensive and self-reproachful, and to Gladstone he appeared so wretchedly alone. 'I've been having these dreams of late,' Soames went on, 'and when I return to consciousness and realise it wasn't real, I feel a sort of emptiness. And the strangers that were once present in the dream … well I suppose one could say that I mourn them.' His eyes began to fill slightly.

Meanwhile, Gladstone grappled with that professional boundary he had so very nearly crossed many times before with patients who had rattled the bulwark. 'You mourn strangers in dreams?' he repeated in an attempt to understand Soames.

But something in Soames shut down instantly, as if he had vouchsafed some highly classified intelligence. 'Yes, it's all frightfully tragic,' he said, half joking and half reasoning himself off. He then changed the subject entirely and Gladstone did not push. 'So, when will you lot be issuing the carte blanche?' he said humorously.

Gladstone, however, cast him a bewildered look.

'Oh, keep pace, Gladers … my get out of jail free card?'

'Ah, right. A couple of weeks or so. Why? Aren't you enjoying your little holiday, courtesy of MI6?'

They exchanged a grin.

'Thing is,' said Soames, 'there's a few bits and bobs I need from the flat. Any chance you could scoot over there and fetch them for me?'

'Of course, Alan. What do you need?'

Soames began reeling off a list of miscellaneous items, which were all camouflage to the immediate focus of his incitement. A hiatus took place, during which Gladstone made notes and Soames paused for thought on how best to tally his request. He did not soften the blow. 'There's some compromising materials that need removing from the premises,' he said.

'Christ, Alan! What sort of compromising materials are we talking about here?'

'It's a file—'

'For God's sake man! How could you operate so irresponsibly? Hell, what were you thinking? You do realise this could complicate matters irrevocably.'

'Yes, I'm fully aware of the eventualities, Gladstone. I'm not a complete fool. In truth, I had forgotten it was there. Now, can you do it or not? Otherwise, I shall have to get my contact to jump in.'

'Now that wouldn't look suspicious at all would it!' retorted Gladstone bitingly. 'What if your place is being watched? Or worse? You're skating on thin ice, Alan. Bloody well plan ahead of the game for once!'

'All right!' Soames barked acerbically. 'Leave it. I'll use an intermediary.'

'No. I'll do it,' said Gladstone abruptly. 'Just tell me where it is.'

12

THE FOLLOWING morning, Mercer was carrying out a routine check on the surveillance equipment he had set up at Soames' flat some weeks before. He had listened in daily and regularly each day, and although he had been given additional responsibilities to shoulder, he had adapted well to their numerous demands.

It was around eleven o'clock when he plugged himself in, but as he was conducting the test, the microphones picked up some activity at the premises. Rutherford had informed him that same morning that Soames was not likely to be released from the clinic for another fortnight at best, so the activity currently taking place was certainly due cause for alarm. All things considered, Mercer threw caution to the wind and made a dash for the property, as it was walking distance from headquarters.

On approaching the property, he acknowledged the two field-glasses stationed there with a swift nod. They were in a beige Ford Cortina several cars up across the street and had been in situ from the start of the surveillance operation, purely as a precautionary measure and largely for peace of mind. Their shifts rotated with the night owls twelve hourly, but nothing had occurred that was seemingly open to doubt and to that end there had been scant to report.

There was a resident leaving the building as Mercer approached the steps, and they politely held the door open for him. On entering the communal lobby, Mercer detected the smell of smoked fish, which lingered in the air from a dish that had evidently been cooked the previous night. A child was practising their scales on the piano and a dog was barking persistently as Mercer ascended the stairs. From another floor, Miles Davis was being played at full volume to emphatically drown out the child's efforts.

Mercer clambered to the top floor, where he finally reached the door to Soames' apartment. He listened attentively for a while and could hear movement coming from within of drawers being opened and the rustling of paper. He cautiously decided to wait for the intruder down in the lobby. Since there was no other means of exiting the premises, he was sure to encounter the person who was rummaging about in the apartment.

It wasn't until a good twenty minutes or so later that there was some activity of someone closing and locking a door, followed by footsteps descending speedily down the stairs and striding across the ceramic floor of the hallway. To Mercer's utter surprise he was suddenly face to face with Rupert Gladstone, who was equally as startled as he.

'Jesus, Mercer! You gave me a fright,' Gladstone said, somewhat precariously.

'Hullo, Rupert. What are you doing here?'

'Well, I could ask the same of you, old chap,' the doctor answered cheerfully.

Their mutual consternation gave rise to an outburst of simultaneous spiel, at which Mercer permitted Gladstone free rein.

'Orders from Soames, matter of fact,' said Gladstone. 'Asked me to gather a few desultory odds and ends for him,' at which point he lifted a small suitcase in his defence.

'Ah, right, of course,' retorted Mercer with amusement. 'Got you running errands for him now, has he?'

'Necessary measures. He'll be with us for another

fortnight at the very least, hence the ad hoc appearance … so here I am. All for God and country, right?' Mercer agreed with a simper. 'And you?' added Gladstone.

'Mm, pretty much the same. Temporary postman I'm afraid. In fact, might as well hand these over to you. Two birds? If you don't mind, Rupert?' he said handing the items over.

'Not at all,' Gladstone replied nervously, taking the small bundle of post. 'Save you a trip.'

Mercer could sense a mild anxiety in Gladstone, which had continued long after their collision. A certain restlessness that, in his mind, was uncalled for. In truth, he could not help thinking that Gladstone's manner had indicated a mild element of paranoia; almost as if he had been caught red-handed. But why? This curious set of events he stored away in the accumulating repository of his mind with the recent evidence he had obtained along the way.

'Incidentally,' enquired Mercer, 'how's he doing? Soames.'

'Well, there have been some improvements, I'm glad to say,' answered Gladstone reluctantly. 'Any more than that, I couldn't really say. Doctor-patient confidentiality, etc. I'm sure you understand,' then he threw Mercer a coy look of diplomacy.

'Quite so. Delighted to hear he's pushing on. I expect he's about ready for a drink round about now.'

'I'll say. Honestly, he's found that particular abstinence something of a challenge. As do many. Not an easy feat to master, cold turkey.'

'No, indeed,' said Mercer subjectively. 'And what of you, Rupert? Not often you're in our neck of the woods. All running smoothly for you? Clare's well, I trust?'

'Yes, thank you, Saul. Good of you to ask. I was sorry to hear of your hiccup.'

'Thanks. Well, all part of the game, isn't it? There aren't many women who can see it through … for the Service I mean. Few are cut out for the residual solitude it demands. Not that I blame her, of course. Just one of those things.'

'You've taken it pretty well on the chin, Saul. No point dwelling, that's the ticket.'

'Quite. Too entombed in work to tarry.'

'Good,' replied Gladstone earnestly. 'We must have that drink sometime but look … sorry, I really must dash. Got a one o'clock. Do give me a shout when you're ready for a tot, won't you Saul? Regards to Rutherford.'

They parted ways with a handshake as Gladstone exited the building in haste. Mercer mulled things over in his mind as he approached the watchers in the car a little way up the street. They were a burly couple of individuals, both red-brick but not any the less efficient for the task at hand. Dennis sat smoking in the driver's seat, while Todd sat in the back seat facing the rear window, camera in hand.

Mercer climbed into the car in the passenger seat. 'Can you give me an ETA of when Gladstone entered the premises,' he asked promptly.

Dennis took a small notebook from the inside pocket of his jacket, then replied, 'Quarter to eleven, Sir. He was in there a good hour I would say.'

'Right … Todd?'

'Well, Sir,' replied Todd, with no small degree of enthusiasm, 'about twenty minutes ago, a gentleman was about to enter the premises of the flats, who I recognised but couldn't put a name to the face. Something seemed to prevent him, Sir … from going in, which I took for him having heard voices he recognised on the other side of the door. Expect he heard you talking, Sir. Well, he waited for a moment or two, then walked back up the road and was joined by another individual. Tall, dubious-looking.'

Then Dennis piped up, 'It was that small Russian émigré, Sir. Used to work in Registry. Oleg something or other.'

'Rodchenko,' added Mercer. Then with urgency he asked, 'Where is he now?'

'He's about thirty yards up the road, Sir,' replied Todd as he operated the zoom lens of the camera. 'In deep conversation by the looks of it. Do you want me to tail them?'

'No need, Todd. Thank you. I'll want that film soon as. Meanwhile, keep a keen eye men.' And at that, Mercer was several yards up the street before anything further could be said.

Mercer tailed Rodchenko and the other man for several blocks, holding back at due distance, where he observed a third man, who joined them briefly for a quick exchange before he doubled back and moved in Mercer's direction. In order to avoid eye contact, Mercer feigned to unlock the door of the nearest residence with a swiftly produced set of keys until the individual had passed him. He then proceeded on his tail of the other two men.

They continued north to a dead-end road, which eventually took them down to Regent's Canal, but at this point it became less innocuous for Mercer to hang back without their noticing his proximity. Rodchenko and his companion then disappeared under a bridge, which was quite a distance from Mercer's current vantage point. They remained there for the best part of ten minutes before emerging in opposite directions. Rodchenko, now in haste, was heading back towards Mercer, who then shrewdly put paid to the likelihood of an encounter by starting back towards the watchers in the Ford Cortina.

Mercer finally resumed his place back in the passenger seat, where Todd briefed him on the new set of developments. 'Shortly after you headed off, Sir, a third individual entered the premises. He couldn't have been more than thirty seconds in the building before he re-emerged. He's disappeared in the opposite direction now, Sir.'

'We crossed paths earlier, as I was making tracks,' said Mercer. 'Do you have it on film, Todd?'

'Yep, all here, Sir.'

'Our friend probably dropped a dead letter. It could have been Rodchenko's objective earlier. They made an exchange up the road before heading north. I'll go and check the mailbox for the drop. Sit tight, men, and be extra vigilant.'

Mercer strode across the street, checking over his shoulder as he contemplated the pieces of the puzzle. Many questions revolved in his mind. Was Soames colluding with an alien intermediary? Was Rodchenko coerced or did he willingly partake? What evidence could there be for such an assertion? No doubt both parties would be duly pumped for information at the appropriate juncture.

Mercer climbed the steps once again and entered the property. He unlocked the mailbox to find a postcard of René Magritte's The Double Secret, a surrealist painting of an impassive male face detached from its head. No inscription. A warning perhaps? Mercer's disquieting conclusions were varied. He returned to the car.

'Anything, Sir?' enquired Dennis discreetly.

'Just a postcard of a Magritte. Nothing on its reverse, but it obviously carries some significance to the recipient. I'll take that film back to headquarters if it's all the same to you, Todd. I want to get it developed soon as.'

13

THE DURATION that followed was chiefly spent in the dark room at D Branch, and Mercer, with guileful inducement, would utilise the converted film for interrogation purposes. A handful of photographs would be all that was needed to soften the respondent, even if it meant hours were to be spent in pursuit of that intelligence. And in his usual sentinel manner he would resort to subtlety and manoeuvre, with an absence of browbeating or potency, for as he had come to learn in his extensive years' tenure in counter-espionage, subtlety was sovereign.

Mercer had decided to travel to his destination on foot, since it was a mild autumn evening and the sunset was dying leisurely. There was a gentle breeze, which scooped up collectively a collage of crisp russet leaves, scuttling them along the pavement then disbanding them chaotically. And, like the leaves, his thoughts were disorderly and unrestrained. He recalled Koshkin and his obliterated skull and his unwarranted end. Then Soames and the ostensible lukewarm patronage he had bestowed upon the Service thus far. And the Magritte from the alien contact and what it meant. But what was forefront in his mind was his lead – Hamilton. He pondered on this for some time, evaluating the when. A window would need to present itself within the process of things, then he would be able to further his enquiry to Lisbon, for this lead, he was certain, had vital information that might, just might disclose the identity of 'Yuri' and his informant. This was all conjecture of course, but the bog-standard surveillance being applied on Soames' release would surely trap him in the company of that alien or, better still, Soviet contact.

It took him approximately twelve minutes to arrive at Montagu Square, where on advancing the apartments, he buzzed flat seven. The tenant's voice came indecisively over the intercom. 'Hello?' said the voice, as if he had never received guests at that hour.

'Rodchenko?' asked Mercer.

'Yes?' he answered quizzically, not recognising the voice on the receiving end.

'Hullo, it's Mercer here. I wonder if I might come in for a moment. Not disturbing your dinner, am I?' he said apologetically.

There was a long pause. 'Mercer? Well ... actually, yes, but—'

'It won't take up too much of your time, Oleg. There's a couple of documents I would like you to assess.'

Then, without verbal response, Rodchenko buzzed him in.

There was a lone bicycle standing in the entrance lobby, chained in slapdash fashion to a drainpipe, which Mercer had to volte-face to proceed into the premises. At the bottom of the staircase sat a long-haired tabby, which greeted him with blandishment and animation before he ascended the stairs. As he climbed the two flights, the cat followed him until he reached the door to flat seven, then it waited patiently for the door to be opened while purring vigorously.

Mercer knocked gently. Despite a delay, which Mercer took for hesitation, the door opened and the cat shot in at an irregular speed.

'Thanks for sparing me a moment, Oleg,' Mercer began compassionately. 'It's just that something has surfaced, and I would appreciate your assistance.'

Rodchenko nodded with a modicum of disconcertion and summoned him in, ushering him into the lounge and prompting him to sit next to an unclad coffee table, where the cat garrisoned itself comfortably between the two men. No sign of a hospitality drink was offered, since Rodchenko was erroneously under the impression that his unsought visit was going to be a brief one. Mercer attempted to break the ice.

'How are things coming along under Menzies? Settling in well at D Branch, I trust?'

'Yes. Thank you very much.'

Rodchenko's unwillingness was now starting to take its toll on Mercer's patience, yet he did not let it show, neither did he allow it to navigate him away from his real point of interest.

'What you wish me look at?' asked Rodchenko impetuously.

'Well, I shall come to that in due course, Oleg. But first, I would like you to give me an account of your movements as of late morning today.'

'My movements?' Rodchenko seemed to speculate this question acutely, as if to determine careful selection of his response. 'Menzies send me on errand, which merge into lunch hour. Why you ask this?'

'Can you tell me where that was exactly?'

'York Street.'

'York Street? Then explain to me how it was that I came to see you in St John's Wood? That's quite a distance, wouldn't you say? At least it is on foot.'

A rut of suspicion formed over Rodchenko's brow, as Mercer detected the warning lights alert behind his eyes.

'What were you doing there?' Mercer enquired collectedly.

'I wasn't there!' Rodchenko answered defensively.

Then with deeply quiet restraint, Mercer added, 'Now one could argue till one was blue in the face, but I would rather cut to the chase, wouldn't you? Pointless denying it. Now what, pray, were you doing there?'

Rodchenko sat silently resistive.

'Come now, Oleg. I'm not here to burn you, I just require an explanation.'

Again, no response.

During this long, drawn-out silence, Mercer picked up the briefcase he had brought with him and opened it up on the coffee table, then proceeded to take out several photographs that lay face down in the case. He closed the case and set it upon the floor next to his feet, before carefully displaying the photographs uppermost for Rodchenko's perusal.

As Rodchenko surveyed the images at his leisure, a look of utter horror darkened over his features and his face reddened with humiliation and distress. With great calm, Mercer began to push him gently for information. 'Who are the two gentlemen in the photographs, Oleg?'

Rodchenko nodded his head with his eyes battened down, as if to attempt expulsion of something he could not control. He then reached into his trouser pocket for his cigarettes and began smoking nervously.

Mercer pressed again. 'Who are they, Oleg?'

At this juncture, Mercer stood slowly and walked towards the window. And there amid that abrasive silence his mind wandered once again to Koshkin. There were two men standing in the trees. Then he recalled, there was a third man who entered from the south side of the park. A third man. But the witness had described him as tall in bearing.

'I just require facts, Oleg,' Mercer continued. 'It's possible I can help you.'

At length, Rodchenko replied with a mere whisper, which Mercer asked him to repeat.

'I don't know who they are,' Rodchenko said with all-out self-reproach.

'Their codenames, Oleg? Surely they vouchsafed those?'

'One of them is called Maxim … that all I know.'

'Who sent them?'

Yet another stinging hiatus followed. Mercer pushed a little further. 'The photographs plainly show your location outside Soames' apartment building. What were you doing there? Were you coerced?' Rodchenko was tugging away on the cigarette feverishly. 'Oleg, I can help you.'

This statement seemed to soften Rodchenko's resolve; however, as he was perspiring incommodiously, he took out from his other trouser pocket a handkerchief, which was used to soak up the residue.

'They're Soviet hoods,' he answered anxiously. 'I can offer you drink, Sir? Tea? Coffee? Vodka?'

'I'm fine thank you, Oleg. Please go on.'

'They approach me several weeks ago. They follow me home one night after chess game with Sergei and force their way in my home.'

Mercer listened observantly and returned to the sofa, next to the impassive cat.

'They tie me to chair in kitchen and ask information about Sergei. Hold knife to my throat all this time.'

'What sort of information?'

'They say he have vital evidence on film of Soviet contact … their case officer and courier … British spy, they say.'

'The Soviet contact? We're now talking of Yuri.'

'Yes, but they no say his name. They all the time press knife to my throat. I terrified. I think they going to kill me. They say I must get evidence from Sergei or they intervene … and better I never been born if they have to intervene.'

Rodchenko stopped for a moment, stood up and started pacing the room with grave agitation. He lit yet another cigarette.

'They say they involve my family in Moscow … threaten them or worse if I don't do what they ask! What could I do? I pushed in corner. They want kill me, my family, these men … so I agree.'

'And Koshkin? Did he know of this?'

'Yes, I tell him, so he say he get rid of photographs and I must say to Soviet spies that Sergei burn all … film, negatives, everything … long time ago, since nobody claim them.'

Mercer's eyes were on Rodchenko with unwavering focus. 'Yet,' he returned, 'he had retained some evidence, otherwise his rendezvous with us would have been utterly redundant, wouldn't you say?' Then he contemplated the evidence Koshkin had left at Scotland Yard: the torn-up photographs and the single negative cut deliberately from the frame. 'So, did they believe you … the intermediaries?'

'No. They start following Sergei. They search his place. Turn everything topsy turvy. Destroy furniture. Terrible mess. Sergei get scared. Then he leave me postcard in dead-letter drop. Then I know. I know he leave me evidence.'

'So, you went to collect it … at the British Museum.'

'I want get there before hoods, so I collect early morning before I go to headquarters.'

'And did it never cross your mind,' said Mercer judicially,

'to let us in on it? Your little scheme with Koshkin? Or the savage measures you had been subjected to? Christ! You could have been killed. You've no idea what these people are capable of, Oleg. Sergei Koshkin was a minor episode in their grand scheme … an insignificant aphorism. They contrive their objectives at great cost. You can't reason with them … they're resolute and uncompromising.'

Mercer had taken several moments to dampen the fire raging within, to eradicate the stoke that latched itself on to the stubbornness of man, like a tick feeding away, all in the name of hatred and its elegiac purpose. For this was not who he was. And what had incensed him most was their reckless barefaced innocence. Their inability to exercise foresight in a world that was brutally unforgiving. Where mistakes are prohibited. Verboten. Vetoed.

Then he at long last enquired, 'So what of the evidence?'

'Sergei leave me one single proof. A negative cut from frame. Just two men in image, but too small, I can't see faces.'

'And can I see it? Or don't you have that either?'

'Soviet spy take it. Maxim. They threaten me. Say they chop off fingers if I no give them!'

At this pinnacle moment, Rodchenko succumbed to his anguish and finally broke down. Tears were rolling down his face as he was rubbing the back of his hand against his forehead, and suddenly he was incapable of controlling the fear that took precedence over his entire being. Saul Mercer permitted him that time composedly. He allowed the moments for Rodchenko to gather up the pieces that had disarmed him without reservation.

'In order to outflank them,' suggested Mercer, 'we shall get you transferred to a safehouse.'

'Tonight?' asked Rodchenko with a measure of relief.

'Tonight,' Mercer answered assuredly. 'Gather some essentials and we'll make tracks.'

14

THE OBJECTIVE underway in the cipher room at D Branch was to broaden their search amid the repository of intercepts chronicling the word 'Yuri'. The wireless intercepts that had been decrypted to date had revealed two clues relating to the Vesna case. The first was of a certain informer who 'continues to be invaluable' yet no codename had been disentangled. The second clue referred to 'our ally, Poli', but no other intercepts had yet mentioned both parties. With this intelligence in circulation, a connection needed to be made between both distinctions and operatives employed at the time of the case, which was in the ballpark of fifteen years prior. So far, one agent had purportedly been connected to the Soviet case officer, Yuri, and schedules of travel needed to be investigated to determine possible trips.

Saul Mercer was focusing his investigation through alternate means of telephone recordings chiefly communicated in Russian. He had spent hours raking through a futile collection of conversations whose subject matter was beyond the context or even framework of intelligence; so much so that he could see no relevance whatsoever to the case. He was beginning to feel as though he had been roped into a wild goose chase, for the whole exercise had generated nothing substantial. All things considered, he had several recordings left to monitor and was not on any account prepared to be clean bowled.

It was now 4.30 p.m., and Mercer sat himself in the listening booth after a quick coffee break, snapped the headphones back on and pressed the play button to re-examine the conversation he had earlier suspended. As the recording played out, he noticed an oddity that was repeated a few times in the thick of the Slav sibilance and laughter – a word that stuck out like a fish in a tree. That word was 'Euclid'. He studied with intensity the text surrounding this word and it was plain that the person leading the conversation was referring to a codename. Furthermore, he had come across in a more recent transcript that Euclid was still active. There was finally solid proof of a Soviet spy operating in their midst.

Mercer next scrutinised all the translated transcripts assigned to those recordings that had established that Euclid to have travelled to Austria for a meet with his intermediary – a third man. Having concrete evidence of dates and frequency of travel during that period, Mercer needed to telephone the travel office to tally which agent fitted the schedule.

On politely requesting to speak with David Carlisle, Mercer was told that Carlisle had regrettably left for the day. So, his next enquiry was to ask who his second was. An interval followed, during which Mercer could hear the friction of paper being sifted through. He was told that it was Tom Langdon and his call was connected.

'Langdon,' said the voice rather sternly.

'Ah, Langdon. Mercer here from D Branch.'

'Saul Mercer?' came the savourous reply. 'Well, here's a bolt from the blue. Spot of digging, is it?'

'I need you to paddle through the archives I'm afraid. Spare the time?'

'How far back are we looking exactly?'

'Ten years – March through to December. What I need you to pinpoint are schedules that include trips to Austria exclusively. Hope I'm not wrestling you down a rabbit hole, Langdon. Appreciate the brawn.'

'It will be a cinch, Saul. About half an hour?'

'Much appreciated, Tom.'

This timescale presented a window for Mercer to, in substance, relay his findings to Menzies before briefing Rutherford. The conversation with Menzies took place in Mercer's office and began with Mercer disclosing the intelligence that Rodchenko had vouchsafed the previous evening.

'Well,' said Menzies conspicuously, 'I think it's safe to assume that the Russian hoods that harried Rodchenko are one and the same culprits who murdered Koshkin.'

'Beyond question,' returned Mercer solemnly. 'Oleg's safe for the time being but I think it prudent to rotate his location intermittently.'

'Where is he now?'

'St Albans. I'll be checking in on him this evening. Do brief the cipher room on my recent findings. Concentrate your efforts on Euclid. Go over old ground if you have to but root it out.'

'We're at a crucial turning point Saul,' said Menzies with excitement. 'Events are in train.'

'Aren't they just. I'm waiting on Langdon to get back to me from the travel office. He's ferreting through archives to drop anchor on the mole's travel schedule. I should have something by the end of the day. What we do know is that regular trips were made to Austria for a rendezvous with an intermediary. Our third man perhaps? Once we've pinpointed Euclid, we'll set a honeytrap. Ruse him into company with his Soviet contact, then bring him in and squeeze.'

Rutherford, on being briefed on the new developments, was by no means down in the mouth; nevertheless, this did not preclude his grinding his unassailable axe.

'So, our man Rodchenko has been bulldozed into jumping ship, hey? Hand in glove with these Soviet hoods? No doubt he was completely unprepared for that fiasco.'

'Bloody reckless if you ask me,' said Mercer somewhat peeved. 'One can't subject a couple of all-fired amateurs to call the signals on two Soviet agents without collecting on some venal counterstrike.'

Rutherford nodded in vague assent. 'You can't blame yourself, Saul. They were neither of them trained in methods of tradecraft. Neither are they field men.'

'But that's precisely my point, Sir!' exclaimed Mercer with substance. 'Both morbidly unqualified, thrown shamelessly in the deep end, and without a damned lifeline. We have a duty of charge, Sir. Koshkin gave us crucial evidence.'

'We can't be certain of that yet, Saul. It could be a Mickey Mouse. In fact, it's more than bloody likely it's a red herring.'

'I disagree. That negative he was about to disclose was an invaluable commodity, and quite possibly the only crowning blow we'll get at revealing the identity of the Soviet handler, Yuri. Not to mention his courier … who is one of us, might I add.'

Rutherford shot him a scolding glance. 'But this is all conjecture, Saul. You're building castles in the air. It won't benefit you, jumping at shadows. These Soviet hoods are tip-and-run agents and we've dealt with their kind before haven't we. They'll soon disappear into oblivion. No. Any intelligence you've recently requisitioned needs to be cogent and validated … you know this. So far, the only commerce this evidence has offered us is death.'

Mercer accrued sobriety as he listened to the chief's half-sighted comments, for not only had it rankled him but it had also offered him no incentive to continue. He did so, nonetheless. 'I do have a lead I would like to follow through.'

'Ah, here comes the rub,' said Rutherford curtly.

'With all due respect, Sir, my lead has come from a reliable source.'

'Mm?' Rutherford answered abruptly. 'Who might that be?'

'Detective Fenhill, Scotland Yard.'

'And?'

Rather grudgingly, Mercer gave his propoundment, yet all he could think about was how and when he was going to escape the room. 'Well, Fenhill alluded to Koshkin's relationship with Chief Superintendent Hamilton,' he began.

'Jeremy Hamilton?'

'Yes, Sir. I understand he's retired now but Fenhill seems to think that Hamilton took Koshkin under his wing somewhat. Formed a bond. A trust. Now, I have reason to believe Koshkin had vested something in secrecy to Hamilton. I believe he could have intelligence relating to this proof of Koshkin's.'

'You mean the proof we don't have?' snapped Rutherford.

Mercer ignored the chief's lack of civility and continued. 'I've lined up a trip in the pipeline. Once I've unriddled the identity of Euclid, I mean to annex my lead.'

'Retired to Portugal, didn't he? Hamilton.' Mercer nodded quietly. 'Right. What do you need? Do you have passports, sundries, etc? I can displace you in Treasury and they'll not bat an eye. Just give me the red flag when you're travelling.'

15

BACK IN HIS office, Mercer waited anxiously for the imminent call-back from Langdon. He almost anticipated the intelligence with dread, for the exposé would not only disband entirely the dynamic among current operatives but disfigure the face of MI6 irreparably. The phone rang and Mercer allowed it to ring several times before answering, to pre-empt his vestige of unease.

'What have you got for me, Langdon?' Mercer asked casually.

'Well, it was a tricky one, Saul. I'll give you that!'

Mercer waited with bated breath.

'Are you there?' enquired Langdon, as a current of static intervened over the telephone line.

'Altogether present, Tom,' replied Mercer in jest.

'Thought you had been cut off there for a moment. As I was saying, it was a bit of an eight-ball quandary, but it finally delivered. The only agent we have whose trips fit those specifications is Alan Soames. Incidentally, his trips to Austria occurred thrice through the month of May that year. France and Berlin became the norm thereafter.'

'Right,' said Mercer impassively. 'Yep, that tallies up. Thanks Tom.'

'Menzies, however, also took one trip to Austria the same month, but none ensuing.'

Mercer pondered on this detail for a while and stored it for later use. Menzies?

'What's this all in aid of then, Saul? Has an absurdly large cat been let out of the bag? Soames been dickering about with expenses or some such?'

'Something like that,' said Mercer with a changing of the guards. 'You know how it is, Tom. Once we're given a whiff of leave, some try their luck and go off radar for a spell. Think it's their birthright or other. Minor discrepancies, nothing untoward.'

'Cheeky blighter!' returned Langdon with a chuckle. This sally confirmed to Mercer that his evasive soft-pedalling had paid off in steering Langdon clear away from the patent perversion of conduct at hand.

'Rap on the knuckles for Soames then, eh?' continued Langdon. 'Heard he was in Harley Street for a turn. Doing all right is he? Poor bugger.'

'Alan seems to have a penchant for self-destruction. That and a tot or two are a bad combination. He's certainly had a tough time of it, but he'll pull through, I'm sure of it.'

'Damned shame. Well, do give him my best, Saul, once he's back in the game.'

'Will do, Tom. And thanks again for your assistance. Much appreciated.'

After replacing the receiver, Mercer speculated on the new-found evidence with gravitas, and although he was assailed by its nucleus, he could not help thinking how obvious a result it was on piecing the circumstances together. Soames' unorthodox behaviour had indicated clear signs of him cracking under pressure but Mercer was jumping ahead of the game, since Soames had not been caught red-handed as yet with his Soviet contact, neither had he been subjected to interrogation. And then there was Menzies, who had also been found to have travelled to Austria that same month. What would be his explanation of his itinerary? Was he the third man? Or their ally, Poli? And who was the operative visible in the negative proof caught in rendezvous with Yuri?

These thoughts rallied through Mercer's mind and were spurred on by Rutherford's blatant incompetence to recognise the obvious. Mercer had concluded, although he held the chief in high regard, that ignorance and arrogance made for a lousy alliance. However spurious the evidence had appeared to Rutherford, Mercer would allay his own doubts by exercising his immutably sound instinct. Having weighed the evidence as it now stood, his assumptions were resolute and qualified and would play a long hand where his co-workers were concerned, since his suspicions were his own until, of course, that moment of expiration.

•

ON COMPLETING some menial paperwork, Mercer found that it was now after six o'clock, and having left his office shortly after, he discovered that the building was virtually empty, bar the night janitors. He made his way down the four flights of stairs, passing a handful of night-owl operatives on the way, who threw him the odd preliminary or harmless gibe in passing. When he reached the night registrar, he greeted Mercer with a hearty smile.

'Good evening Mr Mercer sir. Working late if I might say?'

'Yes, Guthrie,' replied Saul cheerfully. 'Got a little carried away.'

Albert Guthrie was an elderly gentleman, small, thin, and Scottish by birth. He was an amenable, jovial sort of character and quite possibly as old as the Secret Service itself.

'Ah, now, you've got to know when to quit, sir, if I might be so bold. Appreciate the little things in life. Not getting any younger, sir.'

Mercer chuckled. 'No, indeed. How's Mrs Guthrie, Albert? In the pink? Keeping you on your toes?'

'Fiddle as a fit, sir, thank you. Fine woman, no mistaking. Not for everyone though … marriage. I've just been lucky, I guess.'

'Glad to hear it, Guthrie. Do give her my best.' As Mercer turned to leave, the night registrar conceded in wishing him a good night.

Mercer climbed into his convertible MGB and clocked a shady motorcyclist waiting on the corner. Switching on the ignition, Mercer revved the engine gently, and on pulling away he glanced in the rear-view mirror to check whether they would follow. They did. Mercer took an indirect route to St Albans, chiefly in view of shaking off his tail but his efforts offered no great benefit whatsoever, so he ignored it until he reached his destination, by which point the motorbike had veered off.

Mercer parked outside the safehouse, noticing that it was in complete darkness, which seemed odd since the streetlamps and surrounding houses were fully lit. He unlocked the boot of the car, felt about for his torch, then locked the car. The watchers, Dennis and Todd had been assigned to their station as a safety measure from the moment Mercer had moved Rodchenko the previous evening, and they would have flanked themselves at the front and back doors as a precaution. Mercer frisked his way cautiously up the garden path, with the torch beam leading the way until it reached the doorstep, whereupon a body lay groaning in pain. After several moments of inspection, Mercer established that it was Dennis. He attempted to communicate with him but all he could prise out of the man was nonsense, with the odd apology brewed into his disorientation.

Mercer saw no benefit in broadcasting his immediate animus, so he started off towards the side gate, which he found to be unbolted. As he opened it slowly, a cat shrieked at him with an indignant growl then clambered over the neighbouring fence with expedition. He edged himself along the exterior of the house very cautiously then peered his head round to assess the back door and garden. Surveying the area steadily with the torch, it appeared that he was in no imminent danger and he deduced that the bird had already flown.

He could hear a high-pitched whistling that sharpened the closer he got to the back door, which he also found to be open, and as the torchlight guided him into the kitchen, he discovered the kettle screaming on the gas stove. He switched off the gas and moved the kettle, which he sensed by its weight had barely any water left in it to boil. How long has the thing been left boiling? he pondered. As he shuffled further into the kitchen to look for a light switch, his left foot knocked a large, heavy object on the floor, where Todd lay unconscious with his skull bludgeoned and seeping blood. Mercer immediately checked his vitals to ensure that he was still in the land of the living, which mercifully he was. Then on locating the light switch, Mercer tested it several times before concluding that the power had been cut altogether. He made his way into the next room and called out for Rodchenko but there was no response, only silence and darkness.

Climbing the stairs to the first-floor landing, the sound

of intermittent dripping was coming from the bathroom, thudding against the enamelled steel composite. Treading lightly towards the rear bedroom door, Mercer prodded it open with his fist, the door creaking in protest. He scanned the floor with the torch and noted a chair standing in a rather irregular position in the open space. He pointed the torch further into the room and the light caught something ambiguous hanging from the ceiling. He could not quite decipher it at first, but on studying it further, he became jarred to the core. Oleg Rodchenko was hanging with vitriolic intent from a ceiling hook fit for a chandelier. An ultimate blockade from Moscow Centre.

Mercer's revulsion at the sight brought forward a stream of expletives, which fell from his mouth like dominoes. He even reproached himself on this unfortunate eventuality, feeling disparaging guilt, and as he stared at the lifeless face and body of Rodchenko, still sporting his oversized tweed overcoat, he felt entirely outmanoeuvred and circumvented by yet another venal counterblow. An innocent who knew too much. Said too much.

Mercer then hotfooted it down the stairs to see whether Dennis was in a fit enough state to deal with the current can of worms. He found him steadying himself on the doorstep.

'Are you all right, Dennis?' asked Mercer despondently.

'They gave me a proper royalling … back of my head, Sir,' Dennis answered with irritation. Then as he glanced at Mercer, he watched the dejection glaze over his face. 'What is it, Sir? Not Rodchenko?' Mercer nodded. 'Christ! Where's Todd?'

'He's been bludgeoned … back of the head, but he's still with us, thank God. Need you to help me with him. Can you manage?'

They lay Todd out on the sofa carefully, bandaging his head with some torn-off bit of curtain. 'Give me a hand with the fuse box would you Dennis? Need an extra pair of hands. Some light on the subject would be a bloody great help.' And within minutes they had the power back on. Mercer cautioned Dennis about the murder scene prior to their entering the upstairs bedroom.

'Jesus Christ!' exclaimed Dennis in a wretched state of shock. 'Sure it's not suicide, Sir? Does look a bit suspect.'

'Do you not notice anything peculiar about the room?' said Mercer with forethought. 'He couldn't have got up there unaided.'

Dennis assessed the room in search of certain anomalies that were not initially visible to him. 'The chair, Sir. It's yards away from the body. He would have to have kicked it away a damn good distance to succeed in the act.'

'It was a deliberate act of flagrancy. A stone-cold acerbic message from our Soviet friends. What a godawful mess!'

'You mustn't blame yourself, Sir,' said Dennis earnestly. 'If anything, it's down to us. It was our job to protect him and we've ballsed that up good and proper.'

'No, Dennis. What this boils down to is our meagre half-baked resources. It's a disturbingly backward and pitiful sham. There should have been more watchers down the pipe.'

'But what I don't understand is, how did they know he was here? We have umpteen different safehouses scattered across London.'

'By the simple truth, his location was vouchsafed … and by one of us. We have a mole fouling up D Branch, Dennis.'

Dennis cast a dubious look at Mercer as mutual suspicions hung heavy in the air.

'Did you get a good look at them, Dennis?'

'No, Sir. They attacked from behind. Outflanked us proper, like. Didn't even see them coming.'

There was a long and steady silence as the two men surveyed the body while it hung weighted by the rope, defunct and forsaken, then Dennis finally spoke. 'Hadn't we ought to call it in, Sir? Get the establishment in on the scene?'

'We can't involve the police, Dennis. Out of their jurisdiction, I'm afraid. I'll get on to Rutherford … leave it at that.'

16

'WHAT AN APPALLINGLY demeaning setback!' said Rutherford, unreservedly nettled. 'It's like a sodding bird trap. No sooner are we one step ahead than we're cunningly outfoxed and marginalised into a tunnel. I won't have it, Mercer. It's shameful!' Mercer simply listened with reserve in his usual sentinel air while his superior ruptured in a fit of contention, pacing the room like a trapped animal. 'Rodchenko was an innocent and it sickens me to my stomach, it really does.'

'He knew too much, Sir, and he disclosed vital intelligence. He obviously didn't pass muster in their view, so they shut him up with sordid retribution.'

'Well, we'll have to be extra vigilant with our next move Mercer, to avoid running headlong into a quagmire. To be frank, I would rather a stalemate than an outright defeat. British Intelligence can't afford another debacle. We would be the laughing stock, not to mention it sullying ties with our cousins over the pond. No. It won't ruddy do!'

Mercer permitted a short interval for a necessary cooling off on Rutherford's part, while he pondered on a possible plan of action.

'How's your man Todd doing?' Rutherford put in as an afterthought.

'In and out of consciousness, Sir. His skull took a proper beating. Didn't come round for hours. We're lucky we didn't lose him.'

'Well don't hurry him back into the field, Saul. Put him on desk work for a bit, hey? Incidentally, I'll be replacing Rodchenko's spot with Stewart Graves. Make a jolly good batsman in the cipher room. Thought he would do well with Menzies.' Mercer conceded quietly. 'Now, down to the brass tacks. Take a seat Saul, you're making me nervous.'

Mercer complied as Rutherford continued. 'I've been reviewing the decoded transcripts of Vesna regarding Euclid, and I think our best bet would be to demur on bringing Soames in for questioning.' Mercer shot him a questioning frown. 'Only for the time being, Saul. I feel a great deal more would materialise, having him placed under surveillance.' Mercer showed mild disapproval. 'Well, you've got to crack a few eggs to make an omelette and it could lead to uncovering the identity of his Soviet controller, and, hell, possibly to the names of the other moles! I want to catch him bang to rights man. I'll get Special Branch on the case now Harley Street have let Soames go. No doubt he'll catch on fast, have them scurrying on some bootless errand around London, but we'll get our chap, Mercer. We'll get him if it's the last thing I do.'

'Indisputably, Sir.'

While Rutherford removed a fat cigar from the box on the desk, Mercer thought it the opportune moment to proffer his travel plans. 'It's high time I made tracks for Lisbon. I've telephoned the airport ahead of schedule and booked under the name Carlisle. He's seldom used. Thought it appropriate.'

'Right,' returned Rutherford with endorsement. 'When do you fly out?'

'Tonight. Didn't want to waste any more time. Can't imagine much is likely to occur in my absence.'

Rutherford peered over his half-lens glasses with impartiality. 'We'll manage, Saul. Oh, and should you obtain any concrete material, get it sent by diplomatic bag direct to me. Encode it yourself. We can't afford some furtive interception at this stage.'

They parted without a single further word.

•

SAUL MERCER left his studio apartment on Markham Square at 7 p.m. that same evening, from where he found that he was being tailed once again by a motorcyclist. On this occasion, instead of using his usual disjointed artifice, he pulled into a lonely layby, under pretext of carrying out a minor inspection of the engine. The motorcyclist was obliged to continue down the road but waited two miles on at another layby before the chase resumed. It was not until they had reached Heathrow that the futility of the pursuit became evident and the motorcyclist continued their journey in the opposite direction.

It was a little before midnight by the time Mercer arrived at the hotel in Lisbon and settled in with an ample tot, which uniformly induced him into a deep sleep. As arranged on his arrival, he was woken the next morning with a seven-thirty call from reception, which he found on rising took some considerable coaxing. The scene from his window, which could not be seen the evening before, offered panoramic views of São Jorge Castle and the Tagus, a spectacular view to behold.

He breakfasted leisurely on the room's balcony with an inordinate population of squawking seagulls overhead, and he watched the torpid city rise to the tempo of a masterful dawn. He then referred to Koshkin's coded address book and dialled for an outside line. The phone rang three times before it was answered, and a female voice spoke: 'Pronto?' She had a velvety Italian inflection, which Mercer thought both inviting and appeasing; all of which could be detected through just two syllables. He replied eventually, after a short pause, and requested to speak with Jeremy Hamilton, if indeed he was at home. The woman replied graciously, handing the telephone over without enquiring who the caller was.

'This is Hamilton,' said the voice curiously. 'To whom am I speaking?'

'Ah, good morning,' Mercer began amiably. 'This is David Carlisle. I hope it's not impertinent of me to be calling but we have a mutual friend in common.'

'Yes?' countered Hamilton with caution.

'I believe you were his superior at Scotland Yard before your retirement, sir.' Hamilton waited silently. 'It's Sergei Koshkin to whom I refer.'

'And how is it you've come to know him, may I ask?'

'The company I work for is often in a position to employ freelance photographers from time to time, which is seldom a disagreeable arrangement … for both parties involved. He had come highly recommended to us.'

'And how is it I can help you?' Hamilton returned, a measure pointedly. 'I've had no contact with the man, not for some weeks now.'

'I'm sorry to be the bearer of bad news, sir, but I'm afraid Koshkin is dead.'

There was a long and weighted silence before Hamilton could bring himself to speak. 'Dear God!' he muttered ruefully. 'May I ask the cause of death?'

'I'm sorry to say he was shot.'

A jarring gasp followed. 'What the devil did you entangle yourself in, Sergei? Oh, what a monstrously pointless death.'

'I'm sorry … might I suggest we meet if it's not inconvenient for you? There are several important matters I would like to discuss with you further. I appreciate your reticence, Mr Hamilton, but if it helps any, it was in fact Detective Fenhill who nudged me in your direction.'

'Fenhill? All right … well, why don't you come here? I'm sure my wife wouldn't mind offering a little hospitality. I know she relishes in such things. That's to say if you can provide certain materials of distinction.'

'That I can do, sir.'

'Fine. Shall we say midday? If all goes well, you could join us for lunch.'

'That's very kind … much appreciated. And do thank your wife.'

'I assume you have the address?'

'I do, thank you.'

'Just a word of caution. Parking can be a bugger, but more often than not you'll find a spot round the back of the premises.'

'I'll be coming on foot, but thanks all the same. The hotel is walking distance, I believe, plus I'll enjoy observing the local amenities.'

'Well, shout if you get lost.'

•

HAMILTON'S PROPERTY was located in a highly sought-after street in Principe Real, just yards from the botanic gardens. On his route, Mercer passed through a vibrant area of concept stores, restaurants and the luxury boutiques of Avenida da Liberdade. Near the gardens stood the 19th century Museum of Natural History, a grand stone structure with a pillared frontage.

On his arrival at Hamilton's, Mercer was greeted by Mrs Hamilton, a tall, dark, elegant woman with a sensual figure. She wore an embroidered caftan and high-heeled sandals, and a delicate scent of perfume wafted towards him as she opened the door. She was evidently younger than Hamilton, and Mercer estimated her as being in her fifties.

'Mr Carlisle?' she said in a near whisper. 'Welcome.'

'Thank you for accommodating me at such short notice.'

'Not at all,' she answered convivially. 'It's not often we have the opportunity to meet new people. You see, my husband and I prefer a more private lifestyle. But I must admit to enjoying the odd soirée now and then. Come through Mr Carlisle.'

'David, please.'

The apartment was a vast space embellished with marble fixtures and parquet flooring. She led him through a plush living room where he found Hamilton sitting out on the adjoining balcony. There was an impressive view of the river, and as Mercer ingested the scene, Hamilton rose to offer him a cordial handshake.

'Carlisle? Pleasure. So, you've met my delicious wife, Monica. She'll be our hostess for the duration. Drink?'

'Please,' replied Mercer. 'Anything with ice will do.'

Hamilton gestured him to a chair and the two men were left alone. The general feeling between them had become rather sombre, for Hamilton had recalled the real interest of Mercer's visit.

'You said that your company had employed Koshkin on a temporary basis. Had he fulfilled his contract?' Hamilton asked.

'No. Unfortunately not. We had organised a private meet the evening he was shot. It had gone beyond our agreed time when I heard a commotion out in the park adjacent to the building. Naturally, I went to see what was going on. Fenhill and his crew arrived not long after.'

Hamilton gave a wearisome sigh as he gazed out, forlorn and beaten, over the burnished river. 'It's a dreadful thing. He was one of my best men, and one of the ablest of professionals. I just can't believe it.'

'A repatriation was presented him, out of respect, of course.'

'Damned right! Slavsky wasn't offered that privilege.'

'Slavsky?' reacted Mercer, pleading ignorance.

'Another émigré and colleague. A solid and conscientious officer. He and Koshkin worked well together. Fellow comrades if you will.' Then with sympathetic consideration, he added, 'His life was also cut short. Never got to the bottom of it … an elusive case.'

It was at this stage of the conversation that Mercer retrieved from the inside pocket of his jacket the encoded correspondence franked Lisbon that he had found at Koshkin's flat. 'Am I correct in assuming this was sent by yourself?' Mercer handed the memorandum to Hamilton for inspection.

Hamilton picked up his spectacles from the table and peered through them briefly so as to examine the dispatch. 'Correct. This was our final correspondence.'

'In truth, Mr Hamilton, Koshkin was about to disclose photographic evidence to us, which I believe he had secretly dispatched to your good self for … shall we say … discreet preservation.'

There was an intense interval, which disrupted the flow of conversation temporarily, before Hamilton countered discursively. 'If that were the case, Mr Carlisle, certain satisfactory material would need to be produced.'

At that, Mercer reached for the left pocket of his jacket and handed over the first half of Koshkin's postcard from the British Museum. 'Are you in possession of the product, Mr Hamilton?'

'As you've made the match,' Hamilton replied in the spirit of cooperation, 'I am indeed. Although sadly they're not on the premises. The product is, as you say, discreetly preserved.'

'Is it obtainable, sir? Or is it to be got at via extraneous measures?'

'I can get at it but I might need a couple of days in order to do so.'

'Of course,' replied Mercer with incitement. 'Whatever you feel necessary.'

There was a din of rattling glasses coming from within the apartment, and before long Monica re-entered the balcony gracefully, tray in hand. She placed it gently upon the table and poured three ample servings of a citrus libation from a rather large pitcher.

'While you're biding your time, Carlisle,' Hamilton implied, 'I have a source whom I can put you in touch with. I'm certain he'll offer you invaluable information to help further your enquiries.'

17

'A SOURCE?' returned Mercer reflectively. 'Would that be a former colleague?'

'Not exactly a colleague,' replied Hamilton. 'Let's just say our paths crossed sporadically during my service at Scotland Yard. Rafe Hederby ... Foreign Correspondent for The Times. An exemplary journalist and trusted friend.'

Mercer digested the information tentatively, for reasons largely of recollection, and he quickly concluded the name to be unfamiliar to him.

'Shall we discuss this matter over lunch?' continued Hamilton. 'I'm famished. My wife and I often take lunch on our boat. Would you care to join us Carlisle? Unless of course you have a prior engagement you would prefer to concede?'

'I would be delighted, Hamilton. Thank you.'

'Excellent. We'll make headway after our aperitifs. All prepped darling?' Hamilton asked his wife.

'Waiting to be devoured my dear,' she replied affectionately.

Their dialogue continued on the balcony in a conciliatory tone and deviated more in the direction of Fenhill and office politics, for a mutual respect had developed between the two men after such a short acquaintance and they were settling into an easy rapport. The Hamiltons' yacht, The Falcon, was a handsome 62ft flat-bottomed vessel, outfitted with mixed exotic wood. It had been used, in the early part of Hamilton's retirement, for cruising around northern Europe, but chiefly Italy, as Mrs Hamilton still had living relatives there.

The trip they took that warm afternoon was twenty kilometres or thereabouts along the Tagus, inclusive of passing leisurely under the Vasco da Gama Bridge, inspecting the alluring twelfth century Castle of Almourol and lauding the extensive architecture and monuments. All this while the sun reflected a sterling sheen of prismatic light over the skin of the water. They took a light lunch, with a bottle of Chardonnay, and their conversation reverted back to Hamilton's brief mention of his journalist friend.

'As you'll no doubt recall, I referred earlier to Rafe Hederby, so I'll jump right in. Some years back, he had been approached by a defector, I believe she was something of a clerk at the Russian Embassy here in Lisbon, stating she had damning evidence of, shall we say, Soviet proclivity.'

'What sort of evidence?' questioned Mercer temperately.

'Well now, this is often the predicament I'm faced with concerning Hederby, since his reticence had been imposed on him by certain diplomats to a level of crippling discretion. Nevertheless, what he could impart to me alluded to a codebook. She had, in her initial efforts, approached the British Embassy some three kilometres down the road with said documentation but was turned away under the assumption that she was trying to fob them off with false information.'

'And was it false?'

'Not remotely. But on her third attempt at the British Embassy their interest suddenly took an about-turn and they placed her under protective custody. As is usual in such cases, the situation spun itself out of control but they finally released her. The ordeal was less than moderate, from what I gather, and it was at this point that she approached Hederby. Rafe confided that she had been so traumatised by the fiasco that she blew the lid off the whole incident on their first meeting.'

'Who was the diplomat at the British Embassy who sanctioned her claim. Do you know?'

'I couldn't say. Hederby will no doubt have all the nuts and bolts, but there was a frightful brouhaha carrying on between the British and Russian embassies. Then, out of the blue, someone furtively silenced Hederby. Completely road-blocked his running the story. Shut him down … took him off the assignment. And that was that.'

Mercer conveyed lucid consternation before putting his next question forward. 'Is Hederby still in Lisbon? Or has he moved on?'

'No, he's still here. Working his fingers to the bone. Dined with him last week, didn't we darling?' Hamilton then reached into his jacket for his wallet, where he retrieved a business card and handed it over to Mercer with his forefingers. 'Rafe is a cast-iron informant, Carlisle. I would trust no other.'

'Thank you, Hamilton. I'm indebted to you.'

'Not at all, Carlisle. Glad to be of service. You'll invariably find him rambling around the bars near the city square … Terreiro do Paço. If you can't get him by telephone that is.'

And this was precisely Mercer's method of locating him that evening after telephoning the number on the business card; albeit to have Hederby's secretary give him the name of the bar in which he could find him.

•

IT WAS A DARK and rowdy establishment and in dire need of charm, yet the locals were uncharacteristically friendly, which duly compensated for what was lacking. Mercer made an enquiry at the bar briefly to ask where he might find Mr

Hederby, and the barman pointed in the general direction of the farthest point of the room, where the person in question could be distinguished by his beard. In any event, he was the only gentleman to be sporting one on the premises.

Mercer hauled himself through the high-spirited youths and spotted Hederby sitting at a table in the corner, alone. On approaching him, Mercer introduced himself as Carlisle and a recent acquaintance of Jeremy Hamilton, who had given him Hederby's business card. Without hesitation, Hederby invited him to join him and continued to clarify that Hamilton had in fact telephoned ahead of their meet, giving Mercer the green light.

'I'm gratified to hear that I cut the mustard,' said Mercer with an audacious smile.

'Well,' replied Hederby with a chuckle, 'if you've made the grade with Hamilton, it's duck soup thereafter.'

Having manoeuvred their way through the preliminaries, they ordered a set of drinks and settled into mutual ease, bringing to light the true focus of their meeting.

'Hamilton inferred that you were in possession of some intelligence,' said Mercer genially. 'I understand your reluctance in disclosing such furtive material, since you don't know me from Adam. But that being said, I can ensure the utmost discretion on my part, and I feel it would reinforce my position by telling you I'm tenured under the British Government. But if you would prefer to see whether my credentials check out, I can put you in touch with my superior.'

'That won't be necessary, Carlisle. I'm fully prepared. Hamilton is testament enough.' He lit a cigarette and offered the packet to Mercer, which he accepted. Hederby then put a shrewd question forward after downing his single malt. 'I understand you were acquainted with Koshkin?'

This question had come somewhat out of left field, but Mercer was certainly intrigued to see where the conversation was headed. 'That's correct,' he answered. 'Although, if I'm entirely honest, we never met.'

'Appalling business that. He didn't deserve such a butchering.'

'Were you familiar with Koshkin yourself?'

'I was. Rather indirectly,' Hederby replied. Then, taking Mercer into his confidence, he muted his voice to the quietest level possible before becoming almost inaudible in the babel. 'Ten years or so back, I had a tip-off from an informant, whom I shan't name, of a rendezvous about to take place in Prague between a Soviet spy and his British agent. Now, this informant had assigned an officer at Scotland Yard to tail the two spies and obtain photographic evidence of the culprits in situ, only he sidestepped and convinced Koshkin to take the job on. So, the job was done but the officer who was initially assigned got himself dispatched by the Soviets, since they believed him to be the guilty party. It wasn't until much more recently that the Soviets smoked Koshkin out from under a hovel through some British Intelligence operative dropping the ball.'

'That's acutely uncommon of the Soviets to get wise so late in the day,' said Mercer with a measure of irony.

Hederby chuckled. 'Well, I suppose the material got buried somewhere along the way and they thought they were in the clear. Or at least until recent exposure. But, at that same period of events, I had been approached by a defector. She was a cipher clerk at the Russian Embassy here in Lisbon. Beautiful woman. Elena Kozakov. Pensive type. When she first came to me with her story, her mental state was … how shall I put it … compromised. She was a nervous wreck. Spent weeks under interrogation at some camp or other. At any rate, she disclosed all the sordid details of her then current predicament.'

'Had she already turned? Or was she entangled in the process?'

'The intelligence she possessed was her ticket out. But I'll give you the facts as she vouchsafed them. The start of it all was down to her forthcoming time being up at the Russian Embassy, and she didn't want to return to Moscow, so she had hidden some documents of the Soviet propaganda type, which had been released through the media worldwide, and intended to reveal their baseless content. Apparently, the propaganda described a draconian Russia with conditions of near starvation and police brutality, which was a blatant fabrication of course. But the Holy Grail of her evidence was a GRU, Russian Military Intelligence codebook, supposedly listing names of Soviet informers.

'So, off trots Elena to the British Embassy with her little product shoved under her arm, primed to bargain for her asylum. Well, the ruddy lot turned her away twice didn't they, despite all her efforts, so Elena returns home somewhat dejected to find three Russian military attachés trying to force entry to the property. Unbeknown to them, a neighbour had called the police, and while Kozakov was being read the riot act, two officers arrived to break things up. The diplomats were let go but the police report subsequently included their presence at the premises. The following day, our girl decides she won't be crushed underfoot by a couple of pesky Russian hoods, so she grits her teeth and takes her cute little arse back to the British Embassy.'

'So, who was it that sanctioned her claim?' Mercer put in.

'Jane Ashford. Exceptional officer. Had a few run-ins with her over the years. Can't for the life of me think why we didn't have a bit of the other. Hey-ho. Timing I suppose. At any rate, it all went tits up after that for Elena. Found herself in some seriously deep water did little Kozakov.'

Hederby took pause for a moment to light another cigarette then called in yet another round of drinks. The alcohol was certainly proving to have loosened his tongue and his narrative deviated marginally into the sector of his alleged intimacy with Kozakov, but Mercer reeled him back in mildly towards the matter of Jane Ashford.

'Quite right, Carlisle,' said Hederby unruffled, and he pressed on with his tale. 'Elena insisted she speak with a female officer, which was how Ashford managed to get her foot in, and discerning the sensitivity of the documents, she places Kozakov under protective custody and packs her off to some SOE camp on the outskirts of Lisbon. Ashford then knocks up some encoded memorandum to London station, stating that she has retained vital documents from a Russian Embassy clerk who is now in protective custody. Jane's immediate objective was to buy some time while a decision was being made over how to deal with the Russian ambassador.

'He had requested, and not lightly, that Kozakov be returned to his custody since she was guilty of nobbling diplomatic material from the embassy. In any case, the interrogation kicks off and Elena is subjected to techniques of sleep deprivation, denied food and threatened with deportation back into the hands of the Soviets, because her real motive was to plant fake intelligence.'

'Who was Kozakov's inquisitor?' questioned Mercer.

'Some burly chap named Bradshaw.'

'Jim Bradshaw?'

'That's the fellow. Hard as nails. Know him, do you?'

'I know of him. Quite a reputation as it goes.'

'Well, he wasn't letting up. Not by a long chalk. Questioned her for hours. But she stuck to her story good and firm. Said the intelligence she was offering wasn't false and that she was prepared to cooperate with her interlocutors in exchange for being granted asylum in Lisbon.'

'So, did the GRU codebook reveal anyone of importance?' asked Mercer equably.

'Mm, yes. The primary operative was "Alek", the British physicist, Alan Nunn May. No doubt you heard the scandal. Possibly before your time.'

'It's ringing a distant chime, yes.'

'He was assigned to the Manhattan Project, which produced the atomic bomb. Turned out the weasel had been stashing crucial samples of the uranium isotopes and passing them off on the QT to his Russian controller. Got an absurdly short sentence of ten years due to his offering his treachery as quid pro quo to plug holes in the security of British Intelligence. Bloody light sentence if you ask me. Should have lined them all up against a damned bulwark and popped some holes in the lot.'

'Were there any other operatives discovered in the codebook?'

'Well, that's just it. All the evidence decamped. Just upped and walked off after Kozakov had been released. Some

Charlie's got it, no doubt. Still, our Elena had memorised a handful of codes. "I've got a little list," she says. Saving it for a rainy day I expect. In any event, they deadlocked my running of the story. Old Hederby was incommunicado. No sodding scoop. End of the line for muggins here.'

'And what of this Russian handler who Koshkin was assigned to photograph? Do you have any information on him?'

'Tough nut to crack, that one. I tried probing it out of Kozakov, but she wasn't having any of it. Said her head would be on the block if she heralded his identity, and she wasn't prepared to risk her precious asylum for anything. The only scrap she offered me was an alias. He's known as Yuri, but that was all she would give me at the time. It's all linked though, no doubt about that. Koshkin, the photographs, the GRU codebook … only someone's had the foresight to hamper its progress. Put the kibosh on the whole operation before they're all blown. My guess is they've had a bloody good double agent in on it from day one.'

'Well, the case has been dormant for ten years. Chances are there are a few of them doing the legwork to keep that under wraps. Meanwhile, good men have been needlessly squandered.'

'Whichever way you slice it, Carlisle, the Soviets have outdistanced the whole intelligence community. But there'll doubtless be a leak somewhere along the line. These things have a habit of escaping somehow. Just a matter of time.'

'Quite,' agreed Mercer pensively. 'And what of Kozakov? Did she remain in Lisbon?'

'No. It seems our little lot recruited her. Contrived a legend for her … new identity, British passport, the whole package. Works at the British Embassy in London. You might be able to squeeze something out of her now the dust has settled.'

18

THE VERY NEXT morning, while fending off a slight headache, Mercer telephoned the British Embassy, Lisbon, and having given it a great deal of thought decided Jane Ashford would be his first port of call, since she was intrinsic to the Kozakov case. Kozakov he could approach on his return to D Branch if necessary.

Their conversation was brief, and it was readily agreed that a meeting take place at the embassy that afternoon. Given he had a little time to kill, Mercer drafted a memorandum for Rutherford's attention, including chapter and verse thus far.

That afternoon, as Mercer entered the embassy, he passed a former colleague with whom he had been briefly assigned some months before. But the operation in question would forever be forefront in Mercer's mind, since it was the very operation that had preceded the end of his marriage. Flushed and rather chipper, the short and fleshy figure of Samuel Northcott was stood holding the main door to the embassy.

'By jingo!' Northcott said with excitement, 'if it isn't my chum Kit. How the devil are you, Mercer?' Applicable to everyone, Northcott would coin a nickname, and for Mercer he had dubbed him Kit, due to his reputation of invariably carrying essential equipment whenever a tight corner presented itself. This had often been the case during their two months together and Mercer had quickly become familiar with the near fatal absent-mindedness of his cohort.

One or two incidents came to Mercer's mind while Northcott was stood gloating at him from the doorway. One evening, Mercer had returned to their digs to find no Northcott, but a charred gloopy substance still cooking on the gas ring and a bellowing plume of smoke occupying their rooms. The second event was regrettably in the field, when Northcott's wool-gathering had offensively blown their cover, resulting in a rather unsavoury jam. And on pondering it further, Northcott often reminded Mercer of a bungling character from Wodehouse – a loveable walking disaster. How he had passed muster for the Secret Service was beyond Mercer.

'Hullo there Northcott. Been caught in any double binds of late?'

'You know me Mercer. It's rather my forte, what?' and he gave a hearty belly laugh, which echoed through the reception hall, luring a few snooty looks of disapproval. 'Come and have a drink old boy.' Then as an afterthought: 'What the dickens are you doing in these parts? Fag-end of a holiday, surely?'

'Oh, just chasing a lead … minor errand, you know how it is. Grain of chickenfeed most likely. Everything well with you and so forth?'

'More than satisfactory, Saul. Got hold of a feisty little Jag. Must take you for a run in her; convertible E-Type, British Racing Green, black soft-top. Demon ride. Gets her fair share of admirers, I can tell you.' Northcott's eyes gleamed as he spoke.

'Lucky Jim! Sounds like quite a find, Northcott.'

'Oh, she is old boy. Purrs like a kitten. Tempt you to a spin?'

'Afraid I can't old man. Got a briefing shortly. Another time perhaps?'

'How long are you in Lisbon?'

'Difficult to say. Things are far from lucid … get the picture?'

With a portion of disappointment, Northcott sputtered:

'Mm, well … well, can't be helped old chap. Give me a tinkle if you find yourself twiddling your thumbs. Happy to oblige man; happy to oblige.' And at that he bestowed Mercer a playful tap on the shoulder and added, 'Toodle-pip.'

•

THE CHANCERY OFFICE where the briefing was held was on the second floor and overlooking the street below. The late afternoon sun channelled its glory through the spotless windows and the blinds were pulled down to half-light to act as a screen. Commencing with witty preliminaries invoked an easy rapport, since they were already familiar with one another and were comfortable in an instant. For in Mercer's view, Jane Ashford was a handsome woman, with an intellectual endowment to match. She was a dark-haired classic beauty from a middle-class family of emissaries and a hefty Cambridge education to boot. Her prestige as an operative was on par with her superiors, regardless of her gender or rank, and her style of polemic would often cut a heavyweight duly down to size with devastating effect.

Their conversation edged moderately towards the real focus, and Jane's story checked out almost word for word with that of Hederby. As she had had the advantage of stealing a march on the other female cohorts, it had conveniently placed her slap bang in the thick of it all and deeming her a weighty source.

'I've no knowledge,' Ashford announced, 'of who the inane culprits were that turned Kozakov away, but I can make an informed guess. Quite frankly, it wouldn't be worth the candle investigating it.'

'There would be little surprise in discovering Northcott a suspect,' added Mercer.

They laughed heartily.

'The man's an unmitigated fool.' Ashford grinned with relish. 'But I'll give him his due, he does deliver the odd bit of solid intelligence.' There was a short pause before she proceeded. 'Now … brass tacks. I assume your little chat with Hederby didn't quite quench your thirst?'

'Let's just say I would rather you regale me, since you were actually there at the time. Rafe Hederby was very thorough in his appraisal but there were a few blanks that I should like to have clarified.'

'Namely?'

'Jim Bradshaw. The interrogation.'

She threw him a coy smirk. 'You don't ask for much, do you Mercer? Well, it was Bradshaw who considered it prudent to bundle Kozakov off to SOE camp. The moment he clapped eyes on the documents she was carrying, he wanted her out of the Soviets' reach. I argued the toss, but to no purpose, sadly.'

'What would have been your line of action?' Mercer asked calmly.

'Probably cached her off to some quiet safehouse out of harm's way.'

Mercer raised his eyebrows with enquiry.

'Well, damn it, Saul, I certainly wouldn't have thrown her into the lion's den at some primitive training ground just to put the frighteners on her. Sometimes diplomacy is a more effective method.'

'Agreed. And you think Bradshaw was a trifle carriage-and-four?'

'That's putting it mildly. Don't misunderstand me, he's an exceptional inquisitor. I just feel it can't hurt cooling one's heels now and then.'

'So, talk me through it, Jane. From the beginning. And omit nothing.'

'Well, initially, Bradshaw was moderately tame and would nod sympathetically between questions, but as the hours mounted up, he began to plant the odd lethal question to test her resilience. He then started accusing her of planting fake evidence and threatening her with deportation back to Russia if she didn't come clean. Kozakov, although terrified, insisted over and over that the intelligence she was furnishing us with was high priority and not false and that she was prepared to cooperate with us in exchange for asylum.

'Anyone with any sense could see that she was telling the truth, but maybe that's a woman's intuition talking. Call it what you will, it was obvious to me. Bradshaw had pushed all the right buttons to harry her into a corner but she wasn't budging. After that it was a different proposition entirely. He defaulted to more drastic measures. Questioned her more closely. Deprived her of sleep and food. The poor woman was on the verge of becoming a bedlamite. But it was evident Bradshaw had one or two irons in the fire. He was edging towards something far more furtive. Then he came down on her like a ton of bricks.'

'For what motive, exactly?'

'He wanted all the dirt on how things were run … Soviet end. Who was the case officer of the British agents listed in the GRU codebook? Who recruited them and when? Where were they embedded? He sweated her hard.'

'And did she crack?'

'Eventually. Took days of sleep deprivation. More fire and brimstone. You know the drill, Saul.'

'In truth, I've not been a fly on the wall for one of Bradshaw's infamous cabarets.'

'I wish I could say the same.' A solitary pause. 'So, every hour he repeated his modus operandi. The same probing questions: "Who was the Soviet handler for the British operatives? When were they recruited? Where were they placed within MI6?" He wasn't remotely interested in where the moles had been lodged outside of British Intelligence. That was a concern for our cousins across the pond. For days, Kozakov completely shut down. Didn't utter a single syllable. Just stared at the iron table. Entered an impervious state. I tried defusing the situation but by that point she had run out of steam.

'Then again from Bradshaw: "Who was the Soviet handler?" "They call him Yuri," she answered finally. Bradshaw pressed harder: "Who's Yuri? What's his shielded identity?" Her answer remained singular for hours. That was all she would offer. That's when he threatened deportation. And he was very final about it. She broke down. Became hysterical. Then she turned the table on her inquisitor. Said she wouldn't expose Yuri's identity unless she had absolute assurance of her immediate asylum. She was shrewd. Demanded a written declaration, immigration papers, British passport, bank account, the whole nine yards.'

'Did Bradshaw take the bait?'

'Oh, he yielded all right. Handed over the bag of tricks off the bat. Then the floodgates opened. Yuri's identity, she claimed, was known to very few operatives. The select few, his trusted circle. Kozakov had come to know it purely by accident. When she was stationed in the Soviet Union at the GRU, a colleague had blindly let it slip to another cohort while she was attending to records in Registry. Now, this colleague, Vengerov, had been planted as a defector at the Russian Embassy in London since '47. She said his function was to act as intermediary between Yuri and his British agents at MI6. Passed on all the serviceable intelligence … the firewater. He's still stationed there, so I believe.'

Once again there was a suitable silence, which Mercer permitted with ample form.

'Then Kozakov vested the axiom. Yuri, she said, was the head of the Third Directorate of the GRU. A highly placed operative of the Russian Military Intelligence. His name, Alexei Gorokhov. Former veteran of the Red Army. He has cropped up on several occasions over the years during my research. A twelve-cylinder blue-chip hood if ever there was one. An unbridled Trojan dignitary. An unorthodox cutthroat. It's alleged he had his son shot for reasons of nonconformity. I'm sure the pool went a little deeper than that, but by any objective standard, his political assertions are unconstitutional. A fanatic.

'No small wonder Kozakov was duly in fear of her life and demanded a rearguard action. According to Kozakov, he pulled all the strings for the three British spies that were blown in the fifties. Plucked them fresh from Cambridge in the thirties. Placed them strategically across the globe. Uprooted two of them to Russia when their cover was blown. The GRU codebook referred to their replacements, should a witch-hunt or any other blue ruin be incited. These, Kozakov said, were new recruits, and the codebook, for vigorous security measures, listed only their codenames. "Alek", the

British physicist, had been blown through extraneous means, which had merely ratified his identity in the codebook.'

'And what happened to the GRU codebook, Jane? After Kozakov had been processed through the necessary channels.'

'Your guess is as good as mine, Saul. Fallen off radar ... disappeared, like our friend Alexei Gorokhov. Nemo saltat sobrius.'

19

SOAMES SAT glaring out of the large Georgian windows of Rutherford's office in a crippling half-cut state, alone, with the ticking clock harrying his conscience. It was a savage hour of the morning and the scales were now weighted heavily against him – but this was what he wanted wasn't it? He had finally contrived a safe passage out of the quagmire from which he so desperately needed liberation. His train of thought was fixed on his exploits of last evening, along with his noncompliance against the two external sources instructing him to whip up a succession of speeding tickets for the purpose of immediate arrest. For this – although it had had prior success – Soames did not follow through. Instead, his spontaneous actions had unwittingly brought him to the finish line. An agonisingly slow odyssey of discovery and admission. He was coming to terms with the truth, a truth he had obstinately been staving off for the greater part of his life. This path would lead him in one direction only thereafter, and he was prepared for the onslaught of repudiation.

The door to the office opened abruptly, fracturing Soames' flow of thought, and Rutherford entered somewhat morosely. Without comment, he traipsed over to the desk and took out a cigar from the carved wooden box, then offered it to Soames, which he accepted. After a very long silence, Rutherford sat down and began his appraisal temperately.

'It seems we're becoming quite handy at getting you out of scrapes of a spectacular nature, Soames.' A moderate glance of amusement was exchanged. 'But, before we discuss that little incident, I would like to chew over the recent dispatch you received from an alien source.' Soames shot him an unsettled glance. 'Oh yes, Alan, we're fully aware of your skulduggery. You underestimate our abilities. You do know that there's a law against conspiring with enemy agents? Or are you going to deny all knowledge of association?'

Soames said nothing.

'According to a couple of field-glasses assigned to the surveillance of your flat, two undesirables of a Slavic inclination were seen hovering in the vicinity, one of whom made good a dead-letter drop in your very letterbox. What have you to say about that?'

Again, no answer.

'Of course, your cast-iron pretext had you consulting with Dr Gladstone at the time. I assume the correspondence was a tip-off to your being placed under surveillance.'

Rutherford stood at this point and meandered over to the window, where he invariably found it conducive to reflection. He was deep in thought and took ample time to present his next question, and Soames could sense his lack of composure. 'Who are they, Soames?'

Soames sat as quiet as composite, almost as if he were stuck in some godawful waiting room.

'One of the Moscow contacts you're so hugger-mugger with is called Maxim. Who is he?' The air was opaque with suspicion and Rutherford knew he did not have a leg to stand on without valid proof of trapping Soames in Soviet company. For it was all very well acting the judicial emissary and flinging pungent comments left, right and centre, but it was to Soames' advantage that nothing could be imputed on him, and he exploited that fact without omission.

'Your chums are doubtless implicated in lynching

Rodchenko and obliterating Koshkin's skull. Or are we going to plead ignorance on that score as well?'

Feeling the pressure of self-constraint slipping, Rutherford became subject to the slow meddling tug upon the gasket he often struggled to keep a lid on. More militant this time: 'Who is Euclid, Soames? Or Poli? Or the third man?'

Again, Soames concealed his alarm and said nothing.

'Menzies and his army of cryptographers have been most productive while you were on sabbatical. It seems we have a cosy little alliance of Soviet agents fouling things up. Mercer is off grid chasing a vital lead in Lisbon who can shed some light on Koshkin's proofs … or so I'm told. I expect a diplomatic bag of goodies from him any day. But don't concern yourself with the futile procedures of cooperation at this stage, since I have you lined up with Bradshaw tomorrow, who will no doubt sweat the whole kit and caboodle out of that diametric brain of yours. So don't even think about doing a bunk off this godforsaken island, Soames. You stay local, you hear? I've got a team on your back every minute of the day. You'll not get far if you do try your luck.'

It was at this juncture that Soames' noncompliance took a more uncompromising stand, despite the disquieting debriefing imposed upon him. He pocketed the cigar that had been offered him earlier and, in succession, took out a cigarette from its gilded case and lit it.

Rutherford, on the other hand, poured himself a large tot from the whisky decanter but offered no hospitable libation to his subordinate. 'Now on to more pressing matters. I trust you're sober enough to sit through my prattling on. Only you're a rather critical component of the dross I'm about to spill.'

No response was proffered further from Soames' quarter. He merely continued to smoke casually with consecutive indifference.

'I'm in full receipt of a chronicle,' continued Rutherford, 'from Detective Fenhill, who spun a rather florid yarn concerning misdemeanours of your recent and most crowning hours. Additionally, I've had a pithy account from our scouts in the field, which is far less entertaining, I might add. Now, having taken a somewhat indirect route from your flat in St John's Wood to Chelsea Palais, you sought the company of a certain breed of gentleman. After several hours of some serious elbow bending, you took it upon yourself to pull a rent boy of your acquaintance, then you proceeded towards the nearest public lavatories. It was at this setting that you were caught in flagrante delicto with the young gentleman in question and arrested with your trousers down, so to speak.'

A lengthy and awkward pause followed this revelation, yet Soames remained entirely unmoved.

'Far be it from me to cast judgement on your sexual predilections, Alan. It's no business of mine what you get up to out of hours. In fact, it's positively commonplace in one's youth to bat from the pavilion end once in a while. However, it calls for comment to draw your attention to the Sexual Offences Act 1967, which states clearly that although it has been legalised with certain conditions appended, maximum penalties are exercised should those actions fail to meet the strict requirements set out … ergo gross indecency. Now since your miscue falls foul of said requirement, I'm in the hog-tied position to force our hand.'

Soames remained mute and was as responsive as a brick

wall, yet behind those dark stoic eyes of his, he tossed around in his mind the unassailably strong points that were stacking up against him. He tried to process the train of events that had occurred some hours before and questioned who the person was that he had now become. He waited calmly for the other shoe to drop, and Rutherford was as predictable as the night is black.

'In face of your apparent indifference, I think it a bit rum being dragged out of bed at some ungodly hour for the sole purpose of prising you, yet again, from the grip of Scotland Yard. And without any sign of gratitude or compunction from your quarter. But then that's your usual pattern of antics, Soames, isn't it? See how high we can stack things before the whole bloody lot comes crashing down.'

A lethargic sigh was expelled from Soames while he reached for the cigarette case and lit yet another in defiance.

'Damn it, Soames! Bloody well say something, anything, in your defence, blast you.'

'What would you have me say Ruthers? That you've got it all wrong? That my conduct of recent hours was just a farce and I just happened to feel like a bit of the other at the time?'

'Don't be obtuse man! I couldn't give two hoots about your social conformities. I refer to your skulking beyond your legitimate duties. That's what's in question here! Your treachery and your flagrant abuse of diplomatic privilege.'

The tautness in Rutherford's voice invoked a stare of rebuke from Soames and the air was pierced with an accusing silence. Soames said nothing.

'I've stuck my neck out for you on several occasions, not to mention your recent admission to Harley Street. Well, I'm sorry Soames, but your luck has run out. It's against my entreaties to the hierarchy that I must inform you that your tenure has been permanently suspended. It's the end of the line for you, chum.'

20

A MEETING RESUMED between Mercer and Hamilton the day after Mercer's debriefing with Jane Ashford, which was a meeting that had proved highly inciteful. It had been agreed the evening before that Mercer return to the Hamiltons' apartment on Principe Real, where his invitation to dine would convene. Their dining had been excessive, with an ample quantity of cru du Beaujolais, and their banter had continued as it had on the day of their first acquaintance. Following their indulgence, Hamilton led Mercer into his private office, where they would be completely undisturbed for the duration. To begin with, their conversation was moderate, which Hamilton initiated with an accompanying brandy and a cigar.

'So how did your powwow go with Hederby? To your satisfaction, Carlisle, I hope?'

'Yes, most informative thank you. He's very thorough in his intelligence gathering, even if his methods are a little unorthodox.'

'Unorthodox? How so?'

'Bit of a ladies' man,' said Mercer with a savourous grin. And why not? He's a charming enough chap. Make a damn good fieldman.'

Hamilton laughed. 'I dare say he might entertain the idea if things go off course. He was dealt a bad hand concerning that defector. As I said, road-blocked all the way. Unlucky, I guess.'

'Quite. He was certainly rankled by the whole ordeal. Shame. Would have made for great reading. Incidentally, he put me on to an edifying diplomat at the British Embassy.

In actual fact, she was the only attaché with any sense at the time of the incident. Sanctioned the claim. Her appraisal certainly bridged the gap.'

'Pleased to hear you're making headway, Carlisle. It's so gratifying when one has a clearer direction on a case. Makes the albatross of labour far more worthwhile, wouldn't you agree?'

'Entirely. Do I detect a Coleridge buff, Hamilton?'

'"Through the fog it came, as if it had been a Christian soul," or something along those lines. I'm partial to a bit of Coleridge, I must admit.'

'I'm not in the least surprised. I had taken you for an educated man, Hamilton. Are you an Oxonian?'

'That I am. Went straight into the Indian Police just before the war. Quite an eye-opener, I can tell you. Spend any time there yourself, Carlisle? India?'

'Can't say I have, sadly. The Middle East is the nearest I came to India. I was stationed there for a time.'

Hamilton strolled over to a private safe, hidden behind a Turner, and as he opened it, he asked, 'How long were you stationed there?'

'Three-year stint. Quite a wrench leaving it, in truth. Still, one can't very well object about when and where one is sent.'

'Occupational hazard, eh?'

Watching Hamilton remove the evidence, Mercer replied, 'Indeed. I see you've had a spot of luck your end.'

'Standard procedures … but by and large no bother.' Hamilton carried the large brown folder from the safe to the desk, removed the images carefully and placed them uppermost on the surface. 'This,' he continued, 'was the dispatch I received from Koshkin. The terms set out categorically precluded any possibility of acquisition unless the countersignal could be produced. Koshkin was very final on that score.'

Mercer scrutinised the photographs with intensity. A seriousness formed over his brow and his consternation was no pretence. Hamilton watched the staidness darken over Mercer's face with alarm, then asked, 'Would it be impertinent of me to enquire whether they're familiar to you? The men in the photographs?'

It took a little time for Mercer to answer, for he struggled to process the revelation before him. 'Carlisle?' prodded Hamilton with concern.

'Forgive me,' Mercer replied. 'I'm somewhat tongue-tied. Not impertinent at all, Hamilton. There's one gentleman I recognise, yes.'

Hamilton waited firmly for his reply. Then pointing to the tall, dapper figure in the image, Mercer said, 'He's a former colleague. MI6 operative. Spent years in service. Still has his finger in the pie, so to speak.'

Although Mercer had eluded broadcasting the name of the individual, the name chimed over in his mind, inhibiting his thought process from manoeuvring beyond the words: George Dryden. But Guy Menzies was still a possible suspect since his travel schedule had fallen in with Mercer's enquiries. And Mercer could not help thinking that Rutherford was going to have a field day with this lot. He then recalled the deciphered wireless evidence of Euclid and Poli to mind. And the elusive third man. Which role had Dryden been assigned to enact?

'And the other gentleman?' pressed Hamilton mildly.

'Him I don't know. That being said, I have three individuals who confirm that he's the Russian handler known as Yuri. Any more than that, I couldn't say. I assume he's the principal head-hunter.'

'But will the evidence assist in catching your man, Carlisle?'

'Grist to the mill, Hamilton. Thank you for your cooperation. The net is certainly closing in.'

•

THE CONVERSATION that morning was fraught with corrosive testimony and would collate a train of events that would prove adequately shocking. The atmosphere within D Branch was bleak and plagued with uncertainty since the dismissal of Alan Soames, and Rutherford did not react favourably to the topic of discussion incited by Menzies.

'Speak up man!' said Rutherford curtly. 'I haven't the time nor the patience to tolerate your dithering.'

'Well, I'm sorry to have to complicate matters further, Sir, but we have had some rather sticky news from our watchers in St John's Wood.' Menzies took a somewhat reticent pause before he continued, and Rutherford glared at him acerbically. 'It appears Soames has absconded during the night, Sir.'

'He did what!' Rutherford belted out.

'Looks like he had help. Our field scouts followed them to Dover, where they boarded a ferry to France. Dennis tailed them to Provence.'

'Christ! Who the devil is the bogus prig assisting him in his sordid decampment? Must have fabricated a damned passport for the blighter … the whole shooting match! Bloody incompetent lot. How did he manage to slip out from under their noses? The premises was meant to have been well flanked.'

'Dennis confirmed it was Dryden. Couldn't tell at first. George must have cached the escape car at the rear of the property. There's no fire escape, so Soames must have hit the trail from his back window.'

'Dryden?' Rutherford yelled.

'Yes, Sir. We've had our scouts double-check Dryden's on Curzon Street. He's flown the coop. The premises has been completely gutted. Seems he knows something we don't.'

'Who's the bugger tipping them off? Right, as soon as Mercer's back on home turf I'll send him over with Bradshaw and they can spring an abrasive interrogation on the pair of them. That ought to cause a stink.'

That aphorism lay heavy in yet another awkward interval and Rutherford could sense that Menzies had become uncommonly tight-lipped. He finally surmised that he was withholding further misadventure. 'Oh, spit it out, Menzies, for God's sake! I'm not going to buckle at the knees over some illicit activity or whatever unsavoury deployment you have shoved up your sleeve.'

'Well, Sir … Stewart Graves has been sighted in the company of a Soviet attaché from the Russian Embassy … London residency.'

'Graves? Our Stewart Graves? Cipher clerk? Ludicrous.'

'Quite the contrary, Sir. We have photographic evidence to suggest otherwise.'

'It's quite possible, Menzies, that this attaché is a commonplace defector. Perhaps he's playing both ends against the middle. An unmediated communion? Just applying his trade.'

'Ordinarily, Sir, I might be inclined to agree, but the circumstances are far from ordinary, especially in view of recent eventualities.'

'Well, who's the Soviet in question?'

'Dimitri Vengerov … alias Maxim. I've been doing a bit of digging. Turns out he's not quite so pure as the driven. There's a list of discrepancies as long as your arm. Gaps unaccounted for. Caught light-fingering the slush fund.'

'Vengerov? Yes, I know the swine. Defected in '47. Jumped the fence from the GRU. Offered some digestible tidbits over the years. In fact, I received a diplomatic bag from Mercer this morning and the memorandum he scratched out also gives mention to Vengerov. His appraisal ratifies your theory, Guy, or so it would seem. Appears Maxim has a conflict of interest. According to Mercer's source, he's a plant. Aside from straying from his legitimate role at the embassy, his function is to act as leg man between the British operatives and their Soviet handler. Passes on any incendiaries that might prove useful.'

'Well, he's slipped through the net rather lucidly.'

Menzies' polemic quietly rattled Rutherford, almost as if it had been a direct slur on his authority, yet he steadied the buffs moderately.

'Well, quite. Just as easily as the Cambridge Five managed to fool the entire intelligence community … apparently.'

Rutherford's statement resembled humour, but underneath, Menzies sensed a scathing stab. 'Serious steps need to be taken, Guy,' Rutherford continued. 'Bring Graves in for questioning, but don't under any circumstance give him the incentive to suspect your motive of interest. Give him some flummery about the chief lauding his hard graft, blah blah. Bradshaw was slated to interrogate Soames today, so as he's going to be in the building, he can maul Graves in his stead … make the bugger sweat.'

21

IT WAS A SMALL dark room tenanted by three agents: Jim Bradshaw loomed large with his deceptively cool-headed manner, Charles Rutherford silently mediated, taking on his usual regimental air, and lastly the respondent Stewart Graves. The questioning began with banal pleasantries, which did not diminish Graves' anxiety. He merely gawked at his interrogator like a rabbit caught in headlights.

Before the interrogation proceeded, Bradshaw laid out a handful of photographs on the table to invoke a response from Graves, which had in turn fired a motion of self-reproach. He stared at the images for as long as Bradshaw allowed, then Bradshaw delivered his opening gambit: 'In reference to the photographs before you, do you now grasp why you've been sent for?' Graves nodded ruefully. 'Then can you tell us the identity of the person you're seen with in said photographs?'

Graves fastened his attention to a blemish on the floor in the hope of masking his fear, but he knew that his resistance would only foment the grim and corrosive techniques that Bradshaw was known all too well for. Furthermore, Graves was vastly unqualified in methods of deflection.

'It would be wise for you to cooperate,' added Rutherford sternly.

'His name is Maxim,' answered Graves sullenly.

But Bradshaw retorted, 'Maxim is his alias. Who is he, Graves?'

'Dimitri Vengerov. He's an attaché at the Russian Embassy.'

Bradshaw gave a mocking reply: 'But what's his official function for Moscow?'

Graves sat silent once again.

'What were you doing with him? Passing on some appetisers for Yuri?' Bradshaw continued.

At the mention of this name, Graves took on a bilious complexion, which then paved the way for contrition and an influx of wholesome intelligence. 'His function,' he began, 'is to act as courier between the case officer and his British agents.'

'Apart from the obvious,' said Bradshaw stoically, 'who are his agents?' As Graves gave no answer, Bradshaw offered him an unpalatable option: 'Of course, if you prefer, we could put you in solitary to liven things up a bit. A taste of that will either give you a case of verbal diarrhoea or send you entirely off your trolley.'

This dictum inflicted unholy terror within Graves' mind, since he had been subjected to that treat in Korea some years before, and he was not inclined to have that same horror repeated for anything. His answer came discursively, and he was in a very talkative mood. 'Vengerov was planted as a defector at the London residency twenty years ago. Moscow orchestrated a battalion of moles to burrow deep into SIS organisations in the field, not just Anglo and American, and Vengerov would become integral to three major operations during that timeframe.'

'Go on,' incited Bradshaw.

'The first was Operation Stopwatch.'

'For the benefit of Bradshaw's ears,' chimed in Rutherford, 'could you expand on this particular piece of intelligence, since Jim was barely out of short trousers at the time of this death blow.'

Graves elucidated: 'In 1953, MI6 and the CIA wanted

to monitor comms traffic from the Red Army's Central Group headquarters in East Germany, where all military and intelligence data surged to and from Moscow. This enabled Britain and the US to intercept the Warsaw Pact battle plans so as to pre-empt deployment actions of NATO forces. In order to achieve this, expert tunnelling was excavated in West Berlin near the border of the Soviet zone. It tunnelled under the Imperial Hotel, Vienna, which was the headquarters of Soviet Kommandatura, where telecommunication lines linked to Moscow. An operative, whom I shall refer to as Ovid, was 6's director of requirements at the time and took the minutes to all briefings of the operation. A couple of years beforehand, time had come for us both to be posted on a tour of duty overseas, which was the South Korea station. Little time had been spent there before we and other diplomats were seized by North Koreans when they invaded.'

Having made a deliberate breach in his narrative, Graves asked whether he might be permitted to smoke, which was promptly agreed to by both parties. He continued: 'Eventually, 6 pulled their finger out and we were both freed in a prisoner exchange. Ovid returned to London to his new post and I ended up in Cairo. The minutes circulated by Ovid were highly classified and on a need-to-know basis. In truth, they were as sensitive as the plans for the D-Day landings. They included the blueprint of a building in Wünsdorf, which was some sort of radar station for aircraft en route to West Berlin airport. Beneath this structure was a shaft that dropped thirty feet into a tunnel, and above the tunnel, a huge warehouse had been fabricated for the sole purpose of excavating tons of soil, which needed to be transported out in large crates and, if possible, undetected by unfriendly eyes.'

The next interim allowed Graves to reflect deeply on the forthcoming intelligence, and while this was in train, he intensified each draw and every expelled breath on the cigarette he was smoking. His interrogators looked on completely motionless, yet watchful of his every move as he added, 'Fourteen months after the tunnel had been completed, it was discovered by Soviet engineers.'

'You refer to Blake of course. Ovid is George Blake?' enquired Bradshaw with contempt.

'Yes. We had both been recruited by the Soviets during our POW stint in North Korea. In truth, we thought we had been abandoned there … left to rot in that godawful oppressive climate. Blake's first assignment was to penetrate and leak the entire operation back to Moscow.'

There was a debilitating silence, which sat heavy in the room. Bradshaw and Rutherford were collectively static and incensed by Graves' latest axiom.

'So Vengerov was Blake's postman?' asked Bradshaw in a flippant tone, to which Graves nodded remorsefully.

'But what of the other Soviet spies?' interrupted Rutherford impatiently. 'Can we not just cut to the chase and smoke the others out into the open?'

'No, let him speak,' replied Bradshaw mildly. Then with a sympathetic air he asked Graves, 'And the second operation?'

'The second operation,' Graves said, lighting another cigarette, 'was the Suez Canal debacle. And that was an unqualified disaster from the get-go. As you know, the Baghdad Pact was Eden's attempt to arm-twist the governments of the Middle East. This stated that Britain would guarantee defence against an attack, namely the Red Army, who were poised at the ready on Russia's southern border to capture the oil fields of Iraq and Iran. But in order to make this pact stick, Nasser's signature on behalf of Egypt was foremost since it would legitimise keeping British troops in the Canal Zone. The Egyptians utterly resented the occupancy of the British axis, and it was well known that Nasser's hatred for British soldiers had been generated by his own ill-treatment and imprisonment. So, the news of Nasser's outright refusal to sign had trickled through the Soviet channels and it was becoming clear that the Egyptians and the Russians were teaming up; plus he was prepared to allow Egypt to become a Soviet satellite.

'He then ordered the mobilising of the fedayeen in the Gaza Strip to launch an attack on Israel along with an unfriendly gripe with Iraq since Baghdad had signed the Pact. Simultaneously, he signed his first arms deal with the Soviet bloc for 400 million dollars' worth of weapons from Czechoslovakia, including all the toys … fighters, bombers and Soviet tanks. Kermit Roosevelt was ever present in Nasser's entourage and closely advised him on how to handle us British, which fanned the flames of the mounting conflict, to say nothing of our cousins being kept in the dark over the Anglo-French bunco.

'Six months later, Nasser gave diplomatic recognition to Communist China, and Eden spent his remaining months in Downing Street deranged in near obsession over assassinating Nasser … which came to nothing of course.'

At this stage of the interrogation, Rutherford was called out of the room and Graves was left with Bradshaw in what could only be described as a cripplingly taut atmosphere.

'I assume,' said Bradshaw fervently, 'that Vengerov continued to rally between yourself and the agents at 6 during this operation?' Graves nodded. 'And you were passing on the scraps to Yuri in Cairo.' Yet another nod was pledged by Graves. It then followed that before the final section of the questioning would ensue, further intelligence should not be disclosed without the presence of Rutherford, at which point Bradshaw promptly left the room momentarily.

On the eventual return of Rutherford and Bradshaw, a third man, unfamiliar to Graves, entered the room with them. He was an imposing figure and of a similar age to Bradshaw but placed himself directly behind Graves against the back wall, which Graves found inordinately distracting. There was a decided about-turn in their overall manner, which unnerved Graves considerably, yet he knew it would benefit him on more than one point to continue in the loose-lipped method he had proceeded with.

'Right, where were we?' snarled Rutherford as they returned to the table and seated themselves.

'Our friend was about to disclose vital intelligence concerning the other moles, weren't you Stewart?' said Bradshaw inflexibly. Graves countered nothing in response. 'Don't clam up now old boy, especially as you've been dishing out all the spoils like a good Samaritan.'

'Bloody well sweat the man!' retorted Rutherford with derision.

'For your information,' said Bradshaw rigidly, and ignoring Rutherford, 'the fellow just entering the party is David Calum. He's dislodging from 5 over to us on a permanent basis, and I won't lie, he's a quiet yet formidable operative … but don't mind him, he's just here to act as middle. Now, as far as intelligence goes, we have three moles, aside from yourself, of course, whose codenames are known to us bar one. These are all long-serving operatives, all of whom have been manoeuvring far afield of their legitimate duties … wouldn't you say?' Graves did not reply since he took it for a rhetorical question. 'Recent gathered intelligence confirms the identity of Euclid, but I would like you to regale us with an unabridged account of all your illicit activities.'

'But I only know the identities of two of the moles,' said Graves in a redeeming tone.

'Well let's compare notes and we'll shuffle along from there shall we? Give us what you have and perhaps something might have occasion to come loose,' suggested Bradshaw.

The room was completely silent, and the asperity was balanced on a knife-edge.

'Euclid,' Graves began with apprehension, 'is Alan Soames, and as you've just stated, you're fully aware of the fact.'

'And when was he recruited?' asked Bradshaw.

'Both he and Dryden were recruited by Moscow Centre while at Cambridge.'

'Let's focus on Soames for the time being … all right?'

'His function was to convey Anglo-American relations planning for war with the Soviet Union, which he had obtained by way of camera and photocopier then trickled it back to his controller.'

'Via Vengerov,' inferred Rutherford, to which Graves conceded with a nod before continuing.

'His most valuable espionage work was from Washington and Cairo, where he would pass on boxes full of communications and Policy Committee intelligence to Moscow.'

A sudden statement was vented from David Calum from

behind Graves: 'So Soames took up where Maclean left off,' he said flatly.

'Well in a manner of speaking,' replied Graves, again without turning round to face Hunt. 'When Dryden had resigned from service, Alan was ordered to push for Dryden's role at D Branch as Head of Personnel, where he had information of functioning networks, here and overseas, at his fingertips.'

'Then we have Dryden to thank for blowing all our networks to the Soviets up to said point,' said Rutherford with seething rhetoric. 'The bastard! Countless agents inanely squandered … and for what?'

'With all due respect, Sir,' said Bradshaw calmly, 'I feel it our duty to just listen and question. The hostilities can come later.'

Rutherford agreed with simmering silence and refrained from uttering another word post hoc.

'Continue,' prompted Bradshaw.

'Well, Soames was beginning to show signs of breaking under the pressure of it all, long before his more recent exploits came into play. He began shirking his directives from Yuri, demanding he wanted out, so he was put on the back-burner for a time until something could be duly fabricated at an appropriate time. Dryden, on the other hand, became more pivotal in the witch-hunt of our latest intelligence leak.'

'You refer to Koshkin,' inferred Bradshaw.

'Yes. Some intelligence had filtered through to Yuri from an officer at Scotland Yard, stating that a cohort had evidence of Yuri and Dryden at a rendezvous. Photographs, which had been taken ten years ago in Prague. But there had been misinformation at the time regarding the person who had been assigned to the job. The wrong man was dispatched, and our man slipped through the net … until recently. Then our man showed himself here at D Branch just as the Vesna case was resurfacing and our case officer gave orders to bring down the curtain before the wares were out in the open.'

'And what is your function exactly?' enquired Bradshaw dubiously.

'Bit of a dogsbody really. Middleman. Deliver the odd bit of intel to Vengerov or run between Dryden and our Soviet friends. Dryden was placed very neatly of course … his little backstairs operation offered him the ideal front to steam open the traffic coming in and out of his establishment from 6 and other quarters, passing on all the morsels to the receiving channels. Then when Koshkin showed at the dead-letter drop, that was the end. Koshkin put two and two together and Dryden was ordered to take care of him. We couldn't afford for George's association to break cover.'

'And what of Rodchenko? What was he?' Bradshaw said sharply.

'Collateral damage. He knew too much. Talked too much. The three of us were consigned to put paid to that discrepancy.'

Rutherford scoffed abrasively at this information but piloted his disdain.

'The three of us?' pressed Bradshaw.

'Dryden, Vengerov and myself.'

'And who is your other Russian ally? Vengerov's partner in crime.'

'That's Igor. I'll give you nothing more than that.'

'So, was it you who cautioned Soames with the Magritte as to his being placed under surveillance?' countered Bradshaw.

'It was, yes.'

'And the more recent tip-off?'

'No, that was an external source … of whom I know nothing.'

Bradshaw raised his eyebrows disapprovingly and cast Graves a notably hard stare.

'No, I mean I really don't know who that source is!' foiled Graves. 'Absurd as it might sound, I don't happen to know every Soviet spy … on or off grid.'

After an impenetrable silence, which was opaque with mutual hostility, David Calum finally intervened: 'Can we discuss further your knowledge, or lack of, of the others?'

'The others?' replied Graves, somewhat puzzled.

'Namely the third man, Poli and Yuri.'

'Well, I can't help you there old chap,' Graves said, still refusing to turn and look at him.

'Don't flirt with me, Stewart,' returned Calum readily. 'It's academic now but which alias was Dryden using? We'll come to Yuri in a moment.'

'Dryden's codename was Plato, so I haven't the foggiest whose identity Poli is shielding. Of course, there have been countless rumours falling foul of legitimacy … he's an officer at Scotland Yard, a low rank at 5, a high functionary at 6, some diplomat or other in Europe. I simply don't know. Christ, for all I know he could be one of you lot!'

'Don't be absurd, man,' said Bradshaw pointedly.

'I have hard evidence to suggest,' added Calum, 'that there's a fifth man floating.'

'Like I said, Yuri's products are on a need-to-know basis … and well, I don't need to know!' replied Graves maliciously.

'Then let's move on to Yuri, for now, shall we?' said

Calum. 'Now, our source, who was a former officer at the GRU, confirmed the identity of Yuri to be Alexei Gorokhov. Does that check out?'

'Misinformation, I'm afraid.'

'Then would you care to enlighten us?' opposed Bradshaw.

'Gorokhov is a smokescreen … call it a deterrent for chaps like you. It's one of the many aliases he uses for travel purposes and such. His real name is Yuri Linov … head of the Third Directorate at Moscow Centre. He's as cunning and as ruthless as they come. My life was over the moment you bundled me in here.'

'Not if I can help it,' said Bradshaw bitingly. 'You'll be spending the rest of your days behind bars in a British prison for the treachery you've wreaked. Or perhaps an accident will befall you of which we'll plead ignorance. Your chum Blake received the longest sentence ever given to a traitor. Perhaps that same sentence could be extended on you.'

'He escaped last year though, didn't he? Served only five of a forty-two-year sentence. Sitting pretty in Moscow now … so I hear.'

'Don't take that tone with me, Graves!' bellowed Bradshaw. 'You're not out of the woods yet. You'll be strung up by your ears if you're not careful.' There was a long fermenting pause. 'All things considered, you'll be assisting us in trapping Vengerov, and you'll bloody well cooperate. What's your usual rendezvous? We need to conform to pattern as much as possible, so he doesn't sniff us out.'

'Third floor of the Science Museum.'

'And how will you get word to him?'

'Ordinarily it would have been Dryden's, but since that's

off limits it will have to be a mailbox facility we use in East London.'

'Right. We'll compose a memorandum and you'll append any routine signatures you would use for your usual practice of communication. We'll keep it succinct. Give him a couple of days' grace so as to avoid raising any alarm bells. Meanwhile, you'll be detained on the premises. Can't have you wandering off now, can we?'

22

IT WAS ON THAT cold grey Wednesday that Saul Mercer found himself, having returned from Lisbon on the Monday, impedimenta to a body of watchers, strategically placed in the crowd on the third floor of the Science Museum. As he hovered sub rosa along the outer walls he watched the large school group vent mischief while their teacher struggled to keep them in check. There was a small boy of the group sitting alone, intently reading some handouts given to the class for their excursion, and another boy was trying his level best at distracting him, but to no purpose. The small, seated boy looked somewhat undernourished, donning his uniform and cap rather scruffily, almost as if he had got dressed in a hurry and unsupervised by a parent. His spectacles were broken and his tie askew, but this was all trivial to him since he was occupied in that little solitary world of his own making and blind to life around him.

Like the child, Mercer too was occupied with the task at hand, checking Dennis and his watchers were on the ball and ready for the decoy. The getaway cars were stationed at every possible exit in the event their bait was contemplating imminent flight. The board was set. Graves was wired for surveillance and stood motionless inspecting some eighteenth century mechanical object, while the schoolchildren and the public meandered thoughtlessly about the room. Mercer glanced over towards the stairs where Vengerov would enter. He appeared moments later. The game was in play. With a hot sweaty hand, Mercer gripped his gun in his right pocket and cosseted it for some time before he released the catch.

The two men greeted each other in Russian and the

watchers were privy to every word. They exchanged a string of banal sentences between them, at which stage the watchers sauntered into the crowd on a nod from Mercer, closing the net on their objective. Just as Mercer and Dennis were about to flank themselves either side of the two men, Graves said something completely out of context: 'Thin ice.' Vengerov glanced at him instantly, clocked the scattered watchers closing in and started to make a run for it.

While Dennis decked Graves, pinning him to the floor, Mercer and his watchers went after Vengerov. Then in a random fit of panic, Vengerov grabbed the small, seated boy on his way out, hotfooting it down the staircase, child in arm. The boy was screaming as Mercer and his men sprinted after them, and the immediate comms order was to avoid shooting at all costs.

Meanwhile, the flanked operatives outside readied themselves at all the exits. During the pursuit there was a hazardous scramble as they all descended the stairs, causing casualties among the ascending bodies. Random howls of high-pitched terror echoed through the museum as the chase entered the ground floor, with Mercer yelling abruptly for the people to move aside. The watchers at the exits regrouped as Vengerov propelled his way through the crowd and out through the exit doors with the boy still in tow, and as they entered the street a collision ensued with such force that it clean knocked two of the watchers off their feet.

Vengerov then headed for the road as he checked frantically over his shoulder for his pursuers, but during that momentary lapse of caution they were hit head-on by an oncoming lorry. The boy took the brunt of the collision, resulting in fatal head and neck injuries. Vengerov was unconscious but relatively unscathed bar the multiple fractures to his anatomy. Their bodies lay scattered across the road like toy soldiers defeated in unschooled battle and the bystanders stared in utter horror and disbelief as the scene appeared to wind down to a devastating halt.

•

THE BOARDROOM adjoining Rutherford's office was occupied by five retinues and the general feeling in the room was tenebrous and fraught. Nothing was said for an age while they sat smoking and contemplating their losses. Quite aside from this discomfort, Mercer sat analysing the stranger sitting directly across the table from him and pondered the who, what, where and why. Menzies was studying the file in front of him with fixed attention, never lifting his gaze once to the individuals he found himself in congress with. Bradshaw very coolly scrutinised the men in the room while skimming through the documents in the file, and Calum was composed and sentinel, veiling the slightest shred of emotion as he quietly observed those with whom he had been summoned.

As was commonplace, Rutherford stood stiff and regimental at the window, evaluating the current crisis and how best to proceed. As he glared out into nothingness, he finally addressed the men: 'The files, gentlemen, are the Vengerov transcripts submitted last evening from his hospital bed. Apart from a mild concussion he has suffered the odd broken bone and a severely bruised dignity.'

Rutherford continued to speak directly at the window and beyond. 'But before we proceed with his confession, I would like to introduce our new disciple from 5. Mercer?

Menzies? This is David Calum. He'll be joining ranks and will become a permanent fixture at the Bughouse as of next week.' A mutual nod was exchanged between the three of them. 'Since his current fealty has been safeguarding the security of Britain, both his knowledge and experience will be invaluable to us in counter-espionage further afield, of which he has expressed an interest. The transcripts will bring him duly up to speed.'

Rutherford then took a cigar from his pocket, which he lit with a match, cast the dross to the floor then picked up the transcript for reading aloud. He paced the room for the duration and went straight to the nub, reading it as if it were an ingredients label: 'Dimitri Vengerov, codename Maxim, born Moscow, October 17, 1912. "After serving in the Red Army after the war in '45, I joined the GRU, Russian Military Intelligence, from where I was recruited by Yuri Linov, alias Alexei Gorokhov, to become a representative of the Third Directorate. This is an offshoot of Moscow Centre and where most of the tradecraft training takes place." Does that tally with your source in Lisbon, Mercer?'

'In actual fact, Sir, Ashford's source dubs Yuri's true identity as Alexei Gorokhov. But Bradshaw can back that up since he interrogated the source.'

Bradshaw chipped in, 'We've since discovered from Graves that that's a smokescreen, Mercer. Both Vengerov and Graves appear to be on the same page on that score.'

'Well, that's cleared that up,' said Rutherford. 'Proceed? "After a few months as a personnel officer, I was approached by Linov to take on a special task, which was of the utmost secrecy. His instructions were to defect to England and burrow into the London residency as an attaché at the Soviet

Embassy, where my clandestine activity was to oversee the delivery of British Intelligence documents illegally by his British moles at MI6." Everyone all right so far? Fix yourselves drinks chaps.'

He continued: '"This intelligence I was ordered to either deliver by hand or pass through an intermediary who would courier it back to Moscow Centre. Sometimes the intelligence was segmented and couriered by two or three agents to ensure it was protected from interception. This was Linov's handwriting. He absolutely prohibited wireless comms as a means of transmission since he said these could be easily intercepted being that the one-time pad was now part of Britain's arsenal." No doubt he got his fingers burned in the past, eh, Menzies?' Menzies motioned a nod in agreement without bothering to lift his gaze from the script.

'Yes … well … pushing on,' Rutherford continued. '"Linov explained that freedom of travel would need to be essential to my post at the Soviet Embassy and that certain privileges would be granted me, such as cash for travel, etc., and a handsome salary." Any questions, Calum?'

'I'm fine thank you, Rutherford.'

'Vengerov again: "My first task was as courier to George Blake, who was a new recruit and positioned as Director of Requirements at MI6. He would circulate the minutes of Operation Stopwatch directly, which I would courier back to Moscow Centre. This intelligence blew the entire operation along with the location of the tunnel … blah … blah … blah." I don't think we need go over old ground. Turn to page four. "George Dryden was the mole for Operation Kadesh … the Suez Canal crisis. He would give me regular updates on the progress of Eden's treaty and his plots to overthrow Nasser, and being that Dryden was Head of Personnel, he furnished Moscow with the locations of 6's networks in Cairo. Three hundred odd agents were blown, most of which were shot by firing squad." It was a damn sight more than that, the chode! And furthermore, it was our Cairo and Palestine networks that were cemented in the mire … now there's a bloody restrained statement if ever I saw one! Clearly skimming over the facts, what?

'Reading on: "Stewart Graves was a crucial component to the machine. He was often our second and final intermediary and couriered some of our most sensitive intelligence directly back to Moscow. His posting in Cairo was the perfect location for him to carry out his deep-cover activity since it allowed him to hop across the border to Russia with the goods. Alan Soames was also a vital ally, since he was posted in both Cairo and Washington for a time and was able to pass on copious Policy Committee intel to his intermediary."

'Stewart Graves,' said Rutherford peering over his glasses, '"but Soames' discretion would often misfire when he had been drinking, which became a regular occurrence towards the end. He begged Yuri for a demotion, so Yuri eliminated the bulk of his work, largely because he felt Soames' erratic behaviour might constitute a danger to others, so he became Dryden's leg man."'

'So when was Soames hospitalised?' enquired Calum.

'Just as Operation Vesna was picking up speed,' replied Rutherford. 'And directly before the Koshkin-Rodchenko business.'

A solemn pause intervened as they all buried their heads in the script. 'Everyone keeping pace?' said Rutherford firmly, lighting another cigar. No one responded. They either took to lighting their smoking material or scrutinised the script ahead of speed. 'Now we hack through to the bone,' declared Rutherford with enthusiasm, fixing himself a large whisky. 'Back to Vengerov: "I now come to the case of Sergei Koshkin. But I must first refer to the related incident that had occurred ten years before. We had been informed through a source at Scotland Yard that someone had been assigned to follow and acquire photographs of Yuri and Dryden at a rendezvous in Prague. Our source, whom I'll not name, had disclosed said officer to be a man named Slavsky, who was believed to be an émigré. A few days after the rendezvous had taken place, I was ordered to obtain said film and liquidate the officer in question by any means necessary. My comrade and I," I assume he means Igor, "tracked Slavsky down to the Embankment, where we questioned him and he insisted that he had never been assigned to the job in Prague and therefore couldn't help us with the all-important film and photographs. He had flat-out refused to vouchsafe any information pertaining to the rightful culprit, so after a potent and lengthy interrogation, he was liquidated by a sharp snapping of the neck and disposed of in the Thames. The trail went cold and no further leads could be established until ten years after the event." So who's the blasted source at Scotland Yard? That's what I want to know. Anyone shine any light on the matter? Calum? Any morsels at 5?'

'No, nothing. We did have our eye on the former Detective Superintendent Hamilton for a while but it came to nothing. Couldn't pin anything concrete on him. Wild goose chase.'

'Jeremy Hamilton?' piped in Mercer. 'I can't imagine anything untoward coming from that quarter. Just met the chap ... he's as clean as a whistle.'

'Well, whoever their source is,' added Calum, 'he's no doubt a plant from Moscow Centre scattering misinformation to curb our interest. Throw us off the scent.'

'Fly-by-night sources are pedestrian,' said Rutherford with contempt, 'and are as much as not playing both ends against the middle. Push on? "Our source at Scotland Yard then informed us a few months ago of a cohort who was in possession of the very film we had previously failed to track down. This cohort was Sergei Koshkin, a forensic photographer, defected ten or so years before. Koshkin was known personally to Yuri, since they were both former veterans of the Red Army, as was Rodchenko, and their betrayal to Russia needled him acutely. Yuri wasn't prepared to let provocation go unpunished." Bang to right he wasn't! Blasted understatement … dishing those out willy-nilly, isn't he? Diabolical end for both of them. "We were then told Koshkin had approached 6 with said evidence and was arranging to hand them over to assist in Operation Vesna. We then tailed him and Rodchenko for a time, but our incentive was to blackmail Rodchenko into consorting with us to persuade Koshkin to entrust him with the proofs, which he did under duress." Does that check, Mercer?'

'Yes, Sir. They bulldozed him at his flat. Koshkin had cached the proofs in the men's lavatories at the British Museum. He also left one half of a postcard at the dead-letter drop, Dryden's, as a clue for Rodchenko. The other half he posted to Jeremy Hamilton in Lisbon.'

'Why Hamilton?' asked Calum suspiciously.

'On searching Koshkin's flat after the murder, I found an encoded letter postmarked Lisbon, which read: "Items received stop send countersignal stop vital for requisition stop." It was well known that Hamilton was a trusted friend, so I just put two and two together. The postcard was the countersignal for its bearer.'

'And the items received? The film and photographs I assume?' asked Calum.

'Precisely. He had sent everything to Hamilton to stash away in his safe. All bar a couple of odds and ends kept in Koshkin's locker at Scotland Yard.'

'And you know this how exactly?'

'Detective Fenhill gave me permission to inspect the locker.'

'Chug on, shall we?' This was Rutherford's way of saying he was losing interest. 'I want to wrap this up. So: "We knew that a rendezvous was to take place that evening so we," namely he and Igor, "tailed Koshkin from his flat halfway round London until we finally reached Russell Park where he met his end. We had communicated with Dryden between locations, at which point he confirmed Koshkin's recognition of him at the drop."'

Rutherford then paraphrased the remainder of the script in his monotone drawl: 'So, Dryden was the third man in the park. They bump off Koshkin at point-blank range then Rodchenko gets the chop for blabbing to us and is hung by his ears as punishment. The culprits abscond with the proofs, completely unaware of Koshkin's treasure trove in Lisbon and our two moles – Plato and Euclid – or in laymen's terms, Dryden and Soames, bugger off to France. Damned hornets' nest. And we need not revive the Science Museum fiasco … rubbing salt in the wound, eh?' Rutherford peered over his half-lenses again to glean a response. Nothing was offered. Then on glancing over in Menzies' general direction, he exclaimed, 'You're a bit monastic today, Menzies. Cat got your tongue?'

'Am I, Sir? A lot to take in.'

'Yield any more intelligence on Poli in the cipher room? We could do with some good news round about now.'

'Afraid not, Sir. Still chomping at the bit.'

'Meanwhile, Poli is running loose and we haven't the foggiest who the weasel is. Vengerov doesn't utter a single syllable about him in his confession either, blast him.'

'Want me to pump him Ruthers?' chimed in Bradshaw.

'I would rather you gave Dryden and Soames a tongue-lashing first. You might be able to squeeze something out of them on that subject. Vengerov can be haggled in exchange for one of ours on their turf. That's your territory, Mercer. You can handle that business. But first, I want you and Bradshaw to collar our moles in France. Interrogate them … sweat them … do whatever is necessary. We need the identity of Poli. Oh, and you're both booked on a flight to France this evening. Can't afford to squander any more time.'

'They've most likely bolted by now,' countered Bradshaw.

'That's a risk I'm willing to take,' said Rutherford flatly. He then chucked the transcript on the table which made a loud cracking sound, then he sauntered back over to the window, where he returned to his uneasy conscience.

The room was deafeningly silent. Then Rutherford added, 'And Mercer? I want you to take some leave directly after, you hear? You've earned it.'

23

'ARE YOU FAMILIAR with David Calum's reputation?' enquired Bradshaw as he and Mercer queued at customs in the bustling terminal of Avignon Airport. These were the first words spoken between them since their drive to Heathrow that same evening, for it had occurred that their seats on the plane had been placed at opposite ends of the aircraft, which came to be the most rowdy and turbulent of airborne journeys known to either of them.

'David Calum?' Mercer answered. 'Only what I've heard through the vine. He appears to be a very serious sort of chap. I can't read him.'

'No. Well, he's a shrewd fish. Precision-tool brain along with a deceptively impassive outer shell. He's young and brilliant. Never misses a trick. Makes Rutherford's brainpower look rather menial. Still, a worthy opponent, wouldn't you say?'

'Indeed. Put us all to shame. 6 could do with some new blood … in the state of things.'

Some sort of grievance was kicking off at the beginning of the queue, which attracted almost everyone's attention, and the customs officer was trying his level best to remain composed under the circumstances. What appeared to be the loss of a passport, which must have gone astray somewhere between the aircraft and final destination, turned into a complex treasure hunt, causing tiresome delays for all other recently arrived passengers. Conversation seemed to be the only feasible way in which to pass the time, and Mercer was keen on acquainting himself with his respective colleague.

'So, Graves was somewhat chatty I hear? Must have made your job a breeze.'

'Quite. He scarcely needed railroading. The feeble exchange of a few crusty contentions coupled with photographs of him and Vengerov caught red-handed, and that was it … put pedal to the metal. Couldn't stop the man. He was positively flooring it.'

'Incidentally, your reputation is something of a monument … or so I've been told.'

Bradshaw laughed heartily. 'Oh, really? By whom?'

'Jane Ashford, for one.'

'Now there's a delicious little brunette for the taking. Inscrutable brains too.'

'She's a very handsome woman, I must admit,' said Mercer, 'but I'm off women.'

'Never say never, old boy. You shouldn't let some high-maintenance filly dictate your view on the entire female species. Life's too damn short. Or are you unashamedly married to the Service?'

'I'm afraid so. Work is my priority. Always has been. Most likely why I've a failed marriage. Can't seem to get the balance … drift?'

'Life is about choices, old man, and you simply picked a wrong 'un … bottom line. I'll not sugar-coat it. Apologies for my frankness. Just how I see it.'

'No apology necessary, Bradshaw. Those particular traits of yours are evidently why you're so well suited to your job. You wouldn't be a very effective interrogator if you weren't prepared to show the sharp edge of your tongue from time to time. One has to have the right disposition for it, wouldn't you agree?'

'Entirely. Take Rutherford for instance. His no-nonsense ruthless totalitarianism is the wrong tool for the subtle world of intelligence. He's too ham-fisted … shoots from the hip. All very well for the regiment, of course, but he would make a sticky fieldman.'

'Agreed. He can be infuriating at times, I'll not deny it. But I have the utmost respect for the man, nonetheless.'

'Absolutely. He's an old Trojan horse. But he's a thoroughbred. Due a retirement.'

'Mmm … must be looming. Probably retire with a K and spend his remaining days at Lords.' They chuckled.

The queue finally funnelled through and the two of them headed for the hire car, parked in a dark and desolate spot of the airport car park. Bradshaw insisted on driving and their conversation continued from where they had left off.

'Menzies was quiet at the briefing today,' declared Bradshaw. 'Is he usually that pious?' He frisked for the cigarettes in his right pocket, placed one between his teeth, lit it, then offered the box to Mercer. 'He's a bit of an odd fish.'

'Well, he's a man of few words, on the whole, but he was uncharacteristically so today. Unusual for him not to pipe in.'

'Has any suspicion been raised on his allegiance?'

'Well, nothing of currency, but as you mention it, I did come across a minor fluctuation in his schedule when I was examining Soames' travel schedule before Lisbon. Could have been something as rudimentary as leave owing, but I would like to dig deeper all the same. Just haven't had the opportunity with the current developments.'

'Whiff of something in the offing, eh? Think he's our man Poli?'

'Christ, anything's possible I suppose. I must say, Soames came as no real surprise if I'm honest, due to his more recent behaviour … but Menzies would certainly come as a dropped bombshell. Can't see him as the traitor type.'

'But perhaps he has the perfect equipment for a double agent. Quiet, loner type. Pliable. Doesn't mix well in the playground. Father issues. Oxonian wasn't he?'

'Yes.'

'And Dryden and Soames? Cambridge?'

'Yes. As was Rupert Gladstone. The terrible three, so I recall.'

'Was he, by God! Correlation, wouldn't you say? I would put my money on Gladstone. On the periphery … can get his grubby little paws on all sorts of confidential records. Part-time psychiatrist for the royal family. A functionary in high places. The perfect position … Soviet head-hunter perhaps.'

'You could be on to something there, Bradshaw. That's all perfectly viable. He and Soames are very close-knit. We'll have to probe them both on that subject when we're in the throes of interrogation.'

'If they haven't flown the coop, old boy.'

•

IT WAS MIDNIGHT before Bradshaw and Mercer reached the driveway of the property and there was an eerie silence weighted in the cold night air of the hilltop vineyard. The drive was an unmade road comprising an avenue of Aleppo pine trees, which coiled their way up the hill for about half a mile.

'It's not looking promising,' said Bradshaw ominously

as they slowly approached the house that was in full view. It was a traditional rustic farmhouse, pitch black and not a single light illuminating the exterior; not one. Just the bog-standard cat's eyes paving the way up the road. Having parked the car directly outside the front door, they both reached for a torch in their luggage and gingerly proceeded towards the entrance. The door was ajar, and as they entered the house there was an intermittent popping sound of a stuck gramophone needle echoing throughout the building. Bradshaw tried the light switch in the entrance hall, but since it shed no light, he aimed his torch at the chandelier, deducing that no lightbulbs had been supplied, or they had been deliberately removed.

They edged their way steadily through the hallway towards the din, which seemed to be coming from the kitchen. Once again on entering the room, Mercer searched the clammy walls for a light switch, and while he fumbled about in the dark, Bradshaw started towards the French windows, where a chair was curiously placed. To guide his footing, he shone the torch gradually along the cold, stone floor, when he suddenly came across what looked like tar or some undefinable substance beneath and encircling the object. The torch flash lit the chair.

'Oh, dear God!' exclaimed Bradshaw with horror. 'Bloody hell, Mercer! Jesus Christ!' and he clapped his hand to his mouth.

As Mercer spun round, he shot the torch over in Bradshaw's direction, sighting a body strapped to a chair. As he skirted towards it, he could hear Bradshaw retching in the corner of the room, cursing under his breath at intervals. He approached the body. It was Alan Soames – naked, bound and gagged, with his masculinity severed off. A pool of coagulated blood lay beneath him and the appendage was moored to the chair leg. A brutal and hateful assault. He was battered and bruised, his right eye bludgeoned, but the cause of death was evidently haemorrhage. Mercer stared at Soames' contused face lamentably as his eyes glazed over, then he double-checked his vitals for validation.

'Is he dead?' muffled Bradshaw, still coughing and retching.

'He is. Rigor mortis set in hours ago. Bloody heinous way to go. Criminal waste. Christ, what a scrape! We can't have the French police getting involved.' He paused for a moment. 'Rutherford's going to love this,' he said scornfully.

'Moscow Centre, do you think?'

'It has to be. Can't see Dryden pulling this out of the hat, can you? Not after he had fabricated the whole rescue farce. Incidentally, I had better check the property for his whereabouts. Stay put, Bradshaw. I'll manage.'

Bradshaw could hear Mercer ascending the stairs and rummaging about on the floor above. The floorboards cracked and grated during his vigil from room to room. Minutes later, he returned to the kitchen, where putrefaction was in play.

'Anything?' questioned Bradshaw.

'Not a sodding bean.'

'Dryden's run for the hills then. No surprises there.'

'Or the Soviets pulled him out. Either way he's home dry.'

'We had better get on to Ruthers. Send for the clean-up brigade.'

•

THE FOLLOWING afternoon, Bradshaw and Mercer were inundated with a score of windowless vans for the sole purpose of repatriation. Experts, forensics, pathologists, you name it, and Rutherford had sent David Calum in his stead. The estate was vast and remote, which was entirely to their advantage since the nearest neighbouring property was at least three kilometres away. The hounding press and a surge of prying bystanders was the last thing they needed in the circumstances, yet they managed to carry on about their business completely unnoticed and, more favourably, unharried.

'Nothing is to be committed to paper,' advised Calum stoically. 'Orders from the exalted. You're to offer verbal statements to Rutherford and Creagh-West alone.'

There was a staid silence.

'I assume Moscow Centre are responsible?' challenged Calum.

There was another solemn pause, then Mercer responded, 'I wouldn't think Dryden capable of such a—'

'We can't rule out Dryden as a suspect,' countered Calum flatly. 'It's all rather academic now since the culprits have bolted. Nevertheless, it was his furtive little operation getting Soames out, so let's assume he's partly responsible at the very least, which of course he is. And if not him, the Soviet thugs committed the sordid act. We can rule out Vengerov as he currently has round-the-clock babysitters standing guard at the hospital. His accomplice, Igor, is a possibility. Then it could have been some fringe outfit of Moscow Centre … or another corrosive intermediary entirely.'

The three of them stood in deep contemplative thought.

'It's all conjecture, of course, and we may never know the truth,' added Calum.

'There could be several options open to argument,' said Bradshaw. 'But whichever way you look at it, it's a damned awful blow.'

'By any objective standard,' said Calum calmly and emphatically, 'it calls for comment to state we have two Soviet agents under our jurisdiction: Vengerov and Graves. Yuri will want his pawns returned in one piece, if only to dispose of them via a method he deems fit. We're yet to collate further intelligence on our turncoat, Poli, who is now our primary object of interest.'

'There are two possibilities in that precinct,' said Bradshaw with charge, 'namely Gladstone or Menzies.'

'Oh?' replied Calum speculatively. 'How have you arrived at that conclusion?'

'Dr Rupert Gladstone has the advantage of loose illegitimate movement since he's not only psychiatrist to 5 and 6 but is also appointed to the royal family. An invaluable functionary, wouldn't you say? He has access to an athenaeum of confidential intelligence and would assume the role of head-hunter for the Russians most competently.'

The axiom was forming in Calum's mind like an equation, then a look of puzzlement forged into stimulus over his features. 'And Menzies?' he asked, at which Mercer appraised him of his thesis on the discrepancy of Menzies' travel schedule, which he confirmed had occurred at the time of the rendezvous in Prague.

'Both theories have unassailably strong points,' returned Calum. 'Heavy surveillance ought to be installed on both parties on our return to London. We need to act before the situation crystalises.'

•

HIS JOURNEY was extensive and had been pre-booked under the name Carlisle. The first leg was a flight from Avignon to Sofia, of which the duration took a little under six hours. The second leg he found the most agreeable of the two, of which he boarded an overnight sleeper train taking him to his final destination. The train departed at midnight and he settled into his modest cabin for what he hoped would proffer him a restful night's sleep. He took a large tot before bed, setting the alarm clock for a six o'clock start in order to benefit from a good few hours of the reforming landscape en route.

The following morning, he attended breakfast in the restaurant car entirely alone, committing his attention to the everchanging patterns of scenic lakes, mists and architecture of the passing towns and foothills. And as he watched them speed by, he thought of Soames and the terror etched on his bruised and mangled face, and the direst of infractions to be inflicted on a man's sexuality – humiliating, debasing, with inflexible reprobation. For this was a mentality he struggled to comprehend, and it opposed his own paradoxical moral compass. It was a mindset that grew inwards like toenails, and he simply could not fathom the purpose of such a vile crime. Why not use the uniformly inane method of a soft-nosed bullet to punish? For that was their usual procedure. Such barbarity. Such ignorance. It made no sense.

As he turned this over in his mind, he questioned his

own function in the grand scheme of things; the ideology with which he had joined forces as an undergraduate. Then, for some unknown reason, he thought of Turing and the unconscionable method in which the Government had brutally chastised him, despite his unprecedented achievements in bringing a timely dissolution to the war and the Nazi regime. He pondered on the perfidy and moral decline of Britain, and its government set to rule. There are no accolades, he thought, in a world hell-bent on self-destruction.

A multitude of questions surfaced, and Mercer analysed the strengths and weaknesses in every elite and governing system, acknowledging the failures of his own political assertions. He thought of David Calum and their final briefing, which had given him a strong sense that he was concealing his true suspicions on the identity of Poli. He sensed that Calum's compliance was a cunning smokescreen, one that would remain undisclosed for as long as was objectively possible.

Mercer arrived in Istanbul mid-morning and took a taxi to the hotel on the Asiatic shore of the Bosphorus. The din of the city was a riotous assault on the senses, and before checking in, he walked the shoreline of shearwaters and eddies, feeling once again that he was home. For as a young man, Mercer had been stationed there and Istanbul was then the main base for counter-espionage against the Soviet Union and socialist countries. He recalled that from the Inspectorate office in Adrianople, the production of low-grade information from Bulgaria trickled through, and since Istanbul was an active transit area, a large portion of refugees found their way from the Balkans.

The intelligence fabricated through such channels had become an expensive commodity, and it had been Mercer's task to smoke out the wheat from the chaff. He had sent tip-and-run agents into Russia via the Black Sea ports to infiltrate the Soviet Union and set up resistance centres in regions that the Red Army was expected to overrun. East of Ankara, they harried Soviet communications of airborne troops, and for his first major operation it had been incisive and relentless. By contrast to this posting, his current activity was moderately torpid, but his assumption of the Cold War was a subtle, yet acerbic game of variables and its fray had disfigured the face of MI6 dismally.

It was now the early hours of the morning and the Fajr call to prayer lamented across the empty streets. An aroma of freshly ground coffee and pungent spices invaded the hot air, residual from the spice bazaar earlier the previous day. The crowds had dispersed from the backstreets and hidden byways and Mercer made his way leisurely up some solitary cobblestoned steps leading to a sparse sandstone building. He entered a room, which was tenanted by a thin reflective man sitting in complete darkness. There was a table, a second chair and a single candle to furnish the room with light. He was invited to take a seat.

There was silence. The debriefing with his case officer, Yuri Linov, proceeded.

ACKNOWLEDGEMENTS

WHILE SOME of the characters and events that appear in this book are based on historical events and figures, it is important to stress that this manuscript is a work of fiction and that portraits of said characters who appear in it are fictional, as are some of the events and journeys.

Many books were important to me in my research for both the Westerns and spy novel, *Stalemate*. For the historical material on the West, I have drawn from several sources of the *Time-Life Books* on *The Old West*. It is also accurate to state that a portion of my inspiration was drawn from Cormac McCarthy's peerless masterpiece *Blood Meridian*. With *Stalemate*, again I would like to acknowledge both the information and ideas were drawn from several sources on the Cold War period: John Lewis Gaddis' *The Cold War*; Gordon Corera's *MI6: Life And Death In The British Secret Service*; and the superbly written *My Silent War: The*

Autobiography of a Spy by Kim Philby. I wish to humbly express my gratitude to the authors aforementioned, without which this manuscript could not have been achieved to its final state.

Grateful acknowledgement is made to the following for their contributions toward the final draft and physical copy:

Thank you sincerely Eugen Gorean for his extraordinary artwork, *Fake News*.
To Ronald A. Geobey; author and publisher at *Temple Dark Books*, Daniel Wade, author and playwright, Chris Maddix, author, for their wonderful reviews of my work.
To *Troubador Publishing* for an exemplary service.

And finally, to my father for his endlessly generous support.

This book is printed on paper from sustainable sources managed under the Forest Stewardship Council (FSC) scheme.

It has been printed in the UK to reduce transportation miles and their impact upon the environment.

For every new title that Matador publishes, we plant a tree to offset CO_2, partnering with the More Trees scheme.

For more about how Matador offsets its environmental impact, see www.troubador.co.uk/about/